A Mind Polluted

Martin Geraghty

"A very fine debut. Articulates the tensions and pressures of growing up in a fractured family where broken relationships are the catalysts for an unavoidably destructive path. Like spiralling down a Helter-Skelter blindfold, and with a growing sense of foreboding about what might lie at the bottom. "

David F Ross, Author of *The Last Days of Disco*, *The Rise and Fall of the Miraculous Vespas* and *The Man Who Loved Islands.*

"A new name/face on the Scottish Crime Writing scene...Martin Geraghty is one to watch."

Theresa Talbot, BBC Radio Scotland Presenter and author of *This is What I Look Like* and *Penance*.

CROOKED CAT

Copyright © 2018 by Martin Geraghty
Cover Photographer: Eddie McEleney
Design: Soqoqo
Editor: Maureen Vincent-Northam
All rights reserved.

No part of this book may be used or reproduced in any manner whatsoever without written permission of the author or Crooked Cat Books except for brief quotations used for promotion or in reviews. This is a work of fiction. Names, characters, and incidents are used fictitiously.

First Black Edition, Crooked Cat, 2018

Discover us online:
www.crookedcatbooks.com

Join us on facebook:
www.facebook.com/crookedcat

Tweet a photo of yourself holding this book to **@crookedcatbooks** and something nice will happen.

For Kira, Calyn and Louis.
Love the three of you more
than anything in the world.
Dad x

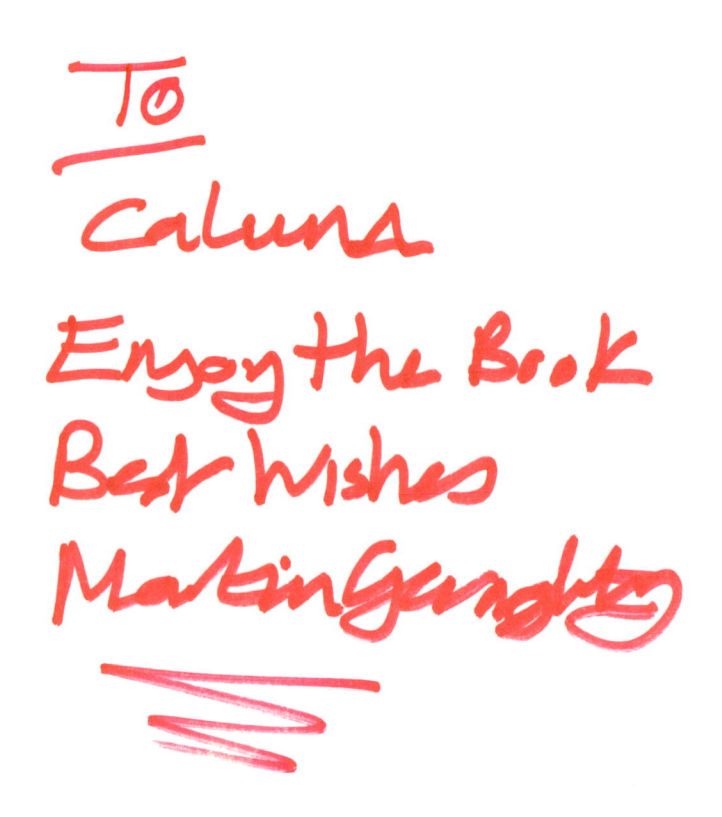

To
Caluna
Enjoy the Book
Best Wishes
Martin Geraghty

About the Author

Martin Geraghty is a forty-five-year-old from Glasgow. He is a self-employed Private Investigator who claims his profession is not remotely as interesting as it may seem. Human beings and how they react to the various curveballs that life throws at them is generally what inspires him to write. He has had work published in various litzines including Razur Cuts and Glove. When not writing or playing amateur detective, he can be found on a golf course or indulging in his chief passions, food, wine and music. A Mind Polluted is his debut novel.

Acknowledgements

For someone with no previous writing experience whatsoever, it would have been impossible for me to arrive at this stage, without lots of help and support. Eternally grateful to the following who helped me along the way: David Pettigrew, Nic O'Neill, Chris McQueer, Emma Mooney, David F Ross, Theresa Talbot & Marc Sherland.

My brother, Mark Geraghty, who along with Vicki, read the manuscript in full-thank you! My wee mum, who instilled a love of books. My late father, his love of words and offloading them with humour was infectious. My sister, Carolann, for taking me to join the library as a young boy, I immediately caught the reading bug. Angie for her humour and smile. My oldest brother, Thomas, for indulging me with my fake synopsis/holiday reads. Kevin Ashcroft, my best buddy, who taught me that boys like us can achieve stuff too.

Thank you to, Susan Maclure, for bringing a beautiful sense of calmness and humour into my life. xx

Massive thanks to everyone at Wooer with Words in Falkirk who gave me a place I felt comfortable reading in, full of lovely, talented and supportive people. Eddie McEleney for his stunning photography.

My crony, Derek Steel, from Razur Cuts. Keep up the fight!

All my fellow Crooked Cat authors for their tremendous help and support. And last, but certainly not least, Laurence and Stephanie at Crooked Cat for taking a chance on me. Your email offering to publish, A Mind Polluted, gave me the biggest rush of my life!

A Mind Polluted

Prologue

Her words were the toxic seeds that polluted my mind. I desperately tried to forget them. My words here on this page are meant for you. Her spoken words were not meant for me. Various traits of my personality can be called into question. I understand that. You will feel the need to pass judgement. It's the human condition. Labelling things or people. Good or bad. Nothing in-between. In my defence, I offer one thing. I defy anyone to accuse me of dishonesty. You can trust my version of events. I promise.

The truth is pounding impatiently at my larynx. Desperate to escape. Bursting with anticipation. It knows its freedom is imminent. Suppressed for too long, its dogged determination is about to prevail.

Apparently, there's nothing stronger than a mother's love. I wouldn't know about that. What I do know is this – that fucked-up day set a destructive chain of events in motion. The Damaged manifested as Damn Rage. I couldn't shake free from it, even when I found the thing that I convinced myself would bring me happiness. How could I have been so naïve to think falling in love was the answer?

Consumed by a fatalistic feeling, I charged towards the inevitable conclusion. And here I am. Ready to set the truth free. Finally.

My name is Connor Boyd. Her truth transformed me into a wandering preta with a rabid, insatiable appetite for self-destruction.

PART ONE

One

A typical teenager with typical teenage dilemmas. I trudged down the lane, heading for home, relieved that I had avoided getting my towel swiped and wishing my body would hurry up and catch up with everyone else. I just wanted to be the same as the others. *Maybe I have something wrong with me?* I couldn't ask Paul though, how embarrassing would that have been? He'd just have laughed at me. I knew I couldn't keep pretending to be sick to avoid PE.

Our street looked like the successful result of a cruel experiment to block all sunlight from reaching the residents. The buildings were built high and faced each other. They were so close together that it appeared as if the residents could open their windows and shake hands with their neighbour opposite. The dearth of light in the street looked as though it matched that of our living room. Approaching our block of flats, I frowned at the unusual sight of the Venetian blinds being closed. Raised but muffled voices emanated from the flat. Stride by stride the restrictive nature of the voices ceded to familiarity. I began to hear Mother's antagonistic tone. Reaching the front door of our ground floor flat, I wiped my feet on the 'We start and end with the family' doormat and smiled as I heard Dad being interrogated.

'Did you go to the job centre yesterday, Gerry?'

'No, hen, I didnae get the chance.'

A sarcastic, false laugh. 'You didn't get the chance? Aye, you've got a lot on your plate ... didnae get the chance!'

I was enjoying this little episode of eavesdropping.

'What the hell was so important that prevented you from going down the job centre and actually trying to get a job for the first time since Dunblane.'

'Wow, did you see that? They've unleashed the scud missiles again, hen.'

'Answer my question, Gerry. NOW!'

The volume and aggressive tone of my mother's voice made me change my mind and think it best that I let my presence be known. Turning the door handle, I heard Dad answer jovially. 'You know Willie Gibb? Well, I got talking to him and he was telling me that he has started racing pigeons and—'

The sound of something smashing off the wall caused me to shudder. My hand separated from the half-opened front door. There was no opportunity to deliberate on what I should do as Mother screamed. 'There's a scud missile for you. Pigeons! Fucking pigeons! What a waste of space you are. I regret the day I first clapped eyes on you … I don't know if I can take much more of this. If it wasn't for falling pregnant with Connor I would be long gone by now. Paul has been big enough and ugly enough to cope with us divorcing for a while. He's got the brains to see you for what you are … a miserable excuse for a man.'

'Come on, Mary—'

'Come on, nothing.'

I stared gormlessly at the closed living room door. A door that separated concealment from revelation.

'I lie in bed at night wishing that I'd had the abortion. I would be free by now.' She was sobbing as she said, 'I wish I had never had Connor. If I knew then what I know now, I wouldn't have thought twice about it. What does that tell you about how I feel about my life with you, Gerry? When I lie in bed at night wishing I'd never had our son?'

I took a backwards step out of the flat and quietly closed the door.

Moving like a sleepwalker, the overheard conversation was on repeat in my head until it came to a sudden halt. One word had taken control.

Abortion.

Abortion.

Abortion.

I was confused, walking aimlessly, when my mind provided some direction. *Library ... I need to go to the library.* I needed a trusted answer to the question that was burning my mind. I refused to believe the answer in my head that was kicking and screaming, demanding my acknowledgement.

From my first visit to the library, the smell of the polished floors and the distinguished aroma of the books had me hooked. While Dad looked for books, I spent my time sitting on a stool flipping through the piles of children's books, front to back, the same way as Mum did when going through her album collection. It was a place of good memories for me. A couple of years previously, I had entered the library to find a poster naming me as the winner of a Roald Dahl Book Collection.

'Excuse me, Missus, do you have a dictionary that I can borrow for a wee minute please?' I asked.

'Of course! It's great to see a boy serious about his schoolwork.' She handed me the dictionary. 'Wait a minute, why are you not at school?'

'Free period.' I walked to the table furthest away from the prying eyes of the librarian and took a seat, placing my school bag on the floor. Opening the dictionary, I flicked to the correct page:

> abortion *noun*
> The intentional ending of a pregnancy; *rare*
> feticide

I placed the dictionary on the table. My head was bowed. As I started to cry, I tried to stifle the sound. My shoulders bobbed up and down in tandem with the sobbing. Thirteen years old. Struggling to breathe.

The realisation pervaded me.

I whispered to myself.

'My mum didn't want me. My mum doesn't want me.'

Strangely, in the past year or so, whenever this scene has returned to haunt me, my mind's eye has added another layer of disturbing imagery. The librarian appears at the table, an outstretched hand full of checked paper like butchers use to wrap their meat. She drops the contents on the desk, blood splashes my school shirt and face. I'm staring at what looks like viscera as the librarian's manic laugh causes others to join in.

Two

When I think back to how I felt in the days after Mother's revelation, I immediately think of one word. Grief. I felt grief-stricken. And I was so confused. Strange ideas began to fill my head. On those first few days afterwards as I walked home from school, I expected to find my clothes and belongings packed. Convincing myself that I would be sent away. Where was I being sent? I didn't know. She didn't want me, so I had to be going somewhere. Days passed with little or no interaction with Mother due to her long shifts and my pretending to go to sleep early in order to avoid her. Then, quite suddenly, everything changed. Around a week after I had digested the information that I'd overheard, I awoke feeling like a different person. The Darkness were booming from the radio alarm clock. Furiously searching for the off button, eventually I succeeded in silencing that ridiculous voice. *Aye, brilliant start to the day. Some clown singing like a woman*, I thought. I tried to figure out what subjects I had that day when a strong current of agitation began swirling through me. I became aware of grinding my teeth. Thinking about the day that lay ahead just made matters worse. Starting to dress, I made far more noise than was necessary. Morphing into the epitome of the disgruntled, chip-on-their-shoulder teenager. Breakfast was eaten in complete silence. Not a single word uttered between me and Dad who sat in front of the television watching *BBC Breakfast*. As I put on my jacket, he broke the silence.

'That you off to school, pal? Have a good day.'

'No, Dad, I'm off to the lab to carry out some ground breaking research into a rare condition you would know all about called lazyitis. Cheerio.'

I was halfway out the front door when I heard the retort, 'Haw, smart-arse! You're a cheeky wee bastard. I'll—' I slammed the front door, drowning him out.

Maths first period was bad enough on a normal day – in my current mood it spelt trouble. I hated the subject at the best of times, had no interest in it and wasn't particularly competent at it. Certain subjects could be spoiled for me by my opinion of the teacher. An opinion that was invariably dependent on their way of communicating, the way they looked or their dress sense. I had a total lack of respect for my maths teacher. The bald-headed, bespectacled, saliva-spraying Mr Toner had an unfortunate lisp that was highly amusing to us. 'Simple subtraction, Samantha' – he sounded like Kaa the snake. He was a total loser who wore corduroy trousers that made a whistling noise when he walked and a tank top with an impeccable attendance record.

'Right, class, today we resume our love affair with algebra.'

Unable to control myself, I pounced. 'How's that gonnae help us get a job, sir? Will I get to use my algebra when I start a job in the bank, or the Whisky Bond, or the supermarket? Maths is a pile of shite.'

'Nobody is asking for your opinion, Boyd! That's enough of that language. How dare you! The majority of your classmates want to learn. Obviously, you don't. I don't know what's got into you this morning but I won't tolerate that sort of outburst in my class. Get out of my classroom. Go and stand at Mrs Kerr's door. I will deal with you later.' Some teachers are fiercely protective of the subject they teach, Toner was one of them. Like I said, he was a total loser. I sprang from my chair, banged into a couple of my classmates' desks on the way out.

Standing in the long, deserted corridor, I tapped my pencil on a radiator hoping that this would gain some attention. Lessons had started and the raised voices of teachers provided some background noise. The radiators were making a groaning sound as the ancient heating system toiled. The walls were decorated with various motivational messages such as: 'Dreams don't work unless you do', 'You've got what it takes but it will take everything you have got' and 'What you were born into does not determine what is in you'. As I read the latter, my thoughts returned to *HER* admission. Hurt and fury coursed through me. Honestly, I felt physically sick anytime I replayed her words in my head. I didn't have a plan or know where I was going, I just started walking.

Down a flight of stairs then through a set of doors which brought me to the cloakrooms. Staring at the contents, I was struck by a simple thought, *I hate that fucking bully, McDonald.* Before I knew it, I was hunting for McDonald's parka jacket. Finding it, I swiped it from the peg, not knowing what I was going to do with it but certain that McDonald wouldn't be wearing it again. As I approached the toilets, it came to me. I pushed my way through the saloon doors and looked around to make sure no one was there. A strong smell of cheap carbolic soap filled the air. Paper towels rolled into balls stuck to the ceiling. No matter the season, the temperature in the toilets always seemed cooler than actually being outside. Opening the cubicle door, I stuffed the jacket down the toilet pan.

As I was about to flush, I heard a voice. 'Boyd, what the hell do you think you're doing?' I must admit, I reacted like a fucking jack-in-the-box. 'Why are you flushing a jacket down the toilet? Is that your jacket? Why are you not in class? What class are you supposed to be in just now?' barked the janitor.

'What's it got to do with you?' I answered. I knew I was in big trouble. The janitor was a joke figure to us. His colleagues called him by his first name, Andy, but we called him Barry Chucklevision. We took great delight in extracting the urine from Barry as regularly as possible. It was pay-back time for him. Barry took me by the scruff of the neck and frogmarched me upstairs to the classroom like I was dangling from a coat hanger. I didn't protest because I didn't care. The janitor knocked at the classroom door while peering through the window to gain Mr Toner's attention.

Mr Toner's instruction could be heard from where we

both stood. 'Right, class, I will be two minutes. I don't want to hear a murmur from any of you.'

'Sorry to disturb you, Mr Toner, I caught this boy in the toilets flushing a jacket down the pan.'

'What in heaven's name are you playing at, Boyd? Whose jacket is it?' He was met with a stubborn silence. I had decided to play the mute.

'You go down and retrieve the jacket, Andy,' ordered Toner. 'I will speak to the boy. Come back up and tell me whose jacket it is please.'

'Will do,' replied the janitor, who was clearly revelling in the diversion from his mundane daily duties.

'Boyd, you are in serious bother, son. It would be best if you just told me whose jacket you've ruined and why. What's wrong, Boyd? This is so out of character; it isn't like you, son. Are you having any problems at home?'

I refused to make eye contact. My shoes had become my focal point. If I had wanted to articulate how I was feeling and why I'd done it, I would have screamed, *'Cos I'm hurting. Everything is ruined so I wanted to ruin something for somebody else. Somebody who actually deserved it ...'*

'Come on, Connor, I'm going to find out in a minute anyway. It would be better if it came from you.' After thirty seconds or so of a pathetic effort at attempting to stare me out, he admitted defeat. 'OK, we will play it your way then but you will need to open that mouth of yours sooner rather than later. It was working perfectly well earlier this morning. That's what got you in trouble in the first place.'

The janitor appeared in the corridor, bursting to tell Mr Toner about his findings. Halfway up the corridor he shouted the name of the jacket's owner. 'I've put it in a black bag. It's in my office when you need it, Mr Toner,' he announced triumphantly as he headed back to his duties.

***

I was given a letter to hand to my parents. Meandering home, I tried to take as long as possible. Remembering that Mother was at work, I wondered what Dad would say.

Entering the living room, it looked like it had been frozen in time since earlier that morning. Dad was sitting in the same seat, in the same position, both arms outstretched on the armrests. The newspapers were still in the same position on the table and my breakfast bowl and glass were still in the same place. 'Busy morning, Dad?'

'What are you doing back, Connor?' I sheepishly handed over the letter. 'What's this all about?'

I watched his expression as he read the letter. Unsure what the reaction would be as I'd never been in trouble of any kind before at school. 'Right, I've to phone the office and make an appointment with the headmaster for tomorrow and you've been suspended for three days. I can't believe this. What have you done? The letter doesn't tell me. I take it that you continued with all that mouthing off you gave me this morning when you left.' Dad reluctantly moved from his chair and stood. 'Your mother is gonnae go ballistic. Tell me right now what you've done so I know the facts and what I'm dealing with tomorrow.'

I was pleased that there hadn't been any screaming and shouting as I provided my answer.

'We'll keep this between you and me for now, Connor. Maybe I can smooth things over tomorrow. Your mother might not need to find out about this.'

***

The head teacher, Mr Lewis, was a giant of a man; at just over six feet five inches, his bald head looked like it had been given the same treatment as his shoes. He was alright as far as head teachers go, hard but fair. He still cut an imposing figure, even when seated, towering over Dad and I. Looking at him, then at Dad, I began to picture Dad dressed as a schoolboy, wearing a school cap, looking like the wee wummin from the Krankies, peering up at Mr Lewis, his eyes pleading for leniency. A business-like voice woke me from my daydream, 'Now then Mr Boyd, I take it Connor has told you what he has done and why he has been suspended for three days.'

'Yes, he has, Mr Lewis, and I have to say I think the punishment far outweighs the crime.'

Mr Lewis stared open-mouthed. 'So, you think a three-day suspension is over the top for taking another pupil's jacket and flushing it down a toilet pan?'

I began to corpse at the scene unfolding in front of me. I genuinely thought I was going to wet myself. Mr Lewis stared incredulously at my father who thought that a three-day suspension was excessive, then to me, the triumphant son.

Mr Lewis was about to launch into a speech when Dad spurted out, 'Flushing a pupil's jacket down the toilet?' He leant over and slapped me hard on the side of the head.

'I presume from that, Mr Boyd, that you were not aware that this was the reason for your son's suspension?'

'Of course not, Mr Lewis, I wouldn't be making statements about three-day suspensions being excessive if I had known about this. He told me he was a bit lippy to his maths teacher about the benefits of algebra to his education.'

'Connor, go and sit outside,' ordered the head. I stood, on my way out I attempted to make eye contact with Dad but he wasn't interested.

Soon as I left the room, I put my ear to the door. 'I am sure that you understand, Mr Boyd, I have a very upset and angry set of parents on my hands. This is completely out of character for your son, however, I need to be seen to uphold our values and rules. If Connor had any history of misbehaving his suspension would have been at least a week, perhaps two. Have there been any changes in the household recently? Anything that you think might be relevant, Mr Boyd?'

'No, nothing at all. To be frank, I am stunned. Rest assured, he will be punished accordingly and we'll reimburse the cost of the jacket. Please accept my apologies, I'm totally embarrassed by this.'

'I appreciate that, Mr Boyd, and I will relay it to Mr and Mrs McDonald. We will see Connor next Monday and we will be monitoring his behaviour. Thanks for your time.' He showed Dad out and I scarpered from my eavesdropping post.

***

We walked in silence. Dad was deep in thought until we were far enough away from the school when he suddenly burst into life. 'Wait till your mother hears about this. I've never been so disappointed in you in my whole life. It's bad enough what you done but to send me in there with a half-baked story to make a fool of myself, that is bang out of order, Connor. Your mother and I will be discussing your punishment tonight. Stuffing a boy's jacket down the toilet … unbelievable.'

Recently, I became aware of a poster that forms one of the intrinsic teachings in Buddhism, the wheel of life. The belief that our existence is a cycle of life, death, rebirth and suffering. At the hub of this wheel of life, a cock which signifies craving and greed, is attempting to bite a snake, who signifies aversion or anger, the snake is attempting to bite the tail of a pig who signifies ignorance. The three animals form a circle as they chase each other. My suspension from school signified the firing of the starting pistol as my parents and I took our positions, each one of us representing one of the three animals. Who played what part? Now, that is a question.

Three

Lying on my bed, staring at the swirl patterned artex ceiling, I could feel the anticipation surge through me. *She* would return from work anytime now. I was at fever pitch about the prospect of hearing her reaction and the confrontation that would ensue. Since overhearing her confession I'd been waiting on this moment. The opportunity to direct my anger at her without revealing the true reason for it. Hearing the front door open, I sat up on my bed, prepared for what was to come. Concentrating on listening to her incredulous, gasping voice.

'He did what, Gerry? He's been suspended?' I heard her frantic, heavy footsteps coming down the hallway towards my bedroom. The door swung open. 'What the hell do you think you are playing at, Connor? I'm disgusted at what you've done.'

'I don't care,' I shrugged nonchalantly, knowing this would light the blue touchpaper.

'You don't care? You don't care? What has got into you?' Her voice was piercing.

'As if you care! Just leave me alone … get out my room.'

'Listen, Connor, I am not going anywhere until you tell me why you are acting like this. Has something happened at school that has bothered you?'

'It's you that's bothering me. I hate you! Get out my rooooommmm.'

'You're grounded for a week!' She nearly succeeded in taking the door with her on leaving.

'Wow, big deal,' I retorted sarcastically.

I lay down on my bed, replaying the conversation in my mind, imbued with a sense of satisfaction. The sight of her shattered face, having just finished a twelve-hour shift, staring disbelievingly at me … it felt like victory. It provided me with some small consolation for how she had made me feel. I wanted to see her hurting. I wanted her to feel the way I felt. I wanted more victories. I wanted to annihilate her.

***

Walking home from school one day, kicking a stone, I found myself thinking of ways to free my anger. It felt like a plague of locusts inside me, bursting for freedom. Being limited physically, taking it out on someone with my fists wasn't an option. I needed to be destructive. A desire to ruin things for others was taking hold of me. Why was I singled out to suffer? Why only me?

It was a cul-de-sac with only three houses on one side of the road and three blocks of flats on the other side. Our street ran parallel, easily a three-minute sprint away. Picking up a stone, I passed it from my left hand to my right and back several times.

As my anger escalated, my mind screened what would turn out to be the first of many images in the years to come that would randomly appear in my head at the most inopportune moment. Mother's sanctimonious face as she nodded her head in approval at Father Edwards sermon. *He that is without sin among you, let him cast the first stone at her*. No thought of whose window it was, whether someone was in the room or what effect my actions would have on them if there was.

I randomly threw the stone as hard as I could at one of the blocks of flats. With all the windows on offer, it would have been harder to miss. Sprinting away, it was no surprise to me when I heard the shattering of glass. I looked over my shoulder as I sprinted nearer our flat. After three or four glances, seeing no one was giving chase, I slowed to walking pace to catch my breath. Walking up the path to our flats, I felt a sense of contentment at satisfying my anger wash over me. Letting myself in, I was delighted to be met with silence. Dad was no doubt down at the bookies while she was still at work. I changed out of my school uniform and began a game of

FIFA.

Even my favourite game was no longer a safe haven from my thoughts as they drifted in and out as I attempted to concentrate on the game. Nearly a week had passed since the confrontation with Mother about my suspension. I now viewed all of the family with suspicion and mistrust. All of them had known how she had felt and they'd been in on the secret. I spent most of my time after school in my bedroom, keeping my distance. A couple of hours of playing FIFA passed when I heard the front door open and my brother shout, 'Alright, Connor,' before sounds of his footsteps made their way to the living room to speak with my parents who had gotten home an hour or so previously.

Five minutes passed before there was a knock at my bedroom door and my brother's head appeared. 'Hi, pal, how was school?'

'Not bad.'

Paul scratched the back of his head. 'Listen, Connor, I know it's difficult at your age. Your body is changing, school can be difficult – if ever you need to speak to me or need advice, I might be able to help.'

'Can you not see I'm playing this game?' *The pathetic bastard has been put up to it by her.*

'I know you're playing, Connor. I'm just offering to help. You've been acting differently recently and I've seen how you look at Mum and Dad and how you speak to them.'

I threw the control at him. 'Look what you made me do!' Game Over was emblazoned across the screen.

'Watch what you're doing, Connor! This is what I mean. Your temper is a joke.'

'Naw, you're a joke, mammy's boy. She sent you in here to talk to me, didn't she? Do you do everything she tells you? Just leave me alone.'

Leaning on the bedroom door, Paul shook his head in frustration, as he offered a warning, 'If your attitude doesn't change, Connor, then you're heading for trouble.'

I picked up the control and resumed the game as if the conversation had never happened.

Four

The troubled kids sought out the kind of friendships that invariably led to more trouble. While 'the brains' pushed one another academically, the bothersome lot immersed themselves in events designed to enhance their reputation. Most of them smoked, it was almost as though they had to, like it was an essential part of the rebellious image they needed to convey. They congregated in a concrete den at a corner of the playground which appeared strategically placed to make it difficult for prying eyes to gauge the activities of the assembled. Whenever a teacher carried out a spot check, we fled like a murder of crows disturbed by gunshot. All evidence destroyed or discarded, leaving a frustrated teacher no evidence of wrongdoing apart from the smell of smoke that they couldn't pin on any one individual.

I had started to frequent the concrete den but the thought of smoking repulsed me. I was beginning to make friends with individuals with similar character traits. My boasting about the window smashing exploits which had now become an almost daily occurrence, meant that word soon spread and a regular group of vandals formed, we took turns each day to smash some poor unsuspecting occupant's window. When it was my turn I would always take it a step further and do two windows.

We began meeting up at night on weekends. At first we just walked the streets looking for trouble and things to do. Carrying out stupid acts like throwing water balloons into Chinese takeaways, jumping over people's hedges into their gardens, and chapping on doors then running away. On one Saturday evening, we were on the bus that went round our scheme. We did this sometimes, depending on what drivers were on shift and what the weather was like. We just sat on the bus out of the cold, having a laugh. My friend Tony McGrory, whose problems seemed to stem from an absent father, his really dark skin and completely different appearance to the rest of his family, pulled out a can of gas lighter fluid.

'Fancy a blast of this, Connor?' he teased.

I didn't have a clue. 'Wit do you mean, Tony?'

'You buzz it, stupid.'

'Wit's it do to you then?'

'Gives you a buzz, Connor. Watch me, I'll go first.'

Tony crouched down on the back seat of the bus, his head just below the seat in front. Apart from us, there were only two elderly women sitting near the front of the bus gabbing away about a neighbour's nocturnal activities. Tony pressed the little red plastic tip against his teeth and held it for around thirty seconds while inhaling the gas.

'Here. Your shot, Connor.' He thrust the can into my hand as if reneging was not an option. I didn't even think twice about it. Grabbing the can I pushed it against my front teeth. The beautiful, intoxicating smell of gas invaded my senses and, within seconds, I had left reality. The contrast between the heaviness I was feeling at the burden of the secret I was shouldering to this weightlessness was beautiful. If it hadn't ended so abruptly, I reckon I'd have cried with happiness at the temporary relief it provided. However, for some reason, I stood and started to make my way down the aisle. Staggering from left to right, right to left, zigzagging my way to the front of the bus whilst grappling at the leather straps that were there to aid the elderly, the unstable or the intoxicated. The doors opened, I managed the first step but missed the second, landing in a heap on the pavement. A stinging sensation on my face. Like a boxer just coming round after the count except instead of a referee hovering over me, I was faced with my so-called friend's malicious grin.

'I'm awright, Tony. That was dynamite … apart from falling aff the bus right enough. Where did you get that stuff anyway?' I struggled to my feet with a little help from Tony.

'My brother gave me it and showed me wit to do. Ants can get us more if we want.'

'Cool. How come you didnae act like me then?'

'Cos I've done it before. Probably hit you more cos it was your first time.'

I had no idea what my face looked like after the fall. Placing my finger on the sore patches I detected a strange sticky liquid seeping from them. A stinging sensation shot across my face through the little pockets of damaged skin. I settled on telling my parents how I had grazed my face but crucially omitting the cause. Paradoxically, although I was in pain, I was happy. Happy because I knew the reaction I would get when arriving home. Happy because I knew she would be upset by the sight of me. Happy because she would be hurt. Happy because I was having the effect on her that I wanted to have. She didn't have a clue that I'd overheard her confession and I would use that to my advantage.

The anticipation re-energised me as I opened the door. Normally, I would have headed straight to my bedroom. But on that night, I stood outside the living room door, regaining my composure. Wiping the smile from my face I walked in. She was sat on the couch in her housecoat, her feet in a basin of water; exhausted looking after a long shift at the factory. I had barely made two strides before she sprang from the sofa, knocking over the basin of water. 'Oh my God, what happened to you?' She covered her mouth with her hands.

'It's no big deal. I fell off the bus,' I replied with a smirk.

'No big deal? Look at the state of your face, how the hell did this happen? Was the driver going too fast?'

'It was my fault. I just tripped on the last step, nothing to do with the driver. I'm going to bed.'

'You're going nowhere, Connor. I'll need to clean that up for you.'

'It doesn't need cleaning up, just leave me alone. I'm tired and want to go to bed.'

'Gerry, get him told,' she screamed.

'Look, Connor, if I need to hold you down while your mother cleans your face then I will. Lose the attitude. Your mother is only trying to help.'

'Hurry up then. I'm sick of this. I'm sick of this house.

I'm sick of you two always on my case.'

She brought in the cotton wool and antiseptic, and ordered me to sit down. Dabbing the liquid on the cotton wool, she placed it on my cheek. She looked in my eyes and I saw that she froze. I knew she could see the hatred emanating from my eyes. As she applied the stinging liquid, I stared straight through her.

She's loving this. She hates me, she didn't even want me. Don't show her it's hurting, I urged myself. Gritting my teeth I maintained eye contact with my mother.

Five

I wiped the condensation from my bedroom window; there was a definite ventilation problem in the house, especially in this room. Patches of white blistered cracks decorated a couple of the walls, creating a pungent, musty smell that could only be rectified by opening a window. The view from my window was grey and hopeless. Square-shaped, the back court was covered with large concrete slabs where grass should have been. There were four poles in each corner which provided the means to hang washing out. Painted a disgusting rusty colour just like the wrought iron fences that separated each tenant from their neighbour. In the back right-hand corner each tenant had a concrete bunker that resembled a bomb shelter. These bunkers housed huge metal bins for the rubbish. Depending on the weather, they emitted varying degrees of air pollution that ranged from slightly obnoxious to the top end of the scale – a rank odour that made you gag.

    I was about to carry out an exercise to see whether it was possible to climb out of my bedroom window then climb back inside. My friends were planning an all-nighter, camping out and getting up to as much mischief as possible. When I asked her if I could join them, she forbade it immediately. There was no way in the world that I was going to be prevented from going. She'd just presented me with another opportunity to gain some revenge. I came up with the plan of coming home as normal at curfew time and then climbing out the bedroom window a few hours later. The bedroom window would be left slightly ajar for me returning early in the morning. Boasting to my friends about the plan had added nicely to the reputation I was gaining.

    Opening the bedroom window, I climbed onto the window

ledge and wriggled my body around so my stomach now rested on the frame before gradually lowering myself to the ground. The drop was barely a few feet. Now that I was out, I was confident that I would get back in. Walking several paces away from the window, enough to build up a little bit of speed, I sprinted towards it. I jumped then slammed my left foot onto the wall giving myself leverage to get my arms on the ledge. Both feet worked furiously as I hoisted myself up and back into the bedroom, landing on the floor with both arms outstretched like an Olympic Diver. The thought of the night ahead and of the impending success of my plan made me tingle with excitement.

***

The tent was pitched in an area known as the Big Backs. Imaginatively named, it was just a large, grassy area situated between two long rows of houses that backed on to it. Its chief uses were football, golf and teenage kissing fuelled by underage drinking. Recently, I'd started to immerse myself in the latter activity. As I approached the tent I heard the voice of Carter, the overweight, red-haired and freckle-faced joke figure of the group. Why the fuck did we even entertain that big cretin? Why was he welcomed into our group with open arms? My only conclusion was that Carter was just so different to anyone else that it made him seem interesting. Opening the zip, I took in the sight of Carter lying in Y-fronts so big that if they hung on a washing line they would block out the sun. Next to him was Tony McGrory, Frankie and Zander – all of whom were fully clothed.

'God's sake, what a sight. Why you lying about in your ma's underwear, Carter?'

'At least my ma wears underwear, ya wee dick.'

Laughter erupted through the tent. I countered by throwing myself on top of Carter gyrating and moaning Carter's mother's name, 'Oh, Margaret, Margaret.'

'Ya wee crackpot, Boyd. So you still on for tonight or are you backing out?' Carter asked between bouts of laughter.

'Am I fuck backing out.'

'Bet you get caught.'

'Bet you a forfeit of my choice, I don't.'

'You're on, and when you show your daft, wee face back here after Trunchbull has finally decided to let you out again, you should be afraid, be very afraid o' what I have in store for you.'

I shot him a knowing smile. 'You're gonnae be making a right tool of yerself the night when I get out, but then what's new, ya big muppet.'

The others just lay back, taking it all in, revelling in the one-upmanship.

***

I headed home at nine thirty in plenty of time for the ten o'clock curfew, racking my brain as to what I would make Carter do for a forfeit. Buzzing at the prospect of having the power to make the big red-headed misfit do something that would make him the talk of the school.

As I entered the living room where that evil bitch sat, watching TV on her own, I saw her face light up at the sight of me. *She's going to try and speak to me, I better nip this in the bud.* Heading straight to the kitchen, I poured myself a glass of water then, without breaking stride or looking in her direction, I announced that I was tired and was going to bed. Just being in the same room as her made me feel angry. I couldn't rest my eyes on her for more than a few seconds as the rage within me would soon take over. It was debilitating. Confusing. Imagine looking at your mother and having those feelings. And all because of her words.

It was a little while later. The room was pitch black. I lay in bed, fully clothed, with the duvet pulled up to my neck. Excitement and anticipation bubbled within, picturing image by image what my friends might be up to. Dad had arrived home five minutes after me and he and Mother had gone to bed around twenty minutes ago. Pressing the light button on my Casio, another hand-me-down from Paul, I saw that it was ten minutes to midnight. *Ten minutes, just ten more minutes*, I thought. Barely a couple of minutes passed before I pulled back the duvet cover. Tiptoeing towards the window in slow motion, like Neil Armstrong's virgin steps on the surface of the moon.

My mind began to play tricks on me; the expectation that the light would go on at any second and I would hear, 'Right, where do you think you're going?'

Opening the curtains enough to let in some light, I gently opened the window and replicated the trial run of earlier that day without a hitch. Standing in the back court, I looked at the striking red sky which turned my thoughts to my big red-headed friend and the impending forfeit. I reached up and closed the window over, leaving it slightly ajar, and began the short journey, looking forward to basking in the admiration of my friends.

***

'No chance, he is aw talk. His ma will have his door locked, she's strict as anything,' said Carter.

'That's wit you're hoping. The wee man will be here,' Tony 'The Gas Man' McGrory remarked.

'He better hurry up, I want tae get some hubcaps tonight and I don't want tae leave it too late,' moaned Zander who was making considerably more stealing hubcaps to order than any of his friends who had paper rounds.

I caught most of the conversation as I crept towards the tent. With my hand on the tent zip, I burst into the tent and shouted, 'Here's Johnny!'

The dramatic entrance was met with three laughing faces and a troubled-looking Carter. 'Told yae, didn't a, Carter? See, your problem is your mouth is as fat as your big, beached-whale body,' I said.

Carter shook his head. 'Shut it, ya wee moron, I'm not doing any forfeit. As if you're gonnae make me, ya fuckin midget.'

He had barely finished his sentence before the others

backed me up. 'Aye, right. If that's your game, you can go back to hanging about with the losers you used to run about with. You're fucking doing it, alright,' warned Frankie.

For a boy who looked like Carter, fitting in was everything. He had no option. 'Calm down, I'll do it. Carter's word is his bond,' he answered with a fake smile.

Zander sprung to his feet. 'Right, let's head down to Spam Valley. I've got my eyes on a few cars there. You can tell us wit you've got planned for big greetin face along the way, Connor.'

Carter was put through emotional turmoil as I ordered him to walk twenty paces or so in front of the rest of us as we whispered and laughed behind him. We made him suffer for fifteen minutes before ordering him to stop. 'Right, Carter, when we get tae just past the pub you're taking your clothes off … that means everything bar your socks and your Travel Fox—'

'No chance,' he interrupted.

Seriously, trying to keep a straight face was a challenge. I remained poker-faced, despite the convulsions of laughter coming from the other three. 'Let me finish… Then you are going to do the Grand National over four hedges while providing a running commentary, then run back up to us.'

'Bang out of order, Connor. I'll get you back for this.'

The pub was closed, it was after one in the morning so there was virtually no one around. Carter took off his T-shirt and shorts, standing in the same Y-fronts as earlier – nasty looking maroon pants with a lemon Y– he grudgingly removed the offending underwear and galloped off with his huge buttocks bobbing up and down like buoys in a choppy sea. 'Red Rum approaching the first,' he commentated. Barely able to lift his leg above knee height, he ploughed through the first hedge with sheer brute force yelling, 'Aaagghhh, my arse! That's fucking sore.' Striding towards the next hedge, he started commentating again. 'A mistake at the first by Red Bum, but he's over the second,' he screamed as he got into his stride.

The four of us had never seen or heard anything so funny

in our lives. The sight of that big oddball of a friend, his balls dangling as he tried to lift his leg and clear the hedge, the sound of him yelping in pain ... this memory is one of the very few good memories that have lived with me for a long time.

'And as they head for the line, it is Red Rum and Red Bum, Red Rum and Red Bum and Red Rum just gets up on the line.' Carter was puffing hard as he finished the final hedge. He bent over, trying to get his breath back.

The living room light of the garden he was in went on, a face appeared between the curtains, squinting and rubbing his eyes. The window opened and a voice pierced the early morning air. 'Whit the fuck ... get the fuck out ma garden, ya dirty wee bastard.'

In an instant, Carter turned into a five furlong sprinter, legging it as fast as he could.

He met us a few hundred yards down the road, flustered and exhausted looking, like Tom McKean's pacemaker. As he dressed, he complained, 'That was out of order, if I had got caught and took back to mine wearing nothing but my trainers and socks ... I don't know what my mum would have done. I'm off up the road. See yiz later.'

I never took to Carter. He was too good a person for me. I wanted to surround myself with rogues. I promised you honesty. The truth is ... I was jealous of the relationship he had with his mother. No one ever knew what happened to his father. He'd never been on the scene. Carter refused to speak about it. Whatever it was, it created a bond between mother and son that I would have died for. I shouted in his direction. 'Aye, away up the road and cuddle into your maw with a cup of Ovaltine, ya big shitebag. Telt yae your mouth is as fat as your gut.'

Zander threw an arm over my shoulder. 'Mon, guys, probably better he disnae come anyway. Imagine if somebody interrupts us. We're aw quick enough to get away, he'd get caught and, judging by him tonight, he'd blab in a minute.'

'Aye, you're right. Wit a laugh though, eh? Wit a scream! I still cannae get o'er his big face when the guy opened the window,' Frankie laughed.

The smell of freshly cut grass still lingered as we headed towards our next adventure. It was a beautiful, quiet night as if Planet Earth had a finger at her lips, urging everyone and everything to be silent. Zander pulled up his T-shirt and checked that he still had the tools tucked in the waistband of his jeans. 'Right, see that silver Escort up there, that's our first of the night. Just walk beside me and keep yer eyes peeled till I get the job done. Any problems, let me know right away. Yiz aw understand?'

'Aye, Zander,' we replied in unison, like three backing singers in a band.

He worked furiously, removing the four hubcaps with consummate ease. 'Job done. Let's go,' he said, winking at us. Two other sets were removed, then we moved on to his last target for the night. 'See that red Astra up there? That's the last one, boys, then we can head back and celebrate.' He removed the first two hubcaps then turned to me. 'My hands are killing me. You do the last two for me.'

'Am not sure wit to dae, Zander.'

'That's crap. You've seen me do it; it's no rocket science, wee man.'

I tried to appear confident, 'Geez it here then, piece o piss.' Meanwhile, I felt like I needed to blow into a brown paper bag.

I started on the first one, working round the rim slowly releasing the hubcap bit by bit. Three quarters of the way through it, I heard the cry of, 'Run, Connor!' I dropped the tools.

Whilst still attempting to get out of the squatting position, I felt my T-shirt being grabbed and my body yanked into the air as if my thumbs had just activated my jet-pack. An irate face was inches away from mine, a drooping moustache, hair long at the sides but none on top, bloodshot eyes. Like a fucking hill-billy from the Hills have Eyes. 'Dirty, thieving, wee bastard,' my captor screamed, saliva spraying over my face.

Less than a minute later I was in his house as the police were called. 'Where do you live?' No answer. 'Do your parents know you are out at this time?' Again, no answer. This freak was getting frustrated with my wall of silence. 'Answer me, ya wee shite. Wit's your pals' names? The police will get it out you, anyway,' he warned.

Thoughts ran amok inside my mind. I couldn't shop my mates in, that wasn't an option. Then the picture of her face seeing me being chaperoned by two coppers flashed in my mind. Guilty of stealing hubcaps in the middle of night when she thought I was in bed. It filled me with absolute, fucking delight. I was taking the rap alright. This was working out better than if I had scripted it myself. This incident would add another layer to my notoriety. I didn't care about the consequences of my actions. I only cared about my loyalty to my friends, my reputation and the police's imminent arrival so I could rub her miserable face right in it.

Six

Sat in the back of the police car next to PC Reid, whom I'd identified as the good cop of the partnership, I watched the curtains twitching at our opposite neighbour's. The appropriately named Mrs McKnight was notorious for her nocturnal nosiness. She claimed to suffer from insomnia, but her neighbours joked that her fear of missing any juicy night-time goings-on was the real cause of her inability to sleep. My thoughts turned to Mother. *Here we go. I can't wait to see her face, see what happens to all the false airs and graces ... she'll be more worried about the neighbours seeing the police at her door than anything I've done*. This would be another battle won in my war against her. Getting out of the car, I couldn't resist waving at our eagle-eyed neighbour. I wished I had a megaphone to announce my return to the whole street. PC McCormack led the way, he checked the nameplate on the ground floor flat door belonging to us then chapped with his closed fist in that rat-a-tat-tat style synonymous with the police. Growing impatient, he had another go, this time with more force.

Some movement could be heard, followed by heavy footsteps. A light from the hallway emanated through the frosted glass panelling of the front door. 'Who is it?' came the disorientated voice of good old Mary Boyd. I felt like a greedy dog getting a steak waved in its face.

'Mrs Boyd, it's PC McCormack and PC Reid, if we could just have a couple of minutes of your time.'

She could be heard hurrying towards the door. 'Oh God, has there been an accident? Is it our Paul?' Her voice was full of fear as she unlocked and swung it open. She was clearly thrown by the sight of the two police officers with me standing between them. She stared in bewilderment at the two uniformed men, then back at me.

'Can we come in, Mrs Boyd?'

'Yes, oh, right, you better come in.' Her distracted manner indicating her struggle to process what was going on.

I was puzzled and disappointed at her reaction, or lack of reaction, then it dawned on me that the fireworks were still to come. I sat on the settee, put my two arms behind my head and clasped my hands together. An attempt at appearing as though I hadn't a care in the world. PC Reid took a seat next to me, leaving his younger colleague standing, facing Mary, with the task of breaking the news to her.

'Mrs Boyd, this morning at around 2 a.m. we received a call from a gentleman in Fairhall Crescent. He had seized your son in the act of removing the hubcaps from his vehicle. Several other youths fled the scene.'

'My Connor, stealing hubcaps, no', she shook her head, 'no chance … you've made a mistake. Connor was here in his bed.'

PC McCormack sighed. 'Mrs Boyd, I think if you check his bedroom window you will find it is open. Your son has already told us he sneaked out of his bedroom around midnight and he's admitted he was out stealing hubcaps. He had tools in his possession which will be used as evidence.'

She looked at me, a pleading look, begging me to tell her it was all a mistake.

My answer burst from me like water from a geyser. 'Yes, Mother, the truth, the whole truth, and nothing but the truth, so help me God,' I beamed, raising my right hand aloft.

Her eyes were fixed on me as her crocodile tears escaped. She turned to the police officers. 'I don't know what to do, officers. I have tried speaking with him, so have his father and brother. He's started getting into all sorts of bother at school – he's been suspended and is on a behaviour sheet.

'I don't recognise my own boy; in a few months he's changed beyond recognition. Look at him! He's revelling in this. He's out of control.'

PC McCormack's response was abrupt. 'We're sorry to

have disturbed you, Mrs Boyd. We'll complete our report and take it from there. I expect you will be hearing from the Children's Panel.'

PC Reid, seeing her distress, much to my irritation, offered up some advice. 'Connor, you're at a fork in the road, son, you can take the route that'll bring you to our attention time and again or you can go the other way and turn things around. You need to think about that, son, before it's too late. Look at what you're putting your mother through and, as for protecting your so-called friends, ask yourself the question, "Would they cover for me?" From my experience, the answer is "No." It's not big and it's not clever what you're doing.'

I stared at him, my expression devoid of emotion.

She showed the officers to the door, then quickly closed it behind them. Marching down the laminate floor of the hallway, she stopped at her bedroom door, 'Gerry, get yer lazy arse out of bed now.' She strode into the living room to find me lying on the settee, hands clasped behind my head, staring contemplatively at the ceiling. Grabbing my T-shirt, she tried to pull me to my feet. I swiped her hand away and stood of my own accord. She lashed out with the hand I'd pushed aside, slapping me hard on the left side of my face. I grabbed her wrist as tightly as I could and screamed in her face, 'That's the first and last time you ever lift yer hands tae me, ya daft cow.'

At that precise moment, Dad entered the living room oblivious to the fact the police had been and gone. Met with the sight of his wife's haunted face, red and bloated from crying and his son's face burning with rage, hand gripping his mother's wrist, he pulled us apart. 'Calm down, the pair of you. What the hell is going on?'

The she-devil examined her wrist. 'I'll tell you what's going on. That little shit climbed out the window tonight, went out stealing hubcaps and was caught. The police brought him back, he confessed to the lot, refused to say who he was with and then lay on the settee there as if he didnae have a care in the world. We've tried speaking to him but nothing is getting through … so I slapped him. He grabbed my wrist and called me a cow. That's about right, isn't it, Connor?'

'Aye, Mary, and you put on a big act for the polis, crocodile tears, the lot,' I answered with a smirk.

Dad tried to defuse the situation. 'Connor, go to your bed, we'll speak about this in the morning. We won't sort anything out like this.'

I have to admit I couldn't get away from her quick enough, I was burning with anger. I felt seconds away from spewing out the monster of a secret that now controlled and directed all my thoughts and actions.

As I made my way out of the room I heard her saying, 'Aye, bury your head in the sand, Gerry. That's the answer, always has been with you. Your son is going off the rails. He flushed a boy's jacket down the toilet, has been suspended, is on a behaviour sheet. He came in a couple of weeks ago, his face in a right mess with a story that I'm not buying. Then tonight he climbs out his bedroom window at midnight and is brought home by the police, caught stealing hubcaps. This is the stuff we know about. Are you so naïve to think he hasn't been up to other tricks?'

'Mary, I know what you're saying but it's best to sleep on it; we'll have a good chat about it in the morning.'

I stood inside my bedroom and listened to her from behind the half-open door, revelling in her obvious distress.

'Sleep? Aye, I'll sleep like a baby tonight, Gerry. You don't have a clue do you? He climbed out the bedroom window and left it open to climb back in when he was finished stealing hubcaps. I'll sleep tonight, Gerry, absolutely. Don't worry if you wake up and your son's not here, Mary. It's fine he'll be back when he's ready. Think of him like the cat – instead of the cat flap, he uses a window. Tell you what, Gerry, you sleep on his bedroom floor and keep an eye on him.' She stormed off to her bedroom.

I threw myself on my bed. I felt overwhelmed. Merging my face into the pillow, I let rip with a guttural scream. My once bright, unprejudiced, tolerant mind was nothing but a dark cavern where everything my family said or did was an attack intended to hurt me. I hadn't done anything to deserve a slap from Mother. The evil cow never wanted me, she hated me, would do anything to be rid of me. Her hand striking my face flashed through my mind. I pictured myself grabbing her face in my outstretched hand, pressing on her cheeks and jawline, then throwing her onto the settee. Contemplating the endless satisfactory conclusions to the scenario if Dad hadn't walked in when he had. As these thoughts passed through my mind, Dad entered the bedroom in his navy blue, shiny, viscose pyjamas with a blanket under his arm.

'Your mother wants me to sleep in here tonight, to keep an eye on you, Connor.' I watched with a look of disgust as he prepared his temporary bed on the floor. 'That's pathetic. I'm no gaun to sneak out, Dad. I don't need you shadowing me.'

'You've only yourself to blame. Do you think I want to be lying on the floor, having to babysit you, especially with my bad back? Just go to sleep and we'll sort everything out tomorrow.'

'Goodnight, Dad,' I said with a sigh, knowing that nothing would be sorted out tomorrow.

Nothing would ever be sorted out with her.

Seven

It was mid-afternoon. The sun had finally made an appearance after absconding for several weeks. Frowns became smiles, outfits and attitudes were transformed. In the scheme, kids played in paddling pools as the adults congregated with friends and neighbours lazily enjoying the sun as Franz Ferdinand boomed from the sound systems.

Meanwhile, my gang and I were on the move yearning for fun and adventure.

Ragtag schemies walking down the avenue of our affluent neighbours, seeking opportunities. Apart from a couple of retired men out cutting their grass, the road was eerily quiet. Most of the residents were at work; in contrast to the scheme where there were always people around. The few people we did pass eyed us with suspicion, the way we spoke and dressed made it obvious we were not from this area.

My speech had changed as part of my attempt to fit in. Mimicking the others, I began to speak more crudely. 'Wit you looking at us like that fir, ya old dafty?' I barked. 'And wit the hell are yae daen wearing a shirt and tie and daft jumper in this heat?'

The octogenarian shook his head and muttered a tut-tut before firing a warning at us, 'I shall be watching you three. You are up to no good, of that I am sure.'

'Oooohhhh, shall you now,' we said in unison, mocking his careful diction. Tony, Zander and I strolled down the road, looking in awe from left to right at the different colours and sizes of the houses. Kicking the empty coke can that Zander discarded, I turned to face him. 'Look at them, total palaces compared tae oor horrible wee hooses. Wit dae yiz think these people work as?'

Tony spat his Hubba Bubba on the pavement. 'Probably school teachers, an doctors, an that.'

I stopped and began to daydream for a moment.'I'm gonnae end up wi a pad like that an when I dae, a won't be letting ma auld man an cow of a ma anywhere near it.'

Zander turned to face me.'Wit you saying that for, Connor? Yer da is cracking and yer ma seems aw-rite even if she's mega strict.'

I reacted without thought. 'Zander, you know nowt about ma da and ma. Don't talk crap aboot stuff ya don't know about.' Regretting my outburst as soon as it left my mouth as Zander's moods were famously volatile.

I watched Zander and Tony look at each other, both pulled a face at the other with their eyebrows raised. Zander laughed. 'A don't think yil need tae worry aboot them coming to your fancy gaff anyhow, Connor, ya wee dafty. There's mer chance o' them visiting yae in the *real* big hoose.'

Halfway down the tree-lined avenue which was at least a mile long, we approached a bend in the road. In the distance, a quaint little greengrocer's, the kind you only saw in affluent areas like this. 'No way, check that wee shop, they're asking fir trouble. Look at the wooden crates wi aw that fruit sitting oot on the pavement. I dare you,' teased Zander, staring at me with a mischievous smile.

I knew immediately what was being inferred. 'Nae botha, I'm up fir that. I'll wait here til yiz get tae the bottom o the road, then I'll make a run fir it an we'll head to the canal.' I had developed a default setting, where I agreed to anything that was asked of me by my friends. Waiting until my sidekicks were a couple of hundred yards away, I scanned the road then began sprinting towards the shop. Focusing on the pineapples, I swiped two without breaking stride. Laughter echoed from Tony and Zander at the sight of me running, both arms outstretched, holding two pineapples like grenades about to explode. Their laughter set me off, the three of us feeding off each others as we ran across the dual carriageway, dodging cars, before crossing the bridge to the canal-side.

Sitting on the grassy verge, the laughter ebbed away as we tried to catch our breath. I turned to Tony, 'Bet you thought pineapples only came from the man from Del Monte.' A thought then suddenly occurred to me, 'How the hell we gonnae eat them?'

'This is how,' said Zander, flashing a pocket knife.

'Wow, wer did ya get that?' Tony asked.

'Never you mind, but if yiz want wan, I can get yiz wan fir a couple o quid.' He grabbed a pineapple from me and began slicing it into edible chunks.

Zander bit into the pineapple, juice dripping all over his hands and his Helly Hansen shorts. 'Connor, do you know the Bannermans?'

'Them that have that fuckin vicious, old dog, Satan?'

Zander threw his knife into the grass. 'Aye, that's them. They live down in Braeside. That sums them up by the way – who calls their dug Satan?'

'Aye, that dug is fucking vicious. If yae go anywhere near it it'll just go fir yae. It should get put doon,' I said.

Zander pulled his knife from the earth. 'Do you know they have a fuckin boat in their back garden and the whole family sit in there sometimes, eating their dinner. Like wan o the fuckers they gave away oan that darts thing, *Bullseye*. Wit's that aw aboot? Sitting in a fuckin boat in yer back garden, eating yer dinner? Can they no just eat it in the hoose like everybody else? They think they're better than everybody. Anyhow, the reason am askin yae is … yi know I wiz blagging hubcaps for them … well the dirty bastards are takin the piss an no paying me. They've totally shafted me.'

I looked at Zander, using my hand like a visor to block out the sun. 'Wit yi gonnae dae?'

'Am working oan it. Did yae hear wit they done tae Pam that runs the ice cream van?' He gave me no time for an answer. 'Yae know they've got the biggest paper round in the whole of the scheme? Well, Pam telt them she wiz going oan holiday and they weren't tae deliver the papers fer a week. They didnae listen an still delivered them. So, she got back and they chapped oan her door askin fir the money. She chased them, told them that she telt them at the time she didnae want the papers fir a week. So, wan time, Davie Bannerman goes to Pam's van. It's scorching, there's a big fuckin queue behind him. Yae know the family is fuckin massive, so he orders tons of stuff … three double nougats, two ninety-niners and two oysters. Pam sticks them in a box. Davie then asks for three cones and three tubs of ice cream. She tells him how much it comes tae an he starts fannyin about in his pockets then says, "Sorry, Pam, a forgot tae bring money out wi me, al be back in a minute." Pam serves the rest of the queue and there's no sign o the bold Davie. She can see the ice cream starting tae melt, so she fires oot the van and chaps on the door. Davie keeps her waiting a couple o minutes then answers the door. She tries to hand over the box and tells him how much he owes her. Davie says, 'Sorry, Pam, a forgot tae tell yae, I didnae want it anymer.' Then he slams the door in her face, bold as that. Pam's left there wi a box o stuff that's basically ruined cos it's aw melting. They're dirty bastards, that family. They think they kin shaft everybody an get away wi it.'

'No way, that's a belter, bet that taught her a fuckin lesson,' said Tony.

'Are yae fuckin stupid, Tony? I'm telling yae these dirty bastards are bumping me fir dough and how they think they can shaft everybody an you're impressed wi them?'

'Am no impressed wi them, am impressed wi how they got their revenge, Zander.'

Zander twirled his knife while staring straight at Tony. 'Am starting to wonder about you.' He sprung to his feet. 'Mon, I've had enough o listening tae this dick, Connor. Let's head.'

The Kabin was a ridiculously small shop that had marginally more floor space than an ice cream van. Enough space for around three people to queue and a counter with various products resting on it. Behind the counter sat large tubs of sweets that were available by the quarter pound upwards. As we three saw the shop in the distance, Zander introduced us to his plan. 'Right, see that wee shop there? It's jist an old wummin behind the counter. Two of us will go in, me an wan o youz. It'll be a doddle. Once we've asked her fir a quarter o something an she rings up the till an opens it, we'll hand her the money... Jist as she goes tae put it in the till, try an get her tae turn an get another quarter o something, awrite?'

'I'll do it,' I jumped in, like the pathetic, approval seeking wee guy I was becoming.

'Right, Tony, you keep watch an if embdy appears, gie us a whistle,' Zander ordered.

We entered the shop, I shook the coins I had in my hand as I approached the counter. Scanning the sweets, I asked, 'Got any pineapple sherbets, Missus?'

'No, son, only strawberry or lemon,' answered the elderly rotund shopkeeper.

Zander stepped forwards, shoulder to shoulder with me as I asked, 'Can I just get a quarter of sweet peanuts then, please?' The shopkeeper weighed out the sweets, placed them into a white paper bag, then rang the till. As I prepared to hand over the money, I said, 'Can I just get a quarter of kola kubes as well please, Missus?' As she shuffled around to get the kola kubes, Zander reached into the till and grabbed three five pound notes. We turned and sprinted from the shop.

Running until we were well out of sight, Zander said, 'Telt yiz, didn't a – piece o piss wizn't it?'

'Aye, total canter,' I laughed. 'Much did yae get?'

'Fifteen quid. This is aw just small fry though, like practice, fir other stuff.' He paused, leaving the 'fir other stuff' hanging in the air, pregnant with possibilities, before adding, 'I need tae see who's got the bottle fer it an who hasnae.' He looked at Tony before turning his attention to me. He playfully punched my bicep. 'You've got it, wee man.' He didn't look in Tony's direction. 'No sure aboot you, Tone-ster.'

'Aye right, Zander, a couple o bits o fruit an helping yae blag fifteen quid oot the Kabin disnae make him Ronnie fuckin Briggs.'

Zander laughed. 'Aye, a know it disnae and it's Ronnie *Biggs* not Briggs. You're as stupid as yae look, Tony. It's a couple o pineapples and fifteen quid mer than you. Mon, let's head up the road, Connor.'

Tragic really, when I think about it now, but those words put me on such a high. Praise from Zander was high praise as far as I was concerned. His words made me feel accepted, appreciated and respected. All of the things I never felt from my family.

We made our way over the dual carriageway, irritating the drivers by nonchalantly walking for as long as possible then sprinting shortly before the motorists had to take evasive action. Meandering along the same road as the shop I had stolen the fruit from, a woman in her early twenties, wearing denim shorts and a vest, walked towards us, wearing headphones.

Tony spoke out of the side of his mouth. 'Check oot that darling.'

As we passed her, the three of us smiled gormlessly while she stared into the distance as though we didn't exist. There isn't much in my life that I regret but this incident is one where I can say, hand on heart, I'm disgusted with myself. 'Stuck-up cow,' I shouted. 'Watch this.' I turned and walked quickly up behind the woman, catching up with her in just a few strides. Zander and Tony looked on, they must have been wondering what I was up to. They watched me put my outstretched arms around both sides of her body, groping her breasts. There wasn't anything sexual in it, I just knew that it was a bad thing to do. I turned and ran before she could catch a glimpse of my face.

She screamed, 'Stop ... Stop ... Stop ... You dirty little creep.'

We needed the safety of the scheme. Through the gap in the wall like rodents fleeing a predator, it took us to the sharp downhill path leading to the pond. Navigating the stepping stones, we cleared the pond before making it up a dirt-covered steep bank which tossed up a cloud of dust that caught at the back of our throats. The silence was broken by fits of coughing as we attempted to clear our throats. Bent over, hands on his thighs, trying to catch his breath, Tony said, 'A can't believe yae did that.'

'She deserved it, fucking looking doon on us like that as if we're pieces of shite oan her shoe. I'm no letting any lassie look at me or treat me like that. Nae chance,' I sneered.

'Well I'll tell yae wit, av had a fuckin great time the day, wit a buzz.' Zander put his arm around me and screamed in my face 'Lege-ennnddddddd.'

Eight

Banging my mucky boots off the ledge at the front door, I dragged them backwards and forwards until I was satisfied they were free from dirt. As I entered the hallway, strange mumblings and banging noises could be heard coming from the living room. Tiptoeing down the hallway, frown lines rippled my forehead. The living room door was slightly ajar. As I approached, I heard Dad mumbling to himself. Peeking through the door, I watched him, hands on his hips, staring at the dining room table that only saw the light of day about twice a year. Cursing himself at his failure to erect it. He was an excuse of a man at times. The table seated up to eight people but, when legs were moved and various parts were manoeuvred, it could shrink to about an eighth of its full size for storage. Dad looked like a contestant from an obscure TV gameshow attempting to solve an esoteric puzzle. A massive grin broke across my face as I watched his pathetic attempt. I waited a minute or so then, seeing no progress being made, I decided to put the man out of his misery.

'Alright, Dad, what you doing?' I asked, as I entered the living room.

'Aye, Connor, just putting the table up. I'm nearly done. Give me a hand.'

I began to adjust the table legs, directing Dad to move various parts into slots here and there. Within ninety seconds the table was fully assembled.

'Wit's the table goin up for anyway, Dad?'

'Your mum wants us to sit down as a family tonight and have dinner together. Your brother will be over in an hour or so.'

'For God's sake, Dad, a can't be bothered with aw this.

I've got stuff to do.'

'Listen, Connor, your mum is worried about you. She just wants the family to sit together and have dinner. Don't make a big deal out of it.'

'Am no the one making a big deal of it, she is. Gettin you to put tables up and aw that fir a stupid dinner.' I couldn't be arsed with all her false, game-playing attempts at playing the dutiful family woman and stormed off into my bedroom.

Aye right! Happy families, all eating dinner together. She can fuck right off. She disnae have a clue ... I'll give her a family dinner to remember, I thought.

Around half an hour later, I heard her arrive home. The sound of the living room door opening carried to my bedroom. It was followed by her voice offering some positive feedback. 'Well done, Gerry. You've got it looking nice. Connor in his room?'

'Aye, Mary, everything's under control,' Dad's voice shouted from the kitchen.

I heard her footsteps grow louder, she knocked on my door and without giving me a chance to respond, she peered in, a strange smile on her face. 'Dinner will be ready in half an hour.'

'OK.' *Poor cow, she's obviously buzzing about her pathetic wee family dinner*.

'Good stuff, it's your favourite dinner,' she said as she left the room.

I joined Dad in the living room. He was glued to his favourite quiz show, *Fifteen to One*. 'In Greek mythology, what two gods were twin brother and sister?'

'Eros and Aphrodite,' he shouted at the TV.

'Wrong!' shouted Paul, as he entered the living room. 'I think you will find it is Apollo and Artemis, Father,' he said arrogantly, just as the quizmaster proved him to be correct.

'What's the point of even knowing that, Paul?' I sneered. 'See when yae finish college an go for an interview, dae yae think you'll get asked that question? Get it right – the job's yours. Get it wrong – back to the job centre.'

'Knowledge is power, Connor. All knowledge, no matter

what. It can all be put to good use, remember that.' He ruffled my hair, knowing I detested it.

'Aye, knowledge can be powerful, you're right, Paul.' The toxic words that mother had expelled to Dad appeared in my mind's eye as if peering through a loupe.

My anger spiralled. *What if I hadn't heard her say all that stuff? But she did say it. At least now I know wit she thinks of me, her plans for me when I was a wee shrimp in her tummy. Aw the misery av caused her.*

'What does the E stand for when using the phrase "E numbers" in food?'

'Europe,' I shouted. Dad and Paul laughed at my answer. 'What you laughing at? You think I'm wrong? Bet you a quid! Mon, hurry up, put your money where your mouth is.'

'You're on,' Paul replied as the presenter said, 'Sorry you are out of time, the answer is Europe.'

I can't begin to tell you how chuffed I was at proving my smart-arse of a brother wrong. I leapt off the sofa. 'Telt yae, telt yae! Mon ... quid,' I thrust my outstretched hand in my brother's direction.

Grudgingly, he handed over the prize.

'*Merci beaucoup,*' I answered, ruffling his hair.

He grabbed me by the neck shoving my face deep into the corner of the sofa. I struggled for breath. My arms were flailing as I tried to break free. After what felt like an eternity, the arse-hole released me.

I gasped for air.'You're a total dick, you could have suffocated me there,' I screamed at the top of my voice.

'Hey you, language! Don't speak to your brother like that again,' Dad warned.

'Language? You kidding me? He nearly suffocated me cos I took a quid aff him.'

Paul fuelled the fire. 'Connor, stop speaking like a ned. Speak properly.'

'This is a joke! I nearly passed oot there an he lectures me bout how I speak. Stick your dinner, I'm gon out,' I shouted, barging past Paul, heading out of the living room.

At the door, I bumped into Mother. 'Where are you

going? What's all the shouting about?'

Unable to make eye contact with any of them, I stared at the ceiling. 'It was yir blue-eyed boy! He nearly smothered me just because a took a pound off him for beating him at that stupid quiz. Then I'm the one that gets a rollicking for complaining aboot it an he gives me a lecture aboot how I speak.'

Ok Connor, calm down.' I pulled away from her touch as if she had placed freezing cold hands on my bare skin. 'Leave me alone. A don't want this stupid dinner; a don't want to play happy families. This is a joke! I'm goin out.'

'Look, you're not going anywhere, Connor. Get yer arse parked on that chair before I kick it,' ordered Dad. I spied Paul who stared straight at me with an idiotic smile on his face. Shaking my head, I sat, mumbling to myself about the unfairness of it all.

'Right, you two, get seated. Dinner will be a couple of minutes,' Mum ordered Dad and Paul.

Paul stuck his hand out offering me a truce. I looked at him suspiciously before tentatively reaching forward. Paul quickly withdrew his hand and ruffled my hair. What had I done in a former life to be burdened with the misfortune of having this pest as my brother?

At this exact moment, Mum entered the living room carrying a large dish held in her oven gloves, just in time to hear me scream, 'fuck right off, Paul.'

'For goodness sake, what's going on now? I don't want to hear you using language like that again, Connor! And you, Paul … I expect better from you. Stop annoying him. Can we just act like a normal family for once … *please*.'

She proceeded to plate up then returned to the kitchen before reappearing with drinks for everyone. Placing the glasses on the table, finally, we were all seated, plates of food before us. Paul and Dad tucked in, I remained still, sat with my hands at my side, staring at the food on my plate.

'What's inside these?' I enquired, pointing at the crispy pancakes on my plate.

Mother Inferior exhaled as she answered, 'You know fine

well, Connor. It's your favourite ... minced beef crispy pancakes.'

'Oh sorry, a can't eat them,' I announced.

'How's that?' she placed her knife and fork back on her plate.

I zoned in on Paul. 'Do you known what's in these things?' It isn't even proper meat an don't get me started oan the E numbers.'

'Just shut up and eat your dinner, Connor,' ordered Paul.

'I've decided to become a vegetarian. It's disgusting how we treat animals. Just taking a life like that.' I clicked my fingers, my eyes darted from Mother to Paul as if I was watching a long rally between Federer and Roddick.

'Since when?' she asked, folding her arms.

'Since yesterday, when we watched a video in school about the sad wee lives of battery hens and learnt about the journey livestock go through, ending at the slaughterhouse.'

Paul and Dad shook their heads looking sympathetically at Mother.

'Everything is a drama with you now, Connor. Anything I try to organise, you just pull the rug from under my feet. Why?' she sighed.

'It's no my fault. It wiz you that organised this. A thought you might have been proud of me, havin good morals, thinking aboot the poor animals,' I said with a smirk.

'Just get out of my sight, Connor. I don't know what your problem is; I don't know why you act like this. I just don't know you anymore.' She smashed her fists on the table. 'I give up.'

'Bit OTT, Mary.' I intentionally knocked over a chair as I left the room.

Nine

Lunchtime was over. Navigating my way past the large puddles that peppered the playground, heading in the direction of my next class, I responded to various acknowledgements that would never have come my way a year ago. 'Awright ... wit's happening, Connor?' a nodding of the head, 'How you doin?' a thumbs up. It was obvious to me that I was now a 'someone' in my peers' estimations. Stories of my escapades had grown arms and legs, embellished beyond belief. When relayed to me, I would laugh them off, playing along, neither affirming nor denying their truth. As I approached the annexe, I became aware of a girl that I didn't recognise standing at the entrance.

'You Connor Boyd?'

Looking her up and down, I answered, 'aye, wit's it got to do wi you?'

'Zander telt me ya had an attitude.' She thrust a bit of paper into my hand. 'A message fae im.'

I quickly unfolded the bit of paper, curious as to what was so important that Zander was sending messages to me at school. Scanning the handwriting, I thought, *Who wrote this, his wee sister? Cannae even spell my name right ... meet him at seven o'clock tonight at the pitches ... weird. Wonder wit he's up tae.*

Rolling the note into a ball, I put it in my rucksack and headed into class. I racked my brain as to what it was all about. I was brought back to the present by the voice of Miss Collinson, 'For the third time, Connor – have you decided what piece you are choosing for exam purposes?'

My concentration levels had really plummeted lately. Before I could regain my proper train of thought I answered,

'*An Officer and a Gentleman*, miss.' Stifled laughter from the rest of the class washed over me. Regaining my composure I answered, 'Sorry, miss, I meant *An Inspector Calls*.'

'I'm sorry we can't cater to your romantic tastes, Connor. Maybe next year we can accommodate you with something like ... *Wuthering Heights*,' she said, flicking her left hand in the air theatrically.

I flashed a fake smile but internally chastised myself for being so stupid.

'OK, class, I am going to read a chapter from *Of Mice and Men* now. Be warned, this week's essay will be a character study based on this chapter so ... concentrate!

'Crooks, the negro stable buck, had his bunk in the harness room; a little shed that leaned off the wall of the barn ... It was Saturday night. Through the open door that led to the barn... "You're nuts," said Crooks. "You're crazy as a wedge..."'

I looked at the clock. *Jesus, this is draggin in*. I raised my arm, 'Miss, miss.'

She looked up from the book and sighed, 'Yes, Connor?'

'Miss, how come sometimes you're doin sumthin ... like say am playing fitbaw and the match lasts eighty minutes ... fore a know it' – I clicked my fingers – 'it's the final whistle? Then other times, like the now, am enjoying the book an aw that, a feel fir big Lenny, but the time is totally dragging in. Why d'ya think that happens, miss?'

'Connor, let me ask *you* a question.' Hands on her hips, she attempted to mimic my voice. 'How come wen am reading a classic novella d'ya think it's aw-rite fir a boy tae totally disrupt us tae ask a stupit irrelevant question?'

'Sorry, miss, it's quite interesting though, yae no think?'

'Well, Connor, I'm your teacher therefore it is my job to try and educate you. I'll offer you some sage advice about time. All of you should pay heed to this. Now, from memory it goes something like this... "You are nothing but a number of days, and whenever a day passes away, a part of you passes away."'

I wasn't impressed. 'Jeeso, miss, that's a bit depressing, is it no?'

She laughed at my reaction. 'OK, Connor, let me think … OK … you'll like this one … "Yesterday's the past, tomorrow is the future, but today is a gift. That's why it's called the present."'

Clapping my hands I looked at my classmates, nodding in encouragement for them to join in. As the school bell rang, I shouted, 'Brilliant, miss. I'm gonnae use that.'

As the pupils rushed by Miss Collinson's desk, she shouted, 'Thank you, class. We will finish the chapter next time, unless the class philosopher interrupts us again.'

I gave her a military style salute. 'You're the best teacher in this school, miss.'

***

I squeezed through the gap in the railings. Staring into the distance, screwing up my eyes to see whether Zander was already there. The pitches were covered in a vast darkness. The lamp posts in a nearby street, a hundred yards away, were the nearest source of light. Halfway across the grass verge that led to the ash football pitches, I heard a whistle. Looking around in response to the sound, I heard Zander, 'Connor, o'er here.' A torch shone in my face, temporarily blinding me.

I laughed. 'Wit's aw this secret squirrel shite about, Zander?'

Zander threw a flurry of playful punches to my abdomen. 'I'm a professional.'

Taking a backwards step I evaded the punches. I didn't want to wait any longer. 'Everything aw-rite, Zander?'

'Aye, buddy, aw good. Av got something a need to ask yae, Connor. A big favour.' He put his arm around my shoulder and we started walking. 'Me and you huv been buddies fir a while noo. Yiv totally impressed me, Connor. Yiv got baws. That's why am askin you an no Tony or Frankie or any of the others. You're the man fir the joab.'

I struggled to speak.'Wit joab?'

'Mind av spoke to yae afore aboot the Bannerman's and

how they bumped me fir the dough fir the hubs. Well, av come up wi a plan. Am gonnae get ma revenge … that's wer you come in, Connor.' I struggled to speak. 'But I…'

'Let me finish, av no telt yae ma plan,' he interrupted, firing a menacing look in my direction. 'Right, you know the youngest Bannerman, Scott – he delivers the *Times* aw o'er the scheme … biggest paper round in the scheme. Every Friday night he collects the money. Can yae imagine the tips fir a round that size? He must hiv at least fifty quid oan him at the end of his round. Av been watchin him fir a few weeks noo. A know his round oaf by heart. Where he starts to where he finishes.'

I was filled with a sense of dread. 'Gonnae just cut to the chase; wit are you wantin me tae dae?'

He removed his arm from my shoulder and spun me around so we faced each other. He looked me straight in the eye. 'Connor, you're gonnae jump him fir the paper money … wi this fir yer protection.' He pulled out a knife, the blade emerged inches from my face.

Frozen to the spot, I stared at the blade. My mind tried to process what was being asked of me. I urged myself to say something but no words came.

'Yae lost yer bottle, wee man? You're awffy quiet.'

'Just thinking, Zander. Yae cannae expect me tae go, "Aye, nae botha, Zander, al jump a guy that's far bigger than mi. A guy fae one of the most mental families in the scheme. And pull a blade oot oan im. C'mon, even their dug is called Satan.'

'A see.' He paused for several seconds. 'Av wasted ma time, av got yae wrong,' he said, turning to walk away.

'Mon, Zander, calm doon. Gies a chance tae think aboot it.'

'So you'll dae it! Magic, wee man. A knew it; a knew ya widnae bottle oot.' The friendly, arm-over-the-shoulder Zander appeared again, 'Mon, wee man, let's head back to mine and al hammer yae at FIFA.'

Ten

The lane consisted of three tenement buildings that faced on to the side of the chapel. The chapel grounds were large, the gardens beautifully maintained. These tenements were a sought-after rarity. The occupants were the only ones in the entire scheme who did not have other tenements facing them. Each building was smaller in height than others, being only three floors high with two flats on each level. This was as good as it got. The only time one of these flats became available was when there was a retirement to a care home or a passing away. Due to the desirable location, they tended to be occupied by the elderly who had graduated steadily from an average street, to a reasonably desirable street, to this utopia. The residents were of a mindset that this was their last move. There was no room for betterment.

Zander and I walked slowly, in silence, from the top of the lane until we stopped at the last tenement. 'This is it, Connor,' whispered Zander. 'This is the second-last street oan his round.' He cupped his ears. 'Listen. Cannae hear a thing. This wee street is full of coffin dodgers ... they're aw probably corned beef. By the time he gets tae here, his joggies are nearly at his ankles wi the weight o aw the coins in his skyrockets. Follow me.' He strode up the small path that led to the entrance. We walked into the tenement until we were level with the front doors to the left and right and facing the stairs. Zander led me down the steps that took us to the back door.

Whispering in my ear, he said, 'Yer in the chapel gardens. Yer watchin him goin in here. Soon as he's in, you get yer arse in here. By the time yae get here, he's awredy collected fae these two on the ground floor and is up the stairs collecting. This is wer yae wait. Yil hear him comin doon the stairs. Soon as he passes yae ... bang ... yae jump him fae the back. Blade at his back, haun o'er his gub. Four words: "Money in bag now." Take yer haun aff his gub. Take the bag aff yer shooder an haud the bag oot for him to put the money in it. Joab done.'

My nerves were shot. I felt physically sick. The creepy whispering in my ear had disturbed me. It really felt like Zander was getting a kick from all of this. *Fuck me, this is just a trial run. How am a gonnae cope wen it comes to the real thing?*

My thoughts were stopped in their tracks as I felt Zander's hand on my shoulder. 'Let's go, wee man.' He ushered me out of the tenement.

We took a right turn as we left the tenement entrance. It was only fifty yards at most until we reached one of the main roads that ran through the entire scheme. As we crossed this road it took us to the Big Backs. 'This is where yae run tae, Connor. It'll be pitch black here ... nae chance o bein seen.' There were two exits, we took the one that led to Laing Street. Zander pointed to a row of houses a short distance away. 'See that hoose there, number twelve, ma uncle Rab lives there. Al be waitin in there lookin oot fir yae. Soon as a see yae, al open the front door. Haun me the rucksack wi the dough in it then bolt up the road. Yae got it?'

'This is aw a bit heavy, Zander, is it no?'

Pouncing on me and brandishing the blade in front of him, he said, 'Nobody shafts me like they huv. Yae think it's acceptable fir them tae bump me? This is aboot putting a marker doon ... revenge. The money is a wee bonus for us. Av got yir back, Connor. Yae better hiv mine.'

'But wit if he tackles me, Zander?'

'You're the wan wi the blade. No him. If you were walking oot a tenement an yae felt a blade in yir back, wid you try an put up a fight?'

'Naw, but am no a Bannerman.'

'He's a dafty, Connor. Get a grip. Yil have a knife, he won't, end of.'

'Wit if he sees ma face, Zander?'

He looked to the sky and shook his head. 'Fuck's sake,

Connor, don't be stupit. Yil be wearin a balaclava. Soon as yae get oot o there, whip it aff, put it in the rucksack. Don't let me doon noo,' he said, raising an eyebrow and glaring until I flinched and looked away.

'Yae worry too much. Mon, al treat yae tae a bag o chips.'

Eleven

Saturday morning. I lay in bed. Another awful night's sleep. Forty-eight hours had passed since I had been given the briefing by Zander. Forty-eight long hours of hell. I felt as if a dark, toxic chemical had entered me. Gaining strength by the minute. Debilitating. Sucking the energy from me. I could think of nothing else. *Six days' time ... six days' time ... backing oot isnae an option ... can't let him down ... don't want tae go back tae being a nothin at school ... al need to screw the heid ... Zander's right ... am the wan wi the knife. A just needed a bit o time tae get my heid roon this ... Don't think aw that whispering in ma ear, laying it oan heavy shite helped. Al go back and check it aw oot on ma own this time. Aye, that's a plan.* Feeling a little more at ease, I picked up the remote control and tuned into *SMTV Live*. Even my infatuation with Cat Deeley failed to provide any lasting respite. I needed to revisit the lane.

What was I thinking? The choice of clothes for the recce were hardly inconspicuous. A bright lemon-yellow Ben Sherman polo shirt with a pair of multi-coloured Air Jordans. Heading towards the Big Backs, I cast a glance at twelve Laing Street where I would hand over the bag to Zander. A large kickabout was underway. I acknowledged a handful of the participants. Crossing the main road, I made my way towards the chapel grounds. Passing through the gothic-style, large, wrought iron gates, I admired the beautifully manicured gardens. *Wit a cracking game o football yae could have on this ... it's like a bowling green.* Numerous oval shaped, colourful flower beds were planted in various parts of the lawn. Making my way over to the side that faced the tenement in question, I spent a few minutes familiarising myself, absorbing the details in my mind. Back through the gates, I turned right onto the lane then walked into the tenement, returning to the exact spot from a couple of days previously. I stood for what seemed to me a minute at most – Zander's whispering voice replayed in my mind. Suddenly, the front door of the flat on the right opened. An elderly woman peeked her head out. 'What you doing in here? Are you the one that's been urinating at the back door? Twice this week I've had to mop it up.'

'Naw missus, a wiz … a wiz … eh … aye … a wiz just looking for my dog an a wiz just seeing if the back door was open.' Head down, I fled by her as fast as I could.

'This isn't a kennels or a urinal either so clear off and don't let me see you in here again,' she shouted at my back.

Aye, magic. Just my luck, a right nosy auld cow.

***

Five long days passed. There had been no sight or word from Zander. Despite clearing my mind and coming to terms with what was being asked of me, a large part of me hoped the plan was scrapped. Some sort of divine intervention. *Maybe he has been caught doing something else.* In my heart I knew it was wishful thinking. *He'll be in touch today, no doubt. Probably just lying low and organising everything.*

Later that afternoon, strolling towards the area that the teachers dubbed 'rogues gallery', I felt a tap on my shoulder that made me jump out of my skin. 'Bottttlllleddddd it.'

'Don't fuckin creep up on people like that.'

'Chill, wee man. Here yae go, another love letter fae yer boyfriend. Catch yae.'

I opened the note. *'Hauf seven the nite at 12 Laing Street, uncle Rab is oot.'*

Eyes closed, I muttered to myself, 'Wish to fuck this was over.'

***

Standing at the front door, I took a sharp intake of breath then emitted our familiar whistle and waited. The door was yanked open. I was met with the sight of a figure holding a knife and wearing a black balaclava with the eyes crudely cut out of it. The balaclava was whipped off, revealing Zander looking somewhat pleased with himself. 'Aw-rite, wee man. Fuckin scary sight intit. Imagine comin doon a flight o stairs an catchin that oot the corner o yer eyes, then ya feel the knife in yer back. Mon in.'

I stepped into a small, square vestibule area with a glass door to my immediate right that led into the living room. Bare floorboards were covered with newspaper pages containing evidence of a dog whose walks were being neglected. I was assaulted by an eye-watering stench. 'Sake, Zander, it's mingin in here. Is there no somewhere else we can go?'

'Aye, it's no a palace but see that letterbox there?' Zander said, pointing at the front door. 'That swallies giros like an auld alky swallies Special Brew. By the way, ma uncle Rab hears yae disrespectin his gaff, you'll be eating that shite, Connor.'

'Gonnae hurry up an tell mi wits wit then, Zander, afore a spew.'

He handed me a black le coq sportif rucksack. 'Everythin yae need is in there.'

Unzipping it, he pulling out a balaclava, then an impressive looking knife which I took no time in familiarising myself with.

'Right, yae got any questions yae want tae ask?'

'Naw ... wait in the chapel grounds ... couple o minutes till he goes up the stairs ... wait in same bit as the other day ... soon as he is doon the stairs ... knife in his back an say, "Money now."'

'Exactly.'

'Actually, a do have a question. Wit if he recognises my voice?'

'Hiv yae ever spoke to him? Naw, a didnae think so. A don't imagine him or any o his family hiv ever took a blind bit o notice of yae, Connor.'

'Wit if he says, "Naw, yer no getting any money"?'

'Wit if… Wit if… C'mon get a grip, Connor. That wilny happen.'

'It's aw-rite fir you, Zander. Yir over a year aulder than me, and a good head bigger than me. Yir stronger than me and yir used tae this kinda stuff.'

'Connor, trust me, havin a knife held at yir back, can turn a big strappin guy intae a gibberin wreck. He's mer likely to shite himself than tackle yae.'

'Right, OK. I'm gonnae head up the road afore a top up the rankomoter in here with a puddle o vomit.' I pinched my nose as I stepped out the front door of that shit-hole. 'See yae here the morra, Zander.'

'Jist keep calm. Stick to wit we've spoke aboot.' Zander gave me a fist bump. 'An mind wit a sed, *don't* let me doon, Connor.'

Twelve

It was four o'clock. I sat on the edge of my bed playing *Doom*. My character had been led to a portal to hell. Gun in hand, he tried to fend off insatiable, greedy, ghost-like figures. My day had been excruciating. Wakened by my body jerking as if on the receiving end of an electric shock. When I opened my eyes, I tried to remember what I'd been dreaming about that had caused me to be jolted from sleep in this manner. As was the norm these last few days, my first cognitive thought of the day was 'the joab' as Zander frequently called it. My only concerns were the two things that were out of my control. Firstly, sheer chance. A workman carrying out work in the tenement. The old curtain twitcher and her neighbour standing at their front doors gossiping or somebody going out to empty their bins. The second was the greater concern. Bannerman's reaction. What if he just ran away as soon as I ordered him to hand over the money. What then? What if he screamed for help? He might attack me. Whilst I knew I was more than capable of keeping my side of the bargain, these external scenarios that played around in my mind unnerved me. No matter how many times I put 'it' to the back of my mind throughout the day, 'it' always regained control.

Totally engrossed in the game, I only became aware that Dad had entered my bedroom when I heard him say, 'If you're not doing anything tonight, I'm going to the greyhound racing if you fancy it?'

I attempted to maintain my concentration on the game, making no eye contact with him. 'Sorry, goin out.'

'OK, no bother. I'll give you a shout when your dinner's ready, son.'

An hour or so later, having finished dinner, I returned to my bedroom to resume the game of *Doom*. I heard Dad walk down the hallway and shout, 'Right, Connor, I'm off to the dogs. Mind and lock the door when you go out and make sure you're back for ten.'

The front door slamming shut was the catalyst for me to spring from bed. Rummaging in the wardrobe, I eventually found the rucksack. In a place so safe I almost couldn't find it. I grabbed the balaclava and went to the mirror to try it on. Satisfied that I could see properly and that it fit, I stuffed it back into the rucksack, then began to dress. It was nearly time.

***

Walking slowly, fully aware that arriving at the chapel too early would increase the wait and therefore the tension, I passed Zander's uncle's house. Convinced I saw someone peeking through the blinds, my thoughts turned to the disgusting living room. *How could Zander spend any time in there and why hadn't he cleaned the place up? Wait a minute, a didnae even see or hear a dog in the hoose. With the amount o shite, there's no way the dog was oot. It obviously disnae get oot. Fuck sakes, Connor, think o something else!*

Heading through the Big Backs, I was relieved to see that it was perfectly quiet with nobody around. A couple of minutes after crossing the main road I arrived at the chapel gates. On entering, another bit of chance that I hadn't thought of came to me. *What if there's something on in the chapel tonight? Confession maybe.* Creeping about in the grounds of the chapel with people coming and going would prove problematic. As I squatted down, peering through the railings at the tenement, I hoped Zander's timings were spot on. *Anything could happen. He might collect his money the morra instead.* I pictured myself in confession. *Bless me, Father for I have sinned. It's been too long fir me tae remember when ma last confession was. Yae see, Father, since a heard ma fuckin hypocritical, church-goin mother confess that she planned on havin an abortion – which am pretty sure isny allowed – a haven't been back. She accepts the Body of Christ inside her. She wisnae so keen on the Body of Connor inside her. No doubt if she comes tae confession and says a few Hail Marys, you'll forgive her. Forgive me, Father, but a can't.* I was roused from my daydream by the sight of Bannerman and his bright orange newspaper-bag. I watched him enter the tenement. Waiting until I saw my target climbing the stairs, I then quickly vaulted the fence and made my way to the tenement entrance. Arriving in position, I searched for the balaclava. The aroma of homemade soup wafted through the building. I heard Bannerman knocking on a door on the floor above.'Paper money please, Mrs Paterson,' I heard, as I pulled the balaclava over my face and adjusted it.

'Sorry, son, you'll need to come back another day.' The door slammed shut. I heard Bannerman mutter something, probably cursing the non-payer but couldn't make out exactly what.

Another door chapped. 'Paper money please, Mrs Grant.'

'Hi, son, I've got it here… There you go, Scott. See you next week.'

'Thanks a lot. See yae next week, Mrs Grant.'

I became aware of the smell of my own breath then felt some moisture forming on my face.

Finally, steps on the stairs. Bannerman was on his way.

I became aware of my breathing becoming more and more audible. I felt claustrophobic. *Stay calm, Connor*, I pleaded with myself, looking at the knife.

As the Adidas Gazelle trainers negotiated the last step, I pounced forwards, prodding the knife against Bannerman's back.'Money, NOW!'

No answer was forthcoming. Ten seconds or so passed before a loud voice that caused me to shudder echoed through the tenement. 'Dae yae know who I am?'

'Money. Now,' I reiterated. Embarrassed at the lack of threat compared to my first effort.

Bannerman was acting like a veteran of this type of situation. 'A … asked … yae … a … question.'

I shook the rucksack, attempting to make Bannerman aware of it. 'Aye a know yer name, put the money in there now, *Bannerman.*'

'Dae yae think yir gony get away wi this? Me and ma

brothers will get yae and wen we dae you're a fuckin deid man.'

I pressed the knife forwards. 'Am no gonnae ask yae again.'

Bannerman laughed. 'You're no gonnae use that knife, *you* know that an *a* know that.'

I trembled. This voice that was taunting was also echoing through the tenement.

I knew I wasn't being taken seriously. My anger soared at the contempt he was showing me. What happened to me being the one with all the power? I gritted my teeth. 'Last chance, am losing patience,' I said, with all the authority I could muster.

'Fuck off … yer no gettin anythin. Tell yae wit, the back door will be open; leave the noo an we'll leave it at that. That's yer only way oot.'

'Don't fuckin tell me wit tae do! I'm the wan in charge here, Bannerman.' I heard my own voice go a pitch higher. Truly pathetic sounding.

'Aye right, so yae are, ya clown.'

At that exact moment a light appeared in the hallway behind the door nearest us. *Fuckin hell, someone's coming*. A black curtain fell across my eyes for a split second. *Do something. Something…anything*. I panicked. The knife plunged into Bannerman's buttocks three times. As the scream echoed through the building, I fled. Pausing briefly at the mouth of the tenement, I heard a door open then an elderly female voice, 'What the hell is going on out here?' I glanced back at the sight that would meet her. Bannerman on his knees, leaning on one elbow, his free hand patting his buttocks, examining the blood on his hand.

Shit. Shit. Oh no. Oh God, wit have a done. Cars travelled in both directions. I sprinted over the main road, dodging them as I disappeared into the Big Backs. I pulled off the balaclava, clutching it in my hand. *Shit, wit ma doin, I'm still holding the knife*. I threw it aimlessly into the distance. *Why did he no just do what he was told? Wit am I gonnae do? Zander. Zander. He'll sort it*. Reaching Laing Street I saw him, my saviour, scurrying around at the front door.

He ushered me in. 'Fuck, fuck, I've stabbed him. He widnae listen to me. A telt yae, Zander. I knew this would happen. Yae should've listened.'

A callous, satisfied smile appeared. Zander threw his arm around my shoulder. 'Slow doon. Wit happened, wee man?'

I shrugged his arm off me, unable to stay still. 'It was fine until he came doon the stairs. He kept telling me a wisnae gonnae dae anythin.' I shuffled from foot to foot. 'He was takin the piss oot o me, then the auld wummin fae the last time's light went oan … an a … an a … a knew she was gonnae open the door … a knew it. A panicked and knifed him in the arse a few times,' I said, gesticulating frantically. 'A threw the knife away in the Big Backs.'

Zander's demeanour changed in a nanosecond. 'Wit yae mean – the old wummin fae the last time?' He took one step forwards.

I was scratching my head as if I had lice. 'Shit, sorry. Oh naw. Zander, a forgot tae tell yae.' I tried to compose myself. 'A went fir a recce a few days ago and the nosy old bastard opened her door an accused me o pishin at her back door.'

Zander grabbed me by the throat. 'Ya stupit little dick. She's seen yae … yae didnae think tae tell me this afore? … and yae jist tossed the knife away in the Big Backs.' He whispered menacingly, as he pinned me against the door, 'This disnae come back tae me. If it diz … it won't be yer arse that a stab. Get the fuck oot o here, ya useless wee dick. Don't come roon here or mine, ever again.' He threw me out and slammed the door shut.

I stood looking at the door. Stunned. My eyes moist with tears, not of self-pity or hurt but anger. The realisation that Zander was discarding me like a piece of shit. *He wiz supposed tae sort it; he wis supposed tae be my mate. We had each other's backs*. I bit on my bottom lip in an effort to stop the tears from flowing.

I turned and ran. I felt like I wanted to run and run and never stop.

No wonder I'm so fucked up.

Thirteen

A curious need for a hot water bottle had been satisfied. *Wonder when I last used one of these*? Trying not to acknowledge the fact I was probably using it as a comforter. I still loved that distinctive smell of hot rubber when pouring the boiling water in. Though the pleasure could be ruined when the bottle neared capacity and started coughing its contents up like Vesuvius. *You should get a pair o industrial worky gloves when you buy wan o these.* I was relieved to come home to an empty house. Dad still at the dogs, Mum at the bingo. I lay in bed digesting everything that had happened. When my parents returned home, I pretended to be asleep.

Hour after hour passed, staring at the ceiling. Numb. In a moment of weakness, I wished I could be comforted by my mother. Perhaps even confide in her. *Get a grip, this is bad, but if I told her, she'd probably shop me in just to try and get rid of me. I can just picture it, 'Hello, Crimestoppers, I've got some information about the assault on the paperboy that got stabbed in the arse. Aye, my name is Mary Boyd.'*

'What is the name of the person you believe carried out the attack, Mrs Boyd?'

'It was Connor Boyd.'

'Daft question, Mrs Boyd, but I take it he's not any relation to yourself?'

'Aye, he's related. He's my son! Anyway, how much do a get for this when he gets found guilty? See the thing is, with him gone, I can leave my idiot of a husband ... so a nice deposit for a flat would be great.'

I chuckled at the scenario. My thoughts turned to Zander. It wasn't on the same level as how I felt about my mum but I felt crushed by my fake pal's actions. As I replayed it in my mind it became worse. Ashamed, as the realisation hit me that I'd been used like a puppet. I tried to think about the possible repercussions, but was clueless as to what kind of punishment I would serve if caught.

Sleep was impossible. Endless thoughts hijacked my mind. Each one more irrational than the last. I slammed my hand against my temple as another, *What if?* rolled through. Checking the alarm clock, I saw that it was quarter to two in the morning. *I can't think straight ... I just need some sleep.* The futility of seeking something resembling peace of mind. Drunks could be heard singing in the distance. As the noise came closer, I got out of bed and looked out the curtains to see one of our neighbours, Tam Campbell, walking as if enduring gale force winds. Campbell was singing, 'Diz yir ma drink wine? Diz she drink it aw the time? Diz she get a funny feeling wen her tits are touching the ceiling? Diz yir ma drink wine?'

The sight of him trying to make it home brought some much-needed relief. Getting back into bed, I realised there was no getting away from what had happened. Sleep was impossible until I cleared my head. *If I can get away with this, I'll get my heid down, keep away from Zander, Mum and anybody else that causes me grief. Aye, I'll stick to myself. People only cause problems. You can't trust anybody. Aye, that's it. If I get caught then so what, it's another thing that'll have her in tears. Aye, sorted ... back to school Monday and get the head doon.* Exhaustion eventually won. I fell into a deep slumber.

***

An uneventful weekend passed quickly. A trip to the game with Dad on Saturday then on Sunday I had most of the morning and early afternoon to myself as Mum and Dad went to chapel, carrying out the pretence that they were a normal loving couple. I pictured her receiving the sacrament and shook my head in disgust. She had given up trying to drag me along to chapel. My parents even had a routine where they would go for a fry-up together afterwards. Sometimes I'd wish

I could be a fly on the wall watching them. Poor Dad trying to spark up a conversation, Mum nipping it in the bud. He would then look for someone he knew or a pair of friendly eyes, engaging in small talk with them. Sunday night dragged in as it always did.

'The telly is rank on a Sunday night,' I complained to my dad. 'Look, Dad … Wan … *Last of the Summer Wine* … Two … some eejit jumping aboot a field whistling at his dug … Three … *London's Burning*—'

'I wish it was, we would be rid of that lot down in Westminster,' he interrupted.

'Four … boring documentary … Five—'

'Aye forget about Five,' he said, snatching the remote from me.

'How come? What's on Five?' I teased.

'Never you mind.'

'Right, am goin tae ma room.'

'Connor, speak properly; you're starting to sound like a ned,' he snapped.

'As you wish, Father. Jolly spiffing weekend I have had, however, I shall retire to bed now as I have somewhat of an early rise tomorrow. Goodnight, Father.'

I ensured I left it as late as possible before leaving for school. The plan was to get there just as the bell went. Straight into class. Lie low at morning break in a different part of the school. Lunch at home. Heading to my first class, I bumped into Tony McGrory. 'Aw-rite Connor, wit's happening?'

'Nowt,' I snapped.

'Whit's up wi yae this morning, ya nippy wee shite?'

'Wit is it, Tony?'

'Yae seen much o Zander?'

My attention was aroused. 'Naw, you?'

'Naw, av no seen him in yonks … wide berth, Connor. A wiz starting to get a bit worried how he wiz acting. A mean we aw like a laff an that but he wiz startin tae take it too far.'

Reaching the classroom, I thought, *Aye, cheers for that, Tony. Bit late for the advice, maybe.*

Morning classes passed without incident. Lunch was a

bowl of cheesy pasta at home whilst watching the snooker at the Crucible with Dad. 'It must be hard for him, Connor, check the size of his chin – it's rubbing off his cue!'

'Quality name though, Dad ... Alain Robidoux.'

'Not a fan, Connor,' he said, between spoonfuls of pasta. 'He looks like a skinnier version of the Yorkshire Ripper.'

'Av heard of Jack the Ripper, not the Yorkshire Ripper.'

'Peter Sutcliffe ... he was a serial killer called the Yorkshire Ripper.'

'Peter Sutcliffe sounds more like a snooker player than Alain Robidoux.' I mimicked whispering Ted Lowe, '"It's Peter Sutcliffe over the black, he has this to reach the quarter finals." Would be a cracking nickname as well, Dad, "It's Jimmy 'The Whirlwind' White v Peter 'The Yorkshire Ripper' Sutcliffe."'

Dad laughed. 'Don't let your mum hear you saying that! It's a wee bit ... a wee bit ... sick. Totally sick. Funny *but* sick.'

Dreading the next period after lunch, I headed back to school. Everyone hated it. Religious Education. Mrs Farrell, the most enthusiastic, jolly-hockey-sticks teacher in the school. A black tight perm and bad acne that looked greasy with Vaseline – not a good combination.

'Good afternoon, boys and girls. We are going to discuss Mother Teresa of Calcutta today,' she said, rubbing her hands, her face radiating with pleasure at the prospect. 'So can anyone tell me anything about Mother Teresa?' Not a single hand raised, as per usual. She was interrupted by a knock on the classroom door. A member of staff from the office beckoned her out of the room. When she returned, she announced that all the boys were to go to the Assembly Hall for some sort of talk. 'Right, boys. Form a line, forget about jackets and bags, let's go. Girls, behave for Miss Mortimer.'

The boys began discussing the likelihood of another sex education lesson. One of my classmates piped up, 'It's gonnae be the auld baws on the spoon and cough malarkey.'

I slapped him on the back of the head. 'Aye, we're aw gonnae get oor baws oot in the middle of the assembly room stupid. It'll be the auld johnny bag discussion, no doubt.'

When we reached the Assembly Hall I saw all the second-year boys coming out of the hall glum-faced. Questions as to what it was all about were rebuffed by the teachers who led their boys back to class. The new batch were made to wait a few minutes before we were escorted into the hall. Chairs, in rows of ten, had been placed with a couple of feet between each row. My class were first in, followed by the other third-year class. As soon as we settled, a tall, suited, polished-looking man appeared and began to make his way to the front, flanked by the head teacher. Murmurings started amongst us before Mr Lewis demanded silence.

'Good afternoon, boys. My name is Detective Inspector Robertson. These are my two colleagues, PC Allan and PC Wilson,' he said, pointing at the door through which we had just entered. 'Now, some of you may be aware that there was an incident involving a local paperboy on Friday night. Our investigations thus far have led us to believe that the person responsible for that attack is a boy around the age of you boys here. The victim is still in hospital, but we have a witness who saw a boy acting suspiciously a few days before the attack, in the exact place the attack occurred. This visit today is part of a visit to all secondary schools of all denominations throughout the area.'

My breathing became frantic. *I'm done for. Shit. Shit.*

'So we are going to bring the witness in and ask that you just sit in your seats and stay *still*. This will take five minutes or so, boys. Thank you for your co-operation.' He nodded to the two PCs. The old curtain twitcher emerged, dressed as if attending Sunday Mass. Her best coat and hat. She walked to the front, an arm locked in one of the PC's.

The giant Assembly Hall had shrunk to the size of a toilet cubicle. The walls were closing in on me. *Please, please don't let her pick me out.* I started fidgeting, struggling to keep my legs still. Hands rested on my knees. Then clasped before shoving them under my thighs in the hope that they would stay still. I lowered my head. The witness stepped forwards and slowly but surely, as if her life depended on it, examined the faces of the first row of ten before advising the inspector that it was a negative thus far. She was led to the second row. Sitting in the row behind, I thought, *This is it. Look how long she is taking, she must have seen me.* Row two was done. The inspector nodded his head, giving the go ahead for the next row. She passed seat one ... seat two ... seat three. 'That's him! That's him, Inspector!' A long bony finger that resembled a twiglet. 'I'm one hundred per cent sure. That's the boy.'

Heads turned and twisted as the boys all panned in on the accused. The head teacher accompanied Detective Inspector Robertson 'Are you sure that you don't want to examine the others as well?' the inspector asked her.

'Inspector, I've told you, *that* is the boy.'

Robertson smiled at her. 'Thank you. You have been a great help.' She was escorted away, holding the arm of the PC.

The head teacher stared at my exhausted but relieved looking face before ordering me to stand. I was steered out of the room by him and D I Robertson.

PART TWO

One

I fantasised about this day for so long. Emerging from the chrysalis of boyhood with a fierce determination to get as far from my mother as quickly as possible. The sooner I moved out and got away from her the better it would be for everyone. My anger hadn't dissipated. If anything it gained strength. Desperate to rid myself of the past and all the baggage that weighed me down. Out of sight, out of mind. A new start. Things could change for people overnight. Look at the attack at Glasgow airport a couple of weeks earlier. John 'Smeato' Smeaton. Just picturing him in my mind makes me smile. What a legend. In the space of twenty-four hours, he went from being a baggage handler to being famous all over the world. *This is Glasgow. We'll just set aboot yae.* Fucking priceless.

Having left school under a cloud with no qualifications, I knew that the first step to freedom was to pass my exams. I enrolled at college and successfully passed six out of six Standard Grade exams which allowed me to enrol in a year-long business, marketing and communications course. The hard work had been done and I was about to head off to college. The one thing I truly craved in life was about to be realised.

It was early afternoon on a Saturday in August. My snider of a Nokia vibrated in my pocket as I finished placing the last of the boxes in the hallway.

'Hi, Greg. How's things? OK, good stuff, just press the buzzer. My gear is ready. Yeah, I'm good to go.'

I shouted towards the living room, 'Dad, that's Greg here. I'm just putting a box across the front door to keep it open, so I can get in and out.'

My parent's appeared in the hallway, offering their help.

'It's fine. I don't have a lot and we've got it covered,' I said, pointing at Greg, who had made his way up the stairs.

'Hi, Mr and Mrs Boyd. Pleased to meet you both,' Greg said, shaking their hands.

Gerry smiled at Greg. 'Pleased to meet you at last, son. I was starting to think Connor had made you up.'

What a fucking red-neck! I looked to the floor, shaking my head.

'Yes, pleased to meet you, Greg,' said a glum-faced Mary. 'Thanks for helping Connor with his stuff. We did offer but I suppose it's not cool to be seen with your parents.'

Greg and I had met at college. Drawn to each other because the other students in our classes were old enough to be our parents. The mature students who had failed first time around didn't interest us. Fair play to them for seeking out another chance but Greg and I bonded over our love of The Klaxons, Kasabian, Football, and the shared excitement of the door to the world being opened to us in a few months when we would both turn eighteen. Greg was confident. Comfortable in his own skin. The type of guy I want to be like. I was happy to listen and learn from my new pal as we breezed through our exams together. Until now, we would hang out at Greg's as I regarded home as a no-go area for friends.

'What's the name of the street you boys are moving to, Greg?' Mary enquired. She didn't miss an opportunity. As cunning as a con artist. I'd been evasive when she had asked me about my address so she chanced her arm with Greg.

'Oh, I forget, Mrs Boyd. It's in the West End, just off Great Western Road. I just know how to get there. I'm from the south side.' I knew her inside out so I'd pre-warned Greg not to give out the address to her, using the ruse that it was because Mother would make regular spot checks.

'I've told you before,' I snapped, 'soon as I'm settled, I'll give you the address. If you need to get a hold of me, you have my mobile number. Right, Greg, let's start with these boxes.'

Reaching Greg's little Renault Turbo, I opened the back door and placed the two boxes inside.

'I'm detecting some friction between you and your mum,' Greg commented, as he took a couple of boxes from me.

'Yeah. We don't exactly see eye to eye. Let's leave it at that, Greg. She isn't going to spoil this day for me. This is going to be a great day.' I threw my arm around Greg's shoulder. 'Right, one more load, then we can go and meet our flatmates.'

Finally, the last of my belongings were safely in the boot of the car. I rolled my eyes. 'Give me a minute, Greg. Better say my goodbyes.'

'Don't even think of getting into my jalopy all red-eyed or bubbling.'

'Tears shall be shed ... tears of joy. Back in a minute.' Bounding up the stairs, two at a time, I was struggling to contain my excitement.

A callous smile spread over my face. *Here we go.* I punched the air.

As I entered the hallway, it was obvious to me that Mother had been crying. Doing her best Bette Davis routine. Dad had his arm around her. His hand clutched her shoulder. I looked at her puffy eyes. *Still putting a show on, eh Mary? Take your mask off. You've been counting down the days for years. Lap up your moment.*

'Right, that's me off, Dad.' Smiling, arms outstretched beckoning him forwards for a hug. We patted one another's backs as if we were choking on food. 'You take care of yourself, son.' Dad released me from the embrace and headed to the living room. Over the years, I had gradually transferred the love I used to have for my mother to my father. My basic human need for love had overpowered the disrespect that I'd previously had for my father's work-shy, doormat-like nature. I was genuinely going to miss my dad.

I approached *her*. Rewarding her with a cold, limp hug as I whispered to her, 'You've got your life back.' As she tried to break from me, I prevented her by holding her as tightly as I could. 'You don't need to worry about me anymore. Enjoy the freedom.' I quickly released her, turned back down the hallway and shouted, 'Bye, Dad.' Slamming the door shut. Closing my eyes, fists clenched, basking in the elation fizzing through me. I imagined Mother frozen to the spot, open-mouthed. A satisfied smile broke out as I sprinted down the stairs.

We drove away, windows down, music pounding to some daft novelty record about dogs woofing. Laughter echoed from the car. I looked out the window, the satisfied smile not yet ready to depart. Delighted with my little speech. *That's it done. No more wasting energy on her.*

'So, Greg, what do you reckon these two flatmates will be like?'

'Not got a clue. Tell you what though. We all need to get on. Get used to each other's habits and stuff. You got any disgusting habits I should know about?'

I laughed. 'You'll soon find out.'

Arriving at the old sandstone tenement building, Greg said, 'Right, fingers crossed, buddy. Let's go and meet them first, make sure they're not a pair of weirdos before we move our gear in.' The flat was on the top floor. The controlled-entry system was redundant as the door had obviously come off second best with an angry keyless tenant. Temporary nameplates in paper form were taped to the various buzzers. Pen marks put through names of former flatmates. A beautiful spiral staircase weaved through the centre of the building. A single row of Rennie-Mackintosh-style wall tiles decorated each landing. The smell of freshly washed stairs and floors pervaded the air as we made our way to the top floor and the next chapter of our lives.

Greg took the lead, chapping on the storm door that led to the front door. We heard the front door open, then the storm door swung back. 'Hi. I'm Greg. This is Connor. We're moving in today.'

'Excellent. The flatmates,' said the guy, shaking imaginary pistols at us. 'Pleased to meet you, guys. I'm Justin.' He waved us into the hallway. We would soon learn that Justin was from Rothesay. He clearly suffered from rosacea. His brown hair was swept straight back, he had a button nose and small beady eyes. His features appeared too small for his face, as though they still had some catching up to do. 'In you come, guys, I'll introduce you to the last member of The Fantastic Four, Luca the Italian Stallion.'

He led us along the dozen yards or so of the hallway into the living room. 'Luca, these are our flatmates, Greg and Connor.'

Luca was one of those guys who made everything look effortlessly cool. His clothes, his messy, jet-black hair. Even his John-Travolta walk.

As we shook hands, Justin said, 'Fancy a wee can to celebrate, guys?' pulling the ring-pull of an imaginary can as he made a psssshhhhtttt sound.

'I think it's our duty,' answered Greg.

Justin returned with four cans of Tennent's. 'Here we go, guys.' He placed them on the table. 'The first of many bevvies,' he announced as he pretended to be drinking from two imaginary pints. The cans were handed out and the small talk began. What course are you on? Where are you from? What team do you support? What music are you into?

When the small talk was over, Luca stood. 'I made a big slab of lasagne, guys. If you are hungry, I can heat it up?'

Greg looked at me then back to Luca. 'I knew we were gonnae get on, Luca.'

'That'd be great, Luca. You into cooking then?' I asked.

'My grandparents are Italian. *Il Cucchiaio d'Argento* and all that. My parents have a couple of restaurants so I was taught how to cook from an early age,' he explained, before he left for the kitchen.

'So, Justin, when did you move in and when did you meet Luca?' I asked.

'I moved in on Thursday and that was the first we met.' He struggled to contain his excitement. 'We've landed on our feet here, guys. Homemade meatballs the size of fucking snooker balls yesterday,' he said, potting an imaginary snooker ball. 'None of the typical student Pot Noodle or beans on toast garbage for us.' He rose from the sofa. 'It's a double dunter for me. He can cook *and* he's a right good-looking guy. So, I'll be eating his grub,' he said, using an imaginary knife and fork, 'then on a night out, I'll be feasting on the crumbs from his table, if you know what I mean.' He placed his hand across his midriff, thrusting his buttocks backwards and forwards.

Greg and I were laughing when Luca re-emerged. 'Twenty minutes, guys. Justin been keeping you entertained?'

'You don't want to know,' I answered.

'Here, guys,' said Luca, flicking his hand through his hair, 'about two minutes after meeting Justin, I thought of his nickname. You two thought of anything yet?'

We looked at each other then, in unison, shouted, 'Action Man.'

'Bullseye, exactly what I was thinking.'

'What's that all about? I don't get it,' asked Justin innocently.

Greg sprang from the armchair. 'You having a laugh, Justin? Who does the dishes here?' Greg mimicked washing an imaginary plate. 'And who takes a Hoover to the carpet?' He strode up and down the living room with an imaginary Hoover as laughter erupted throughout the room.

Two

Opening my eyes, I tried to make sense of my surroundings. My eyeballs felt as though someone was playing ping-pong with them. Stretching my arms upwards, I became aware of my tongue which felt like it was glued to the roof of my mouth. The realisation that I was in bed in my new home, made me smile as a favourite song of mine about being free to do whatever the hell I wanted popped into my head. The smell of bacon wafted through the air. For me, it felt like getting a cuddle and being told everything was going to be alright. I slid out of bed in slow motion and got dressed. Opening the bedroom door, I heard the crackling of the frying pan and the voice of Action Man emanating from the kitchen. The few steps from my bedroom to the kitchen felt like an expedition.

'Whoa, Connor, you look rough. You sleep alright?' Justin tilted his head resting it on the imaginary pillow that was his hands.

I did a double take. A cat's face and a pair of spectacles, coloured in with a black marker pen, adorned Justin's face. I had no recollection of who had carried out the defacement or when. Eventually, I answered, 'I've felt better, that's for sure.' Speaking was a chore for me. I sat at the kitchen table, facing Justin. Luca appeared, looking fresh. 'Morning, buddy. Full Scottish to sort you out?'

Music to my ears. 'You're a legend, Luca.'

'I've just woken Greg, breakfast will be a couple of minutes,' he said, then started to sing about what a beautiful day it was.

'Not in my world, it's not,' I moaned.

Justin puffed his chest out. 'See what happens when you drink with the Rothesay boys.'

'What dirty bastard was sick in the bathroom sink and didn't clean it up?' Greg shouted, entering the kitchen and stifling a laugh when he noticed Justin's feline features.

'Wasn't me,' I answered.

'Nor me,' confirmed Luca.

The three of us looked at Justin.

'Sorry, guys, I was sick during the night. I'll clean it up after breakfast. I think it was that lasagne.'

Luca shot him a sideways glance, raised an eyebrow. 'Insult an Italian's cooking? You'll be sleeping with the fishes.'

Despite feeling awful, I couldn't help himself. 'See what happens when you drink with the Glasgow boys.'

'How you feeling, Greg?' asked Justin.

'Cat-atonic, pal. You?'

'Yeah fine. I had a scream last night.'

'Here we go, men.' Luca placed two plates of what looked like manna from heaven on the table, before returning with another two as he took a seat.

Greg patted him on the back. 'You'll make somebody a great wife one day, big guy.'

'Uuuhhh man, this is dynamite,' said Justin.

I looked at Justin. 'Right, let's have a sweep on how long biscuit-arse can hold on to this fry-up.'

Justin paused, his fork, embedded in a link sausage, pointing to the ceiling. 'No chance. This is staying put. This will act as a sponge for the drink at Manfred's party tonight.'

'You two coming?' asked Luca.

I shook my head. 'We've never met him. We can't just turn up at his party.'

'Don't be daft. Luca's never met him either. Friends of mine, are friends of Manfred's. C'mon it will be good for you to meet him.'

Placing my knife and fork on top of my unfinished food, I resigned myself to defeat. 'What's the name all about?'

Justin chuckled. 'Two minutes tops and it will soon become clear.'

We discussed the highlights from the previous night, then

Justin stood and placed his hands together in prayer.'Right, I'm off to chapel.'

Greg dipped a slice of toast in a small pool of tomato ketchup. 'Listen, don't worry about the sink, I'll clean it up. You get yourself to chapel, Justin.'

'You're a star, Greg. Right, I'm off then. See you guys later.' As the front door closed, the laughter began.

'Imagine the priest. He lifts the bread.' Luca was laughing so much he was struggling to finish his sentence. 'He looks up … he looks up … to see that eejit with his face painted as a cat wearing specs!'

'I can't believe he hasn't brushed his teeth. He can't have or he'd have seen his face. It's gonnae be interesting when he gets back,' I chipped in.

Greg took a large swig from the carton of fresh orange. 'Tell you what, that was an amazing job I did, considering how smashed I was.'

I headed back to my bedroom and searched my jeans pockets for my Nokia. Lying in bed, I checked my messages. Two messages.

Messaging
Paul
Hope the move went well Connor. Look after yourself. Keep in touch.
MILK
What was that all about? Don't know why u r thinking like that bout me. What have I done to make u say those things 2 me? I'm ur mum and I'll always b here 4 u. Please keep in touch. Luv Mum X

I'd saved my mum's number under MILK (Mother I'd Love to Kill) Sick but funny. I threw my mobile onto the carpet.

There was a knock on the bedroom door and Greg entered. 'Good guys aren't they?'

'Yeah. Big Luca is a different class and Justin cracks me

up.'

'Totally. You up for going to this party tonight then?'

'Absolutely. Going to get a few hours kip then I'll be up for it. We'll get Luca some beers for tonight to thank him for feeding us. I don't want him to think we are a pair of spongers.'

'Good idea, Connor. That's a nice touch. Right, see you later, buddy.'

***

The music was blaring. The party was in full swing, judging by the noise as we entered the tenement. Justin knocked on the door of the ground-floor flat. The door was opened by a guy wearing a South Park T-Shirt and black jeans. Long, thick, frizzy red hair tied back in a ponytail. He was extremely tall and thin with a giraffe-like neck. His brain appeared to suffer from a slow processing speed. 'Justin maaaaaan, good to see you,' he said in a sloth-like manner. 'Mon innnn.'

Justin embraced him and made the introductions. Manfred turned to me. 'So, maaaaan, how are you getting on together in the flat. Everything cooooool?'

'Yeah, all good, pal. Justin had a bit of a carry on at chapel today though, didn't you, mate?'

Before he could answer, Greg interrupted, 'Before you describe the carry *on*, is there somewhere I can put this carry-*oot*?'

'Course, maaaaaan, stick it on the kitchen worktop there. The fridge is full, maaaaan.'

Honestly, this guy was on a different time zone to everyone else. Beer would go flat by the time he finished his sentence. 'So, I'll cut it short,' said Justin. 'Massive session all day yesterday. Was pat and mick during the night. Gets up this morning, Luca has fry-up sorted for all of us. Fly man, Greg, distracts me from the bathroom, saying he'll clean up the mess I left in the sink, so I don't see a mirror before heading to chapel. Not many people about but the ones that are look at me funny. Into chapel, everything's fine. I get to the front of the queue for communion. Priest says 'Body of Christ' then looks at my face ... the bread is just hovering in no man's land, halfway between him and me. I've got my tongue out and I'm leaning forwards, trying to get it, straining my fucking neck. He's just looking at my face, not making any effort to put the bread in my mouth. I'm thinking, *This is weird*, so I just stuck my hands out and he put it in my hands. I go into the shop for a paper on the way home. Daft lassie is laughing. "You want some milk? You want some Whiskas? You fe-line OK?" So, I knew something was up. She fronts up and gives me a mirror from her handbag and I look like some psychedelic Cat in the Hat, minus the hat. One of these rogues has face painted me as a cat wearing specs.'

'So you went to chapel like that, maaaaaaan. No waaaaaay. Belter, maaaaan.'

Greg returned with the lager. Greg, Luca and I headed to the living room leaving the other two to their conversation.

The living room was huge. Easily over twenty people chatting or dancing.

A dance track boomed from the sound system amidst a healthy mix of males and females. Greg and Luca smiled at each other as I nervously scanned the room. 'I feel like a fucking jockey standing next to you two,' I shouted at my two friends who towered over me.

'Well, fingers crossed you're doing a bit of riding tonight, Frankie Dettori,' laughed Greg.

I had virtually no experience when it came to girls. What do you even talk about? I felt awkward around them. Had no idea where to start. My friends were the opposite. Watching them from afar, I wondered what their opening line was. What did they chat about? How did they know when a girl was interested? I checked out big Luca working his charm on probably the best-looking girl here. It's alright when you look like him though, isn't it. I told myself just to stay in the background, watch and learn, watch and learn.

A few minutes passed and I made my way into the kitchen for another drink. A girl stood leaning against the sink. Cigarette in hand, looking thoroughly miserable. *Nobody's watching. No time like the present. Give it a go, Connor*, I said to myself. 'Hi, how you doin? Can I get you a drink?' I asked, as I grabbed a beer.

'Yeah, on you go then. Vodka and coke please.'

Rummaging in the cupboards for a glass, I told myself to just be natural. Pouring the vodka, I turned to her. 'I'm Connor, by the way. What's your name?'

'Hi Connor, pleased to meet you. I'm Claire. Who you here with?'

I poured the coke into the glass then handed it to her. 'A few of my mates, there's four of us. We're all sharing a flat together for the year. You?'

'My friend, Mandy, dragged me along. She's in there playing tonsil tennis, no doubt. So, I'm left on my own in the kitchen having a quick puff, talking to strangers.'

I was just happy to be speaking to someone. 'Your friend the only person you know here?'

'Yeah.' She rolled her eyes.

I smiled at her. 'Well, you know me now, Claire.'

'Aaaaww, that's nice. So, what you studying, Connor?'

'Business, marketing and communications.'

She stubbed her cigarette out in the ashtray. 'I'm doing art.'

'Hey, coincidence or what,' Greg said, as he entered the kitchen with his conquest.

'So, you're back then,' Claire said to her friend.

Greg did the introductions. 'Connor, this is Mandy. Mandy, this is Connor.'

'Ohhh, hiya, Connor.' She turned to Greg. 'Your friend is a wee cutie, but not as cute as you.' She grabbed Greg's face in her hands and kissed him.

Eventually, she reluctantly pulled away. 'So, you two getting on alright, Claire?'

'Fine.'

'Cheers, handsome,' Mandy said as Greg handed her a shot which she threw down her throat then grabbed his hand. 'Let's go, big boy. I want to dance.' As he was led away, he winked at me.

'Unbelievable. She brings me to a party to try and cheer me up then dumps me barely half an hour after getting here.'
'She's enjoying herself. Why do you need cheering up?'
'Well, it's a long story but my boyfriend Blair…'
Oh man, I had so much to learn.

Three

There was no lightshade to soften the migraine-inducing brightness of the bulb dangling from the ceiling. Slumped on the worn and cracked black leather sofa, the *News at Six* providing some background noise, I turned to Greg, 'What're the people in your classes like, Greg?'

'Yeah OK, I suppose.'

'You should see some of the misfits in my class. Honestly. There's Billy, he must be about early forties. Face like a rat, moustache, big thick glasses. A right weird shape. You know that way when people look like they have a cushion stuffed down the front of their trousers below the belly. There's no way in the world he can see his boaby. He's got a horrible snorting laugh. To top it off, I kid you not, I've never smelt anything like it in my life … he smells like the worst toilet you've ever walked into in your life. I can barely focus when he chats to me. I zone out and just want him to do one.'

'Nasty,' said Greg laughing. 'Anybody else?'

I moved my legs from the sofa, stretched them out, rested my feet on the coffee table. 'Aye, wee Raymy but I call him Percy.'

Greg pulled off a sock and began clipping his toenails. 'Why Percy?'

'I'll give you an example of a standard phrase he uses in just about every lecture we're in. So according to Maynard Keynes, it's not an increase in spending *per se* that blah blah. It's not divorce *per se* that affects kids, it's the parents' behaviour. Honestly, it does my nut in. Percy this, Percy that. A few weeks ago, me and Gaz started betting each other a quid on how many times in the one week he'd say it. Last week he broke his record with a baker's dozen. Hey! Pick that up!' I said, as a toenail pinged in my direction.

'Calm down, Connor, it's only a toenail,' Greg said, laughing.

'Aye, but it's gross. Anyway, back to what I was talking about. There's an old guy called Andy. Must be about mid-fifties. What's he even doing at college at his age? He makes me look like I'm the height of Michael Jordan. He's like one of those weeble wobbles. Going bald but keeps that daft wee strand of hair in a dodgy side-parting. Tell you what though, he's some table-tennis player. The old shit beats me every day. Then there's big Gordon, he looks like a Greek god. Must be a total disappointment to his parents – he's from the Mearns yet he's at college with misfits like me, Billy and Andy. He's thick as mince, like that Tim Nice-But-Dim character.'

'Connor, you're so opinionated and fixated on what people look like. And ageist into the bargain.'

'I'm only having a laugh. Then there's Gaz. How he gets into his jeans is a mystery. They're painted on. Every single day, the same outfit. Winklepickers, black jeans, black biker jacket, and long hair tied back in a ponytail. All he talks about is Fields of the Nephilim or sex. Right moody shit as well. All sugar or shite. You don't know what you're getting from one day to the next. Moods wise, I mean, cos you do know what you're getting every day – the same outfit, that fucking Fields of the Nephilim crap and constant chat about him pumping his bird. If she even exists.'

My mobile phone rang, an incoming call from MILK. Looking to the ceiling, I shook my head and placed it back on the armrest.

Greg sniggered. 'Was that Billy phoning to see if you wanted to go for a pint?'

'I'd rather eat your toenails in a sandwich. We're going to the District Court tomorrow to sit and observe cases for our legal framework module. Might be interesting.'

'It's all the little petty cases that's heard there though,' Greg said, yawning.

'Petty can still be interesting. The extraordinary is in the ordinary. Where did I read that?' I asked myself aloud.

'Oprah Winfrey's autobiography. That's where all your little pearls of wisdom originate.'

'Where does this verbal diarrhoea come from, Greg?'

Smirking, Greg asked, 'What do you think you'll do at the end of the year?'

'Go straight to the HNC or HND, depending on my results.'

We heard a key in the door. 'Hope that's Luca so we can get dinner. I'm hank,' said Greg.

'Hey mambro, Luca Di Mambro … Hey mambro, Luca Di Mambro … Hey mambro … Luca Di Mambro,' we both sang as Luca entered the living room.

Luca shook his head. 'Let me guess. You two are waiting on me to organise dinner.'

'Don't be like that, big guy. Work your magic and we'll take you to the Union for a few pints as a thank you,' I offered.

'I've got stuff on tonight so I'll need to pass. I'll rustle up something quick.' He headed to the kitchen.

'Greg, maybe we should start taking our turn with the cooking. I don't want Luca thinking we're taking the piss. He doesn't look too happy.'

'Right, guys, rigatoni in a spicy pesto sauce. It'll be ready in half an hour,' Luca shouted from the kitchen.

Greg and I looked at each other and laughed. 'Scrap that,' I said. 'Rigatoni in a spicy pesto sauce. If Carlsberg did flatmates…'

***

I had ignored numerous calls from Mum and a couple from Dad. A couple of text messages each confirming all was well had failed to placate them. Two months had passed since I'd moved out. The thought of having to appease them with a visit felt like anticipating a trip to the dentist. My flatmates made no demands on me. There was no baggage. No history. Everything was easy-going and relaxed. A visit back home would try my patience. My stomach churned at the thought of it. This new life of mine was all that mattered to me. A trip to the dogs or to a match with Dad would have been fine. But no, he told me she wanted to see me. The machine-gun questioning that she fired at me tipped me over the edge; it got my blood boiling. I knew I needed to get it over with. A quick visit with the excuse that I need to do some studying. That was the plan.

As the bus made its way over the bridge to the south side of the city, a certain melancholy overcame me. The flat I shared with the lads was in a vibrant, bustling area with lots of students and young professionals. Now, as I viewed the area of the city I'd lived in for around three years, it seemed drab. Lifeless. Getting through the day looks like a chore for these people, I thought. I watched a leaf fall from a tree and land on the pavement. Analysing the many leaves glued to the pavement I turned my attention to the tree and the stubborn leaves that refused to let go. *Wonder why some of them jump ship and others hang on for dear life. Suppose it's the same as everything else in life, self-preservation. Survival of the fittest. Aahh,* I smiled. *Turning over a new leaf, that's where that phrase comes from.* My thoughts turned to my brother. I just couldn't help the way I felt. I tried. It was impossible to get over the fact that Paul was wanted. The blue-eyed boy, whereas I knew I was 'the accident'. An unwelcome addition to the family. When it came to Paul, I admit, at times, my judgement was clouded by envy and injustice. I kept him at arm's-length, despite Paul's best efforts. Paul being four inches taller than me didn't help matters.

Five minutes later, I walked meditatively along my parents' street, trying to avoid walking on the fallen leaves that decorated the pavement. My earlier musings had convinced me that they were animate objects. The sheer volume of them made avoidance an impossible task though so I satisfied myself with the crackling sound as I gave up and trod on the dry, brittle leaves. Trudging up the stairs I thought of the day, a few months ago, when I moved out. Despite having my own set of keys, I decided not to bring them. I wanted 'her' to feel like I was a visitor. I wanted to feel like a visitor. This wasn't home any more. Chapping the letterbox, I took a deep breath and waited. She answered, her face lit up at the sight of me. As fake as a stepford wife pretending to be pleased at finishing behind her bitter rival in an apple-pie baking contest. 'Oh, Connor!' she cried, throwing her arms around me.

'Hi, Mum,' I answered, giving her a miserly, half-hearted embrace. The realisation dawned on me that I despised uttering the word 'Mum'.

She looked me up and down. 'You look great.'

'Thanks, I'm eating better than I ever have. My flatmate Luca's parents are Italian. His cooking is a different class.'

I walked to the living room. Dad and Paul were sitting watching *Emmerdale*.

Paul rose from the sofa and we shook hands. Pangs of guilt nagged at me like toothache. None of this was his fault, it was hers. But still, it made me feel torn in two directions. 'How's student life treating you, wee fella?'

'I'm absolutely loving it thanks.'

'Alright, son, good to see you,' said Dad, stepping forwards to embrace me.

'You too, Dad.' We hugged then I took a seat next to him. He got up to turn the TV off.

'How's the job?'

'Fine, Dad. It's a little deli, selling all kinds of what you call "foreign muck". Full of Hooray Henrys with bad attitudes and bad dress sense. Were you at the game on Saturday?'

'Aye, we're getting entertained for a change, son. They're playing some good stuff the now.'

Mary returned, walking like a toddler, holding a large, wicker-basket-effect tray. Her expression showing that she was fiercely determined not to spoil her spread. Pulling out all the stops. Pots of tea and coffee with an assortment of cakes and biscuits. She poured Dad his tea then handed him the cup and saucer. Dad and Paul looked at each other, smirking at the seldom-seen, fancy tea set being brought out. 'Coffee, Connor?' she asked.

'Please.'

She poured my drink then offered a large plate, full of cakes and biscuits.

I raised my left hand, palm facing her. 'No thanks, I'm full. I've just had a massive plate of pasta. I couldn't eat another thing.' My pettiness knew no bounds. Fully aware of the trouble she went to and that she was trying to do the 'mother thing'.

She cocked her head. 'Surely you can make room for a cake or a biscuit, Connor?'

I shook my head. 'No thanks.'

Mary sat, crossed her legs, forced a smile. 'So, what're your new flatmates like, son?'

'Great. You've met Greg. Luca is the one that does the cooking and the other guy is Justin.'

'That doesn't tell me anything about them, son. What are they like?'

My eyes scanned the various framed family pictures throughout the living room. I was present in one solitary picture whereas Paul was omnipresent. 'They're nice.'

'How vague is that? Tell me a bit about them. Where are they from and stuff?'

I quickly turned to face her, the sheer tokenism of one solitary picture still on my mind. 'Jesus, what are you wanting? Photos and a copy of their CVs?' They're cracking guys, we get on great. Justin's from Rothesay and Luca is from Balfron.'

'Keep your hair on. I'm only asking, Connor.'

I turned to Dad, but she interrupted with another question.

'How are you finding college?'

'Yeah, great thanks.' *This is worse than I thought it'd be, surely, she'll run out of questions in a minute.*

'What's your neighbours like, Connor? Are they all students?' she asked.

I kept looking at the family photos, refusing to make eye contact. 'There's a mix, I think. We just mind our own business. We don't see much of them.'

Sensing my annoyance, Dad butted in, 'What was that question you were about to ask?'

'You still going to the dogs, Dad?'

'Aye, I was there a couple of weeks ago. We'll get a wee

night organised if you fancy it? You up for that, Paul?'

'Yeah that'd be good,' replied Paul, thumbing through *Empire* magazine.

Mother fiddled about in her handbag, eventually pulling out a diary and pen. 'What's your address? I'll stick it in my address book.'

'Why do you need my address? None of my flatmate's mums harass them for their address.'

'Connor, I've asked you for it numerous times. It's just peace of mind for me.'

'Well it's just a piece of nonsense for me. Be done with it and stick a tag on my ankle. Tell you what, we'll get a little video camera in the flat so you can keep an eye on me. You make me feel like Winston fucking Smith.'

'Calm down. You're so over the top. I'm only asking for your address. I'm not going to start showing up. And what's that old Rangers manager got to do with it?'

Dad and Paul tittered.

'It's Walter Smith, not Winston Smith, that was the Rangers manager, hen,' Gerry explained.

'Who's Winston Smith then?'

'*1984*, George Orwell,' said Paul.

Mary shook her head. 'OK, whatever.'

Dad turned to face me. 'Don't use language like that to your mum again. She's perfectly entitled to want a note of your address.'

I stood, then headed to the kitchen with my cup, returning with my jacket in my hand.

Mary looked up. 'Aaawww, Connor! You're not going already? You've only been here ten minutes.'

'I've got studying to do,' I answered robotically.

I watched Paul and Dad swap looks, disappointment on their faces. 'Maybe I'll see you two in a few weeks at the dogs,' I said, heading to the front door.

'Sure. See you later. Take care, Connor,' Paul shouted, his voice fading as I tried to disappear down the hallway.

My parents followed me. I was in no mood for cuddles or a long goodbye. Opening the front door, I half turned, waving them goodbye before they had reached the end of the hallway, and shouted, 'Goodnight! See you in a few weeks, Dad.'

Heading down the stairs, I shook my head, annoyed I'd let her get under my skin again. *I'll not be visiting there again for a while*, I thought.

Four

Years of unfavourable politics, mismanagement and neglect had relegated, what was previously one of the top stadiums in the city, to a dilapidated mess. Now it was reduced to hosting minority sports events and car boot sales. Dad, Paul and I made our way down the steps towards the resident bookmakers who pitched in a straight line like soldiers preparing to charge into battle. Ready to rifle the pockets of the punters. Dad's face bore the look of the proud father. 'Right, this is my usual pitch. Don't move from here. This is the first time you've been here as an adult, Connor, so I can buy you a pint. Lager, boys?'

'Yeah, thanks, Dad,' we both answered.

It was a cold, crisp December evening, a night for the diehards, I had felt I couldn't renege on my promise to Dad. The veil of fog that had hung around throughout the day like a guest outstaying their welcome had finally cleared, allowing the meeting to go ahead. Paul turned to face me as I was standing on the step above him. 'Connor, I need to ask you something. What is your problem with Mum?'

Enjoying being at eye-level with my brother instead of looking up at him for once, I responded, 'Why do you ask?'

'It's a bad day when she feels like she can't ask you herself. She can't even ask you how things are at college without you turning into a puffer fish.'

'You're older than me, Paul, so you should know better. All families are different. Different people have different relationships. You and Mum have a different relationship to the one I have with her. It's simple. You're the model son and I'm not.'

Paul cocked his head, frowning. 'But why?'

'Why? I've just told you why. You get on with people that I don't and vice versa. It would be bloody boring if we felt the same way about everybody.'

'You're out of order with her. You might not get on as well with her as I do but that's down to you. She shouldn't be walking on eggshells with you. You think it's right that she can't even ask you a question for fear of you exploding? Why are you so emotionally violent towards her?'

The shite he spouted at times never failed to make me laugh. 'Have you been reading those self-help books again, Paul? Get a grip with your daft Americanisms. Emotionally violent!' I shook my head in disgust.

'I'll use whatever phrases I like and it sums you up. That's what you're like with her. She's a nervous wreck around you.'

I was starting to lose patience. 'Look Paul, she rubs me up the wrong way. It's like David fucking Dimbleby whenever I see her. I can't even come to the dogs with you and Dad and still she's spoiling things.'

I watched as Dad negotiated the steps in slow motion with the three pints between his two hands. 'Here's Dad coming back, or is he in on this as well?'

Paul ignored the question, waiting on our father to negotiate the last couple of steps.

'Here we go, boys,' Gerry said, handing over the pints.

Paul took his pint then began shuffling from foot to foot as though holding the pint had reminded him of how cold it was. 'Dad, I was just asking Connor what his problem is with Mum and he was telling me all families are different, she rubs him up the wrong way, is constantly asking him questions.'

Dad took a sip from his pint. 'It's painful for us to watch, son. Your mum loves you and is trying so hard. You get so irritated with whatever she says, it breaks her heart. We are just asking you to make more of an effort.'

I closed my eyes, inwardly counting to five to keep my temper in check. 'This is fucking brilliant … get Connor to the dogs for a night out, lay it on thick. Poor Mum, she tries so hard. I'll say this once. Tell her not to expect anything from me, then she won't be disappointed. As for you two, if this is the way it's going to be, then I'll just be keeping my distance in the future. I mean that, OK?'

Dad and Paul looked at each other, shaking their heads in mutual frustration. Paul placed his pint on the concrete, between his feet, then pulled a beanie hat from his jacket pocket. 'I don't understand you,' he said as he placed the hat on his head, trying to straighten the North Face logo on it as best he could without a mirror.

'I don't understand you either. But I don't go on at you and question you about it.'

Paul scrunched his eyebrows. 'What do you not understand about me?'

'Why do you put Mum on such a pedestal?' I pulled a bookies pen from my pocket, pointing it like a darts player preparing to throw. Forwards and backwards the pen was thrust as I emphasised each point. 'What has she done to merit such reverence? She's even got you doing her dirty work tonight. She works you like a puppet. Why do you let her? C'mon, tell me. I must be missing something. Or are you just easily pleased?'

'She's my mum. She has brought us up well and worked hard all her life. She had to flee the scheme she lived in for most of her life and move to the other side of the city because of you. Remember that? She deserves more than you give her. She deserves respect. She deserves—'

I interrupted. 'She deserves, she deserves. Listen to yourself. Grow a set. Stand up for yourself. Like I said ... we all have different experiences, perceptions and expectations. Probably best to agree to disagree.'

'So are you going to come for Christmas dinner?' asked Paul.

Shaking my head, I took a step forwards. 'You've not listened to a word I've said, have you? Let me think... Do what I want, when I want. Watch what I want on the box, when I want. Eat and drink what I want, when I want. Have a laugh with my mates or have dinner with you three? You playing the perfect son and Dad getting told what to do constantly. She even tells you when you're allowed to speak,

Dad. You should start acting like a man. Why do you let her speak to you the way she does? I came across a word the other day in a book that sums you two up when it comes to her. Milksop. You're a pair of milksops.' I laughed loudly.

Dad made a shushing gesture. 'Calm down. People are watching. Listen, Connor, you might understand when *you're* married. Sometimes you need to pick your battles, son.'

'Well, if that's marriage, count me out. And you talk about battles? You lost the war years ago. So, in answer to your question, Paul, if that's your idea of a cracking day, then fill your boots. It's not for me. Now, can I drink my pint in peace.' I looked at them both. Satisfied with myself as I witnessed Dad's look of weary resignation.

Paul was not so easily rebuffed though, he refused to let it go. 'Do you not think I've got stuff I could be doing? You can do that stuff with your mates every day of the year. Christmas is supposed to be about family. It's not asking too much that one day of the year we sit down together and have a nice relaxing day.'

That was it, I snapped. 'Yes, it is asking too much and I've had enough of listening to your pathetic, fucking whingeing.' I tossed the lager from my pint towards the wall, stamping my foot on the empty, plastic tumbler.

'Sorry, Dad, I've got better things to do than listen to this. See you later.' As I walked away, I turned to Paul. 'You're getting more and more like Niles from *Frasier*, every time I see you.'

My exaggerated laugh was drowned out by the excited punters cheering the greyhounds home.

Five

Greg placed his pint glass on the glass coffee table. 'If I don't see you with your tongue down some girl's throat, tonight of all nights, Connor, I'm going to start a whispering campaign about you. Plus, I've seen the way you look at me in the showers after fives.'

I placed my copy of *NME* on the armrest. 'That'll be right, even if I were that way inclined, it'd be big Luca I'd be all over like a rash. You wouldn't get a look in.'

'By the way, Luca, have you seen the size of the wee man's not so wee man?' asked Greg.

Luca's eyes remained fixed on his mobile phone.'Yeah, couldn't miss it. Size of a Christmas cracker. Shame it only gets used as many times a year as a Christmas cracker.'

We had started early. Drink as much as possible in the flat was the plan so we didn't have to buy many drinks in the Union. For Luca and Greg this was foolproof, for Justin and me – utterly flawed. We both continued to sink drink after drink.

Justin was sprawled out on his prized sumo beanbag, munching on a bag of jumbo-sized peanuts. 'Right, guys, I know some think it's a lot of shite but let's hear our New Year's resolutions.'

'Is it not bad luck to tell, especially when it's not even here yet?' I replied.

Justin threw a peanut at me.'Get a grip, ya wee fishwife.'

I growled as the peanut landed squarely on my temple.'Hope to fuck yours is that you're going to stop acting like a twat.'

'Aye, I'll rap doing that when you man up and stop letting lassies greet on your shoulder about their boyfriends,' he said, mimicking someone crying. 'Or listen to any other shit that you let them pollute your ears with.'

'Boys, boys, c'mon it's Hogmanay. Stop bickering,' warned Luca.

Justin riled me at times but I miss him.

I leapt off the sofa and offered him a fist bump. Peace was restored.

'Right, I'll start then,' announced Greg. 'My New Year's resolution is to get a part-time job and save up for a car to replace René.'

'How tedious,' shouted Justin.

'On you go then, your turn, Mr Exciting. Sorry to bore you,' Greg responded.

'Right, don't laugh, I'm deadly serious. My New Year's resolution is … I'm taking up yoga.'

I had just taken a gulp from my drink. On hearing Justin's resolution, the lager sprayed from my mouth. Fizzy beer shot up my nose causing me to cough and splutter. The other two were rolling about on the carpet, laughing.

Justin shook his head in disgust.'Fuckin small-minded imbeciles.'

'Yoga! That dafty, doing yoga?' I bellowed, trying to compose myself after the spurting fit.

A short silence followed while we gathered like hyenas circling a vulnerable target. It was time to start scavenging. Luca struggled to contain his excitement, 'So how did this come about then, Justin?'

'So I was walking down Woodlands Road' – Action Man made an appearance – from the beanbag, he made a poor attempt at mimicking a walking motion. 'I saw three right good-looking girls going into this building as I was approaching it—'

'Might have known that'd be what it's about. Being led by your wee pecker again?' interrupted Greg.

'Let me finish, ignoramus. I knew this building wasn't a gym or anything. So, I asked them what class they were going to. They told me it was yoga and invited me in. Soraya told me a bit about chakras and—'

'Is that her that sang "I Feel For You",' I asked, prompting Greg and I to chant, 'Chakras Khan, Chakras Khan, Chakras Khan,' while pretending to mix a record.

Justin kicked the slipper off his left foot in our direction and shouted, 'Oh, forget it.'

'Sorry, buddy. That was an open goal. C'mon finish the story,' pleaded Greg.

'That's it. They showed me a few moves. I've signed up for a six-week course. It starts the first week in January. I guarantee I'll have more fun at it than getting a wee part-time job and replacing René.'

'What kind of moves? Like the lotus position?' asked Greg, feigning actual interest.

'Yeah, just a couple of basic moves.'

Making a dent in my pint I then placed it on one of the loudspeakers. 'So, have you been interested in eastern teachings for a while? Have you thought about trying anything else?'

'I've read a bit about Tibet; I'm fascinated by it. The west could learn a lot from the eastern teachings.'

Luca mimicked Justin as he did a few pelvic thrusts while asking, 'Are you hoping it will improve your love-making perhaps?'

'You've changed, Justin. Not even six months in the big smoke and you're turning into something a don't recognise. What's next, origami?' asked Greg.

'Fuck off. Open your minds.'

Greg stood to change the CD. 'Tell you what, Yogi Bear, that daft thing you're sitting on isn't helping your posture for your yoga.'

I elbowed Luca. 'What do yae think the rothesoneri would have to say about this?'

'I don't give a monkey's. I left that parochial shithole to get away from Neanderthals like you lot. The thing about that island is that it's split into three groups. One, the rothesoneri as you lot like to call them. They won't hear a bad word about the place. Will never leave the place. They revel in knowing everybody and knowing their business. Two, people like me who if they were forced to live their life on that island, they would be found hanging by the neck one day' – Justin mimicked a rope pulling on an imaginary neck – 'They can't handle the small-mindedness so they leave. Or they've left, fucked up, and had to come back and are gutted about it. Three, the worst of the lot. They're like agnostics in religion, fence-sitters, depending on their mood or the weather, they change like chameleons. One day they are with the rothesoneri and the next they can't stand the place. They swap sides depending on what is in it for them and to curry favour with people that they deem important—'

'And that was a tourist information broadcast from the Isle of Bute Tourist Board,' I interrupted.

As the laughter ceased, the three of us wrestled Justin from the bean bag. 'Well I'm glad you left the suicide capital of Scotland,' joked Greg, 'cos you're one of the funniest guys I know.'

'Don't try and patter me up like one of your daft conquests,' slammed Justin.

'I mean it, buddy. I'm no blowin smoke up yer arse.' Greg's language, like mine, became more slang when we drank. 'What I love about you is that you don't try and be funny. It's effortless. You're just … being you.'

'Cheers, pal,' Justin responded sheepishly, avoiding eye contact.

'Right, Luca, you're up next. New Year's resolution?' Justin asked, trying to change the subject.

Luca took a deep breath. 'I could bullshit the three of you and just make a joke but I'll be honest. I'm taking up yoga with Justin. No, my New Year's resolution is to regain the trust and respect of my family.' A silence followed. We waited on the punchline. Nothing was forthcoming. Luca shook his head.'Thanks, guys, I open up a bit and I get bashed in the coupon with a wall of silence.'

'Sorry, Luca, I was waiting on a punchline; it's not like you to be serious. Sorry about that,' I answered.

'Aye, sorry Luca,' the other two joined in.

'Don't be daft. It's fine, no big deal. You're up, Connor.'

'Well, as Action Man eloquently explained earlier, my New Year's resolution will be to tell any girl who tries to use me as a fuckin agony aunt, to do one and then pull out my Christmas cracker in front of her.' We laughed like drunks do, as if we had just heard the funniest thing ever.

'This requires a toast. Wait a minute, guys,' Justin said, running to the kitchen.

Greg shook his head in disbelief. 'Yoga. That madman doing yoga. Wit next. Imagine the mad shit you'd come across if yae could peek inside his heid for five minutes.'

'Fucking bonkers,' I added.

Justin returned with four miniature glasses of Aftershock. We stood and raised the drinks for a toast, 'To Justin and his creepy, poofy new hobby,' said Luca.

'To Greg and his' – Justin stifled a yawn – 'René replacement.'

'To Luca and new found trust and respect,' said Greg.

'To me and my Christmas cracker,' I toasted, as we threw the red fireball liquid down our throats. Four faces and bodies contorted and winced as for some the drink worked it's magic while for others it sowed the seeds of havoc.

Showered and dressed, taxi on the way, full of expectation for the night ahead, Greg went to the CD system. As the song started, Greg arranged us in a huddle. Bouncing up and down, we sang a Smashing Pumpkins song that we played religiously.

When I look back on this moment, I can recognise that this was the first time in my adult life that I could remember truly being happy. Lost in a moment. For me, a beautiful moment. It almost made me cry with happiness then, and now.

***

The DJ whipped the crowd up to a crescendo.'Ten, nine, eight, seven, six, five, four, three, two, one … Happy New Year!' The piper signalled the arrival of a new year as Justin and I preyed on the goodwill of girls we deemed single, planting lingering kisses then moving on to our next target. When the well was dry, we searched for Greg and Luca. The four of us took turns wishing each other a Happy New Year. 'I just want to shay guys … this past six months … this past six months … hiv been the best of ma life … the best … a mean it,' I shouted, trying to make myself heard.

'Fuck me, you must have had a right shitty life,' retorted Justin.

Putting my arm around Justin's shoulder I manoeuvred us away from the huddle. 'Justin, I notisssed this earlier, buddy, when Greg gave yae a compliment… Av jist gave yae a compliment… See when yer mates are being sincere and heartfelt yae shouldn't feel the need to crack a joke. Why is it when yae get a confidante yae turn intae a puffer fish?' I felt very pleased with myself for recycling my brother's annoying analogy.

'See, the thing is, buddy,' Justin answered, as we swayed a further few feet away from where the conversation had begun. 'Am no used to it. Condiments make me feel uncomfortable.'

'A no wit ya mean,' I added, wagging a solitary finger at Justin's face, 'we're aw a produce of oor environment, eh?'

'Aye, eh … wit was a saying, Connor?'

'Fucked if a remember, Justification,' I laughed.

'Here … here's a cracker … this is a cracker,' Justin laughed uncontrollably which resulted in me joining in.

Composing himself, Justin continued, 'You know those daft Americans use daft names for celebrities, like Jennifer Lopez is J-Lo. That twishite couple were called Robsten. Well, you're Connor Boyd … CoBo,' he said laughing. 'An yer tiny.'

I frowned, my neck seemed to be losing control of my head. 'Hey, less o rat shite, yer only a couple o inches bigger than me.'

'Aye, so … so … you're the littlest Cobo,' Justin said, again laughing uncontrollably at his own joke.

I put my arm around Justin's shoulder. We both pointed into the distance and sang,

'There's a voice that keeps on calling me

Doon the road is where al always be
Every stop a make, a make a new friend
Can't stay for long then am oaf again
Maybe the morra I'll want ti settle down
Until the morra, al just keep moving oan—'

Until Justin, leaning too heavily on me, caused us both to fall in a heap.

We lay there laughing and laughing. A bouncer appeared, looking down on us, shaking his head. 'Right, guys, I think you've had enough. Time to hit the road.' He helped the pair of us to our feet.

'Aye, time ti hit the road, littlest Cobo. Keep on movin oan. New adventure lies aroon the bend,' Justin sang.

'C'mon, pal, it's New Year, don't be like rat, we're just enjoying oorself.' I attempted to embrace the bouncer.

'Yeah, buddy, it's New Year and I don't want to be here until crazy o'clock waiting on a *paramedic* for you two *paralytics*, cos you've cracked your skulls on the floor.'

'Aaagghh, a poet and a bouncer. See wit he done there, Justin? Para … para … para. Uck, you're too seriezzz, buddy. Mon, it's New Year, let me get the poet a moet. A wee glass of bubbly, that's wit yi drink at the bells, a wee glass of moet.' Shuffling from foot to foot, I struggled to focus.

'No arguments, guys. I know you're regulars. Don't jeopardise that. You'll thank me for it in the morning,' the doorman reasoned.

'Fair enough, big guy. Yir a gentleman. Let's go, Connor.'

I tried pointing a finger at the bouncer but my finger waved around like a magician's wand. 'Am no leaving cos yer tellin me tae. Am jist heading wi ma buddy here,' I said, throwing my arm around Justin's shoulder.

We descended the steps together like our legs were tied together. Stumbling into the New Year air, we managed to turn what should have been a ten-minute walk into a lengthy orienteering course.

Six

Time marched on, advancing like the wind. I absorbed lessons in growing up while cementing my place within my social group. All that mattered to me was successfully completing all my modules so I could move on to a higher course while maintaining the fantastic friendships I'd forged. Life's simple if you keep it simple. I thought if I kept close to the things and people that made me happy and if I gave 'her' and that fucking excuse of a brother of mine a wide berth, I'd be fine.

How pathetically naïve could I have been.

Spring had sprung. Birds made their presence felt, effectively becoming uncalled-for alarm clocks with their songs of sunrise. I marvelled at the soothing sound despite being wakened by the songbirds a couple of hours before my artificial alarm had been due to wake me. The half-light of dawn had failed to penetrate the thick, garish, gold-coloured bedroom curtains yet. I enjoyed this quiet time, just letting my thoughts flow. Silence was anathema to my flatmates. Closing my eyes, I imagined myself lying in a small boat just drifting on a small stretch of still water. No rush. Nowhere to go. Nothing to do. Staring at the cloudless sky. Enjoying just being. I daydreamed about books and how imagination can take you anywhere. Sounds as well. I thought about childhood. The sound of a lawnmower on a summer's morning. A trumpet signalling the arrival of the rag-and-bone man. (*Fucking conmen! Imagine struggling out with two black bags worth of clothes and getting handed a plastic kazoo for your trouble. Then, over-usage of the aforementioned kazoo resulted in several slaps to the back of the head before it was snatched from your mouth never to be seen again.*) Coming out of the swimming baths smelling of chlorine, then a visit to the chippy and the smell of vinegar overpowering the chlorine as you opened the bag. Songs, like a time machine taking you back to certain moments. Like New Year. Tonight, Tonight – brilliant.

The vibration of my mobile phone against the cheap, ash bedside table stirred me from my daydreaming.

Picking up my mobile, I was curious as to who was texting me at this time.

> **Messaging**
> MILK
> Brilliant news. Just heard from Maggie Adams. Bannermans got shifted down to Ayrshire. Irvine apparently. One complaint too many. Handed an ASBO. PS Just got to work. Willie the 4man sacked y-day after I had finished my shift. Caught drinkin on the job! Luv Mum x
> **Sent Messages**
> MILK
> That's magic!!!!!! Plenty of water down there to sail their feckin boat! PS No way, wee willie the wino! Who caught him!
> **Messaging**
> MILK
> LOL. MD was in toilets, herd noises, looks in, willie on his knees with screwdriver moving a wooden panel under the sink wer he had his stash! Tried to make out wasn't his! X
> **Sent Messages**
> MILK
> Lol. Wily old Willie! U shud try 4 his job. U r 4ever sayn u cud do better. Nothin 2 lose?
> **Messaging**
> MILK
> U no wat. Ur rite. I might do that. Thanks son. Luv u x.

Give her an inch and she takes a mile. A snippet of advice and she thinks she can weasel her way back in with me. Stupidly, when I couldn't hear her irritating voice or see her, occasionally I would text her on auto-pilot. Faceless meant thoughtless on my part. I switched my mobile off and went back to sleep.

***

I quickly forgot about the innocuous advice I'd offered. A week later I received a text saying that she was the new forewoman of her section. That just about sums it up. She hadn't done a thing for me. I can't think of one decent piece of advice from her. I gave her one little bit of encouragement for something that she wouldn't have even thought of doing herself. She acts upon it, and bingo, a promotion. I laughed half-heartedly as I picked up my mobile and began typing.

> **Sent Messages**
> MILK
> Congratulations
> **Messaging**
> MILK
> Thanks! Wouldn't hav went 4 it without ur advice. Wud luv u 2 come 4 a chinese wi me ur dad n paul to celebrate. Next Friday 7ish Wok n Roll'?
> **Sent Messages**
> MILK
> Soz. Party at good friend of mine's Friday. Enjoy. Say hello to paul n dad

The falseness of it all. Contrived. Oh Mary, you're brilliant. Well done, hen. Mum, I'm proud of you. Pass me the prawn crackers. Those two are blind to her scheming. I just left them to it.

Messaging
MILK
We'll leave it 2 wen u can make it. Wen suits? X

I tossed the phone onto my bed. 'Aaaaarrrgghhhh, she does my head in!' It felt like repeatedly trying to force a fucking agitated dog (me) back into a corner with a stick (her). Picking up my newly laundered clothes from my bed I began hanging them up in my wardrobe.

Luca peeked his head around the door. 'You OK, buddy? I heard you having a few words with yourself.'

I placed the remaining garments back on my bed. 'Yeah, just my old dear doing her usual,' I said.

Luca sat on the archaic, multi-coloured carpet. 'Do you two not get on?'

'No. It's complicated. Things happened. She just annoys me. I try to forget about the past, but I can't.' I felt a sense of relief when I finished the sentence. This monster that I constantly had to force back into its box was like an indefatigable Michael Myers. So, when Luca offered his ear, I needed to talk.

'You don't need to go into it if you don't want to. But, if you do, you know what you tell me remains between us.'

I sat on the edge of my bed. 'Thanks, Luca. I know that.'

'Forgive and forget. Sounds easy. But it's not. Mind that New Year's resolution to regain my parent's trust and respect? That's about two years now and although I'm making progress, they still don't fully forgive or trust me. I can't blame them. I stole from them to feed my drug habit. Don't know how I got away with it for so long. Taking cash from my mother's purse. Stealing credit cards. Pawning jewellery.'

I was stunned. 'I would never believe that if I hadn't heard it from you directly, Luca. Didnae think you were capable of that kinda shit.'

'Drugs make you desperate, buddy. I resented all the pressure they put me under before I sat my exams, so I rebelled. Instead of studying for exams I studied the effect skunk can have on a fragile boy's brain,' he laughed. 'Anyway, enough about me,' he waved his hand, 'I know your problem will be different to mine, but listen to somebody that's trying to atone for their mistakes. It's hard. The guilt and stuff when you know you've let people down.'

I scratched my scalp. Despite needing to talk, I struggled to express myself. 'Well, thing is. The thing is, she doesn't even know what's she done. Sorry, she doesn't know, that I know.'

Luca frowned. 'So, if she doesn't know. How can she make up for it?'

'I don't want her to *make up* for it. She was telling the truth. I don't want her excuses. To watch her trying to squirm out of it, lying about it, probably telling me that because I was a wee boy at the time that I misunderstood what I heard. I don't want her … her … pity.'

'It's obviously really bad what you heard, Connor. I can see that. I know you said you don't want her excuses and pity but if it's as bad as you say – would it not be wise for you to confront her? Would you telling her what you heard really hurt her?'

I took a moment to reflect before answering. 'It would hurt her, Luca. I've pictured it in my head so many times. The tears, the shock, the drama, but it always comes back to the same thing. Her face. Staring at me. The look in her eyes. Pity. That look. Her pity would fucking destroy me.' I averted my gaze from Luca to the carpet.

'The only advice I can give you then is don't let it consume you. That'd be letting her win.'

I digested his advice before leaping from the bed. I briefly felt a sense of elation at offloading some words about my situation. 'You're spot on,' I said animatedly. 'I won't let her win. Thanks for listening, pal. I really appreciate it.'

'Any time.' Luca extended his arms out wide, beckoning me forwards. 'Mon, time for a man hug.'

The chat with Luca was like taking a couple of paracetamol for a fractured skull.

Seven

The first year at college was coming to an end. The results, which I knew were a formality, would be in the post later in the summer. I was progreessing to the next level in my education. The friendship I enjoyed with Greg and the friendships forged with Luca and Justin meant the world to me. Brotherhood gave me something that family hadn't. Safety. A feeling of people covering each others' backs. Knowing that we'd all be staying on together for another year, looking out for each other, sharing experiences, making more memories and remaining in our cocoon, soothed my mind.

Affluent tree-lined avenues surrounded the West End park on all sides. Architects, dental practices, accountants and law practices mixed with residential properties. Greg and I lay on the grass, enjoying the sun and atmosphere. Hundreds of people were spread all over the park. Serious sun worshippers topped up their tans while book-readers sought shade under the trees. If you closed your eyes you could be forgiven for thinking you were abroad. Various accents from all over the world could be heard. Overseas students were taking full advantage of the very un-Scottish weather. The sun transformed the city. Everything looked, smelt and sounded different on days like this. Cheap, throwaway barbecues were out in force, drawing enviable glances from the hungry. The unusual sight of a man practising funambulism. An elasticated, thin stretch of fabric tied between two trees, thirty yards apart. Small barefooted steps, his arms like a child pretending to be an aeroplane. Desperately committed to avoiding separation from the tightrope. The fascinating sight and curious sound of a group of Asian males playing kabaddi. A group of Chinese girls taking a walk with umbrellas for protection from the sun, causing bare-chested men to frown. The boating lake, tennis courts and bowling green full to their capacities with queues stretching further by the minute. Endorphins released by exposure to the sun resulting in adults reintroducing themselves to sports neglected for years.

'I reckon I would be so much happier if I lived somewhere that had weather like this most of the year, Connor. The outdoor life. Girls in bikinis or at least skimpier outfits than duffel coats and wellies. Eating al fresco. Time spent at the beach. It's a no-brainer.'

I yearned to speak about something that was bothering me but felt that I had to humour him before broaching the subject. 'It's got its plus points for sure. Tell you what I can't get my head around though. Christmas Day in Australia. It's plain weird. You see the Aussies on the beach on Christmas Day. That's just alien to us. We're dubbed up in the house, wearing novelty sweaters and eating our own body weight in turkey and selection boxes. Can you imagine being on the beach, opening your prezzies while wearing shorts and a vest?'

'I could get used to it very quickly. On the beach, swapping presents, sun shining. Fit girls everywhere. Nightmare. You can keep the bad Christmas jumpers and sprouts.'

I knew the longer I left it the worse it would get. I tended to let little things build up within me, let them get out of control. Blowing things out of proportion. Just ask him the question. No big deal, I berated myself. I was relieved I had my sunglasses on. I looked around to make sure no one was within earshot. 'Why do you think girls don't take me seriously?'

'Jeeso. Swift change of subject or what! What makes you ask that, buddy?'

'Come on, Greg. You know fine well what I mean. I'm sick of, "Wee Connor's a great listener. Wee Connor is like a wee brother to me. A pal to me." Blah. Blah. Blah. All that shit.'

'Don't be so hard on yourself. This is the way I see it, right… When it comes to girls I think you're too serious. Too intense maybe. You need to relax. Do you look at them as a potential girlfriend? Maybe they sense that from you. You think too much. If you just acted the way you do with me and the boys, then you'd get on better.'

'But I don't want to shag my mates. That's the difference.'

Greg smiled.'See, that's what I mean. That was funny and sharp. Just be natural. You're like Pinocchio.'

'Wit you mean Pinocchio? I don't turn into a mad liar!'

Greg threw an acorn, hitting my right ear. 'Wooden! You act a bit wooden! I suppose it's like everything else – practice makes perfect. When we go to parties, you skulk away in a corner. Talk to girls, but not with all this planning and overthinking. Be natural. Be you. You're a cracking guy. You're the only one that doesn't realise that. Girls wanting to talk to you, saying you're cute, a pal, etc. is better than them saying, Connor's a creepy wee guy.'

'I know what you mean, I just find it a bit awkward. It's a lack of confidence. A lack of self-esteem.'

'I know, buddy. Trust me, confidence is the difference between success and failure in most things. You need to work on it. Act like you're confident, even if you're really shitting yourself. But why are you shitting yourself in the first place? It's only one human being talking to another human being. Just chill out and relax.'

'Yeah, you're right. I'm glad I got it off my chest though. It's been annoying me.'

'I'm glad you felt like you could talk to me about it. Leave your brain in your trousers. Give yourself a break. Stop worrying. End of advice.'

I clapped my hands together. 'Right, c'mon. I owe you a beer or two. There's nothing better than sitting in a beer garden on a sunny day with an ice-cold pint.'

Greg threw his arm around my shoulder. 'Worry yourself silly and seek me out for advice as much as you want if that's how you're going to reward me.'

'Let's go drink beer. It's a perfect day to put your advice into practice.'

Heading towards the gates, taking in the sights, I said, 'On a separate note. I heard Indians, Chinese and Italians in here today. I saw people playing with frisbees, playing football, tennis. Even a guy doing the tightrope. What I didn't see once was something you see people doing in parks every other day, but not today. What am I talking about?'

'People drinking?'

'No. I didn't see one person walking their dog.'

Greg stopped walking and shook his head. 'See that advice I just gave you, Connor. Add improving your conversational skills to it. What a fucking mundane observation! I'm checking out the talent and you're checking out how many dog walkers you can spot.' He laughed. 'I despair of you sometimes, Boyd.'

Eight

It was rush hour. The car crawled through one of the main arteries of the West End. I sat in the front of Greg's little Renault which still hadn't been replaced. Poor René was starting to show signs of old age. Forgetting to start first time. Age spots of rust clearly visible. Justin and Luca sat in the back. We were making our way home from college. I was becoming impatient. 'Why do they call it rush hour when clearly it's anything but? It's nearly as contradictory as Tim Henman's nickname – Tiger Tim. Aye, right. Fucking wet drip.'

'You're clearly confused about Tiger Tim's battling qualities,' shouted Justin from the back seat.

'Very funny. You go back to being busy doing nothing.'

Watching the world go by I felt a sense of pride that this was where I now called home. A beautiful display in the front window of the florist's. Various restaurants offering cuisine from all over the world. Vintage clothes shops. Small bookshops. A row of stunning townhouses set above street level. I was shaken from my daydream by a question that I'd been meaning to ask. 'Do any of you lot fancy going to a club in town for a change at the weekend? I'm sick of the Union. It's the same people, doing the same things, in the same spot, every week. I need a change.'

Luca, who'd sat in silence for the entire journey, suddenly found his voice. 'Count me in.'

'I knew I could rely on you, Luca. You've bled that place dry anyway. It'll be a fresh challenge for you.'

Greg piped up. 'I'm in as well so that makes three of us. Justin?'

'And it's a no from me. It's too expensive. Full of

pretentious twats. No, I'll stick to the Union.'

I turned to make eye contact. 'You're so parochial. That's the wee rothesoneri attitude in you.'

'I know what I like. That's why I'm happy. Searching for something better all the time only leads to disappointment.'

'Jesus, don't need to go all Zen on us. He's going to test us with a koan in a minute,' joked Greg.

I rubbed my hands together in excitement. 'Right that's sorted, a wee change of scenery will be great. Maybe get myself a new rig-out for it.'

Justin laughed. 'Baby Gap has some nice stuff the now.'

I took the bait.'What is it with you and this height thing? You're lucky if you're two inches taller than me. Hardly a giant yourself, Justin.'

'Key difference though – I'm comfortable in my own skin. You hate being Mini-Me.'

Luca and Greg lapped it up, enjoying watching Justin and me engaged in another battle to avoid the wooden spoon amongst the group.

Placing my hand on my forehead, I said, 'Never argue with an idiot as they will only drag you down to their level and beat you with their experience.'

'Wow, Connor, another *midget* gem of wisdom.'

I gritted my teeth.

Greg prodded me. 'C'mon, you need to admit, that was funny ... midget gem.'

I wished there was an eject button in the car. I hated Justin getting the better of me in our verbal ping-pong.

I resigned myself to defeat, changing the subject, I asked, 'What's for dinner, Luca?'

Before Luca could answer, Justin jumped in, 'Shrimp with baby gem lettuce for you, wee man.'

I slammed my fist on the dashboard. 'Shut the fuck up you, you're doing my head in. You've milked your wee jokes dry.'

'Deary me, such a *short* temper.'

Luca and Greg's laughter made matters worse. I slumped lower into my seat. *I'm going to fucking chin him one of these days*. As Greg pulled into our street, I couldn't wait to get out.

I headed straight to my room for some peace.

***

The taxi pulled up outside the club. A small line of clubbers already formed a queue. Luca and Greg strutted down the line like peacocks, surveying all before them. I tucked in behind them. Luca moaned, 'Tell you what, I wouldn't fancy this every week – standing freezing your nuts off just for the pleasure of paying to get into a club to drink overpriced alcohol.'

'You're a big prima donna, Di Mambro,' I answered, patting him on the back.

We listened to the two bouncers and their charm offensive. 'Hiya, darling, great to see you. Have a great night. How you doin, Amanda? Looking as beautiful as ever. I'll try and catch up with you later for a drink.' Bomber jackets one size too small. The shape making it difficult to decide whether they had been lifting too many weights or were simply overweight. The awful combination of short-cropped hair, teeth like bits of chalk, too much jewellery and overexposure to sunbeds. When we stepped to the front of the queue, two different animals appeared from nowhere. They eyed us suspiciously, holding our gaze for around ten seconds. Amateur psychology in action. Finally, the taller of the two said, 'Where have you boys been tonight?'

'Nowhere, just had a couple of beers in the flat, then a taxi over here,' I answered, as if I had a gun pointed at my head.

'Not seen yiz afore. Where dae yiz usually go?'

I jumped in, 'Usually the Student Union but we heard this place was amazing so we thought we'd check it out.'

The smaller of the two flicked his head to usher us in as if he was doing us a massive favour. 'Have a good night, gentlemen.'

As we descended the stairs to the club, Greg turned to face me, 'What was that all about? Talk about a fuckin power trip. What a pair of dicks. Trying to stare us out. I felt like telling them to stick their club up their fat arses. And you, Connor. That was fuckin desperate. If they asked you to unbuckle your belt and put your trousers at your ankles, I reckon you would have.'

I tried to calm him down, 'I felt responsible cos it was my idea to come. I didn't want us getting turned away. We're in now. Forget about those two clowns. Let's get drunk, buddy.'

We bounded down the stairs into the bowels of the dark, cavernous club. As Luca opened the door we were exposed to a wall of sound so powerful it shocked us into silence. Not a word was spoken as we meandered to the large, rectangular bar, jostling our way through the masses. Exposed brickwork and pipework gave it an industrial look, like an old derelict warehouse. The two dance floors either side of the bar buzzed with energy, hands in the air, bodies moving to the beat of the tunes. Luca pursed his lips and nodded his head in approval. Greg and I smiled as if Luca giving his stamp of approval was a guarantee that it was going to be a good night. Drinks in hand, we circled the club twice, getting our bearings. Luca pulled us closer. 'The Union is Albion Rovers, this place is Barca. Look at the quantity and quality of the girls in here. This is a different ball game. This calls for GPS.'

I frowned. 'What the fuck is GPS?'

'In the Union, you're lucky if there is one or two that you fancy. So, you just go over and have a go with them. In here, the pickings are rich so it's time for GPS. Groundwork, preparation, success. So, I'll do a few laps, draw up a shortlist of half a dozen. Keep tabs on them, then I'll steam in.'

I laughed, 'How about we just get drunk and enjoy ourselves?' We moved to the other side of the bar, I took my turn to get a round in. Greg leaned in. 'Action Man is missing out.'

'You know fine well though, we're going to go back to a cracking story. It's never a straightforward night with Justin.'

We watched Luca eyeing some girls with his familiar imperious grin. A roar went up at the opening lines of a Rhianna song.

Greg and Luca were intent on doing as many laps of the

club as possible. Taking mental notes of their potential targets. 'C'mon, guys, the only thing you two are missing is a fuckin clipboard each. Yiz are creeping about like insurance assessors.'

Greg nudged Luca. 'Aye, we're no assessing dry rot though. We're assessing who's getting a dry ride.'

I shook my head. We downed two shots in a row. Finally, I had enough Dutch courage to hit the dance floor. Handing Greg my bottle of lager, I disappeared into the crowd. Surprisingly, dancing was one of the few activities where I didn't care what people thought of me. Alcohol and dancing, two things in my life that broke the shackles of my self-consciousness. Dancing was pure escapism. It helped me forget my problems. After dancing for a couple of songs, I met the gaze of a small female with bobbed black hair, big eyes like a cartoon character. A Glaswegian Betty Boo. She definitely wasn't scary looking though. As she smiled at me, I noticed how her smile made her even more attractive. The others on the dance floor became non-existent as we danced. Circling around each other, laughing as we took turns doing silly dance moves, egging each other on to copy. She leant in to me. 'Hi! My name's Ella. What's your name?'

'Hi, Ella. I'm Connor.' I said, as I kissed her on the cheek.

'Well, Connor,' she leant forwards and to the timing of the song we were dancing to, she sang in my ear, 'I like the way you mooooove.'

I wrapped my arms around her, lifting her off the floor and spinning her around. 'Fancy a drink, Ella?'

She took my hand, stared at me with her big beaming smile. 'Yeah, let's go.'

She led me to the bar. I scanned the area where I'd been standing earlier with Luca and Greg, finally spotting them chatting to two girls. Ella turned to face me. 'What can I get you?' I asked.

'I'll have a Woo Woo, please.'

I liked how she was so animated and full of life. I ordered the drinks then turned to face her. 'So, who are you here with, Ella?'

'I was here with my friends, they're over there somewhere.' She pointed to the far corner then looked at me with a playful smile. 'But I'm here with you now.'

I handed the drink to her. 'Cheers, I can live with that. Lucky me. You have an amazing smile, Ella.'

'A good dancer and charming.' She leant over and kissed me. A proper, lengthy, passionate kiss. I tasted peach schnapps and orange from her lips.

'Where do you live, Connor?'

'Over in the West End with my three flatmates, two of them are over there somewhere.' I pointed in their direction.

'OK, back to mine it is then. I'm just over the bridge, five minutes tops in a taxi. Fancy going after our drink?'

I couldn't believe my luck. I thought I was going to self-combust. *Ya beauty. This night just gets better.* 'Yeah, I'll let my friends know when we finish our drinks.' I kissed her, to make sure this was real, that it really was OK to do so. She laughed at me draining my bottle of lager like a desperado. Taking her by the hand, we wound our way over to Greg and Luca. I tapped Luca on the shoulder, a silly grin on my face. My two friends looked at me like proud big brothers. 'I'm heading now, guys, so I'll see you back at the flat later. Enjoy the rest of the night.'

Greg gave me a fist bump. 'Off already, Connor? Right, OK. Enjoy the rest of the night, pal.'

Ella smiled at them. 'Don't worry, boys, I'll look after him.' She winked as we turned to leave.

I laughed at the shocked looks on their faces. *Aye guys, I'm as shocked as you two.*

We ran upstairs, holding hands. The cloakroom was free of punters. She handed over her ticket and took her jacket before we headed into the cold night to look for a taxi.

Heading in the direction of the south side of the city, towards the bridge, I spotted a taxi. Waving frantically I succeeded in flagging it down. As it pulled up, I opened the door for Ella then followed her in. Ella gave the directions to the driver and snuggled into me. 'What age are you, Connor?' she whispered in my ear.

'Twenty.'

She spoke suggestively, her hand on my thigh, 'Oh, do you know what you've let yourself in for, going home with an older woman?'

I could feel my right leg and foot twitching. Like someone trying to kick-start a motorbike. I grinned. 'How old are you? Twenty-one?'

'Twenty-five … charmer.' She kissed me, slow and rhythmical.

After a minute or so she pulled away. I was buzzing. Shit like this didn't happen to me. 'So, you've got your own place then, Ella?'

She reapplied her Bobbi Brown lipstick.'Yeah, I've been living in the flat for a couple of years now. My brother and I are close, he stays over now and again but I love having my own space.'

'Must be great. Me and my mates all get on but it would be good to have my own space at times. Where do you work?'

'*The Herald* and *Evening Times*, in advertising. It's a great job. Great … sorry, Connor. That's us just here, driver … on the right behind the white car, thanks.'

I paid the taxi then we headed into the block of flats. She rummaged in her bag for her keys. I had my hand around her waist. As we stepped into the dark hallway, she slammed the door closed. Pushing me against the door, she kissed me frantically, nibbling on my bottom lip. Undoing my belt, she took my hand. 'Let's go to bed.' Opening the bedroom door, she pushed the dimmer switch setting it to an acceptable level for her. Just enough to see what we were doing. She pushed me on to the bed, laughing as she straddled me. 'Do you have something on you?'

I frowned. 'What do you mean?'

She laughed at my naïvety. 'Protection, Connor. That's what I mean!' She went to the chest of drawers, rustled around in a bag before closing the top drawer. Unzipping her skirt, she shimmied out of it, kicking it in the air then watching it land on the carpet a few feet away. Lifting her top over her head, it was launched in the direction of her retro Hollywood make-up mirror. Climbing back on top, she kissed me, thrusting herself against me. My jeans buttons were popped open by her nimble fingers then she helped me take them off. I pulled my boxer shorts off while she tore at the little foil wrapper. Placing her hand on me she slowly began to fit the condom. Laughing, she said, 'Wow, I won't look at short guys in the same light after tonight, Connor!'

***

I was being shaken vigorously. My mind refused to spark into action. 'Hurry. Hurry. Get dressed. My man's back early from night shift. Connor. Connor. C'mon, get your arse in gear!'

My mind was working like a child piecing a jigsaw together. Finally, I jumped out of bed. 'Fuck's sake, what's going on?'

I was met with the sight of an irate-looking guy a few years older than me, pointing at me. 'Get your clothes on, PRONTO! I'm out working my arse aff on the night shift and you're in here messing with my missus. Ya dirty wee bastard! Get dressed NOW! Me and you are going for a walk.'

I looked at Ella. She had the duvet pulled up to her neck, the beautiful transfixing smile was nowhere to be seen. A pair of large, sad-looking eyes gazed at me apologetically.

'Wait a minute here pal—'

'I'm not your fucking *pal*, get your gear on nowwwwww!'

I looked at Ella pleadingly. 'I ... I didn't know about any boyfriend. Tell him, Ella, you didn't tell me about any boyfriend or I'd never have come back.'

'I told you he might come back early, you should have listened to me. You've ruined everything.'

'This is fucking mental. Why are you saying that? Fucking don't believe this.' I grabbed my jeans, tried to put my leg in and fell over.

A deep, rumbling laugh echoed through the bedroom. I got to my feet. Ella and her man were laughing uncontrollably. 'Sorry, Connor, it was his idea. Blame him. This is my little brother Jamie. Jamie, this is Connor.'

'What? This was a wind-up?' I looked at them as they nodded their heads in confirmation. I slumped to the floor on my knees and buried my head in the duvet. I let out a massive sigh of relief. 'Jesus, I thought I was going to be having soup through a straw for a few months. You two are sick.' I laughed, shaking my head in disbelief.

'Sorry, Connor, I heard Jamie coming in and I called to him that I had brought someone back; you were sleeping like the dead. He peeked his head in and then told me to play along. Sicko.'

'That was a belter. Sorry, buddy, I couldn't resist it.'

That fucking nasally voice is even more annoying than your fucking heart-attack inducing japes, I thought.

Jamie gave us a thumbs up. 'Right, I've had a right boring ten-hour shift. I'm shattered; I'm off to bed.'

Ella looked at me then smiled. Pulling the duvet back, she patted the bed. 'C'mon back in and let me make it up to you.'

I got back into bed and snuggled up against her bottom. The beautiful sensation of a soft-skinned female against my naked skin. I didn't want to leave. I felt safe.

The goodbye was more awkward than necessary. I stood in the hallway at the front door facing Ella. 'Thanks for a great night, Ella.'

She cuddled me. 'You're a lovely guy, Connor. It was a great night.'

She turned the handle of the door. I stood still, my hands in my pockets. She looked at me. I stood there staring back at her. 'Will I see you again, Ella?'

'Suppose we might bump into each other at some point,' she said vaguely.

'Can I give you my number and maybe we could meet up?'

'Eh, yeah, right. I'll get a pen and paper.'

She walked into the kitchen, returning with paper and pen, handing them to me. I wrote down my mobile number then handed them back to her.

'Thanks, Connor, I'll see you then,' she said, opening the

door.

'Bye then, Ella.' I walked away like a reluctant child leaving his parents for boarding school.

Pathetic, aren't I?

***

Opening the front door of the flat, I heard them sing some shitty Girls Aloud song.

It was followed by Greg and Luca's laughter. As I opened the living room door, they started it up again.

I put my finger to my lips. 'Right, enough, guys.'

Greg, arms outstretched, hands spread wide, motioned to me. 'Well? How'd it go?'

A smile spread from ear to ear. 'Immense.'

I noticed Justin sitting with a sullen look. 'How was your night, Justin?'

'Aye great, had a laugh, you know that…'

My thoughts drifted to Ella.

'What do you make of that, Connor?' Justin asked.

I said the first thing that came into my head, 'That's good.'

Justin snapped. 'You've not been listening to a fucking word I've said, have you?'

I laughed. 'No, to be honest.'

'One bit of luck and you're away with the fairies, not listening to your mates even though you asked them a question in the first place.'

Greg and Luca looked at each other, then Greg said, 'Calm down, Justin.'

'Calm down?' He pointed at me. 'He suddenly thinks he's fucking Hugh Hefner.'

I pounced on this remark, 'Wow, big mistake, Justin. You've finally shown your Achilles heel. For a guy that doesn't care about anything, you're getting awffy worked up about nothing. Are you sexually frustrated? Do you want me to give you a few phone numbers. Let me help you out.'

'Fuck off. The only numbers you've got are for The

Samaritans and Childline.'

'Ohhhhhhhhhh,' the three of us shouted in unison.

Justin stood, visibly riled. 'They two said she was a right minger anyway.'

'Liar,' Luca said.

'She was like a fucking zombie from the "Thriller" video,' Justin dragged his right foot behind the rest of his body, his tongue hanging out, eyes closed, both arms stretched out in front of him. He started to stagger about the living room singing,

> *'It's close to midnight and something's lurking from the dark*
> *On the dance floor you see something that almost stops your heart*
> *You try to scream—'*

I interrupted him, 'Fucking Bryan Ferry you should be singing, you clown, cos I'm just a "Jealous Guy".'

The room filled with laughter. Justin and I high-fived each other and slumped onto the couch.

Nine

Two weeks passed. No communication from Ella. I knew there wasn't going to be any now. *Why did I not get her number, then I would be the one in control.* I turned to Greg to get things off my chest. 'She was different. Grown up, full of life, funny. The girls in the Union are so serious. We know most people in there now. I liked the anonymity of that club. You could have a good time without being judged. I feel like you get judged in the Union. It's stifling. Apart from the odd few pints during the week, I'm not going there anymore.'

'Connor, "*do you realise that everyone you know someday will die—*"'

I was in no mood for jokes. 'Greg, now isn't the time for singing Flaming Lips lyrics!'

Greg reached for the remote control and turned the TV off. 'Do you realise that it isn't going to be like the night you had a couple of weeks ago every time you go into town?'

'Of course. I'm not daft. I know I'm not going to have nights like that every time. It's not about that. Do you not feel like we've outgrown the Union?'

'I get where you're coming from, but you need to chill out. You had a cracking night with that girl. Why do you want to see her again?'

'Cos I liked her.'

'Aye, but where was it gonnae go? She was a nice girl but obviously not girlfriend material. Anyway, you shouldn't be looking for a girlfriend. We're too young for all that.'

'Everybody's different. Maybe we have different ideas. Just because you don't want to go out with anyone doesn't mean everybody else is like that. I wouldn't mind going out with someone.'

'Well, that's up to you, Connor. My advice would be to steer clear. Just enjoy yourself, buddy. There's plenty of time for all the serious stuff.'

I still felt rejected. I couldn't help taking it to heart. She had been so nice to me. Why did she not feel the same way?

***

A fortnight later, we made another trip to the club. Justin bit the bullet this time and joined us. Standing in the small queue, Greg nudged Justin. 'Listen to they two fannies, trying to patter up the lassies. The last time we came, they tried to stare us out, acted like a right pair of knobs.'

As the girls in front of them headed inside, we were greeted by the same two bouncers as last time. 'Evening, gentlemen. Regulars now, are we?'

'Didn't think you'd remember us,' I answered.

'Couldn't forget the big man there,' the taller of the two bouncers said, pointing at Luca. 'He walked down the queue a couple of weeks back like a big model walking down the catwalk.' Laughter erupted amongst them. 'Have a good night, lads.'

Waiting to pay their admission, Greg clasped his hand around my wrist. 'Can you believe that? What a fucking transformation! Best of mates now. Fucking bipolar behaviour if ever I saw it.'

We headed straight to the bar. 'Beers and bombs?' asked Justin.

Passing the bottles of lager and the shots to us, he shook his head. 'What a fucking rip-off! That just cost me over seventeen quid.'

I laughed. 'Much do you reckon it would cost in the Union?'

'That would come to … fourteen eighty.'

'So, you're moaning about two quid twenty.' I searched in my pocket handing two pounds to him.

Justin couldn't put the money in his pocket quickly enough. 'Very kind of you, Connor.'

'I can't believe you took it. What a tight-arse. I was trying to shame you.'

Justin laughed. 'Right, boys, who's going to show me around?'

We did two circuits then headed back to the bar. Happy to join in with the circuits this time, I scanned the club hoping to see Ella. Luca tapped Justin on the shoulder. 'What do you think, Justin? Don't get talent like this in the Union, do you?'

'Aye and you don't get prices like it either,' he moaned.

Greg patted Luca on the back. 'There's those two we got aff wae the last time.'

'She's a last resort for me, Greg.'

'Aye, me too with her pal.'

I butted in. 'They're human beings, not fucking commodities. Honestly, you two should listen to yourselves.'

'Here, don't get lippy with us cos you haven't spotted your wee bird,' snapped Greg.

I took a step towards Greg. 'Don't talk shite. I'm not looking for anybody.'

'Aye right, your head's nearly doing a three-sixty like that wee evil lassie from *The Exorcist*,' Greg said, laughing.

'Fuck off, Greg.'

'Get a grip of yourself, Connor, and don't fucking speak to me like that again.'

'C'mon, guys, simmer down,' Luca said, as he grabbed us forcing both of us together to shake hands.

'Sorry, Greg, I was acting like a twat.'

Greg rubbed the back of my head. 'No problem, buddy. Let's get a shot.'

Stood at the bar, Greg turned to me. 'I know what you're like, Connor. Put her to the back of your mind and enjoy yourself.'

I threw the shot down my throat in one go. 'You're right as usual, cheers.'

Strolling to the dance floor, I began to dance but I wasn't losing myself in it like last time. I was too preoccupied. Back at the bar, I couldn't see my friends so I ordered a drink. As I ordered a bottle of lager, I heard, 'And a Woo Woo, please.'

I turned to see Ella smiling at me. 'Hey, Connor, how are you?' She hugged me like a long-lost friend.

'Good, Ella. Better for seeing you.' I leant forwards, trying to kiss her lips. Ella turned her head to take my kiss on the cheek. I felt crestfallen. She looked at me, a sad expression on her face. I handed her drink to her. 'Great seeing you. Why didn't you call me? Did I do something wrong?'

A sympathetic look met my stare. 'No, don't be daft. We had a great night, but that's all. I'm not looking for a boyfriend or anything serious. You're really sweet and you're too young to get all serious anyway.'

'Who said anything about getting all serious?'

'C'mon, Connor, I've seen it before. I'm older than you. We both might go into it not wanting anything serious, but one of us would end up getting hurt. We had a great night together, just remember that.'

'You're right,' I grudgingly agreed. 'I really liked you, I mean, I really like you. You're different to the other girls I've met.'

'A bloody charmer and you don't even know it. That's what I like about you, Connor. You're a great guy. Have a bit of confidence in yourself. You've got a lot to offer.'

I sniggered as I raised my eyebrows. 'Obviously not enough.'

'Timing, Connor. That's all. Timing. Thanks for the drink.' She put her hand on my shoulder. 'Friends, right?'

'Friends,' I said through gritted teeth. 'But I would still like a repeat performance,' I laughed.

'That's better.' We hugged as she whispered in my ear, 'Now go and give some other girl a treat.'

Breaking from the cuddle, I said, 'You're an amazing girl, now beat it before I fall for you even more than I already have.'

She kissed my cheek gently. 'Bye, Charmer.'

Leaning against the bar, mixed emotions ran through me. *Timing. My fucking enemy. Story of my sad excuse for a life. Aye, I know all about bad timing.*

Ten

A family visit couldn't be put off any longer. *I wouldn't put it past 'her' to show up at college.* Months had passed since I had seen any of them. I knew I needed to show my face again. *Meet them to show face, drop off Christmas presents. Job done. Lets them know I'm not coming over at Christmas or New Year.* The idea of a neutral venue appealed to me. *Hope that daft brother doesn't start the same garbage as last year, rattling on about families at Christmas. No, he knows better after last time.* I reasoned with myself that surely Paul and 'her' wouldn't air any of the family's dirty laundry in public. Texting Dad, I proposed that we meet at a Chinese restaurant in town as I would be going out afterwards.

Opening the restaurant door, I spotted the three of them sitting at a small booth. Handing my jacket to the waiter, I asked him to look after the presents then I made my way over. Attempting to avoid embraces, I quickly took a seat. Shaking hands with Dad and Paul I then leant over giving Mother an awkward hug. The table separating us made it difficult to give a proper one, much to my relief.

I rubbed my hands on my thighs. 'How we all doing then?'

'Aye great, son. The job's going great. I was a bit apprehensive going from working with people for years to being their boss. They've been good as gold though. I know the job off by heart so a think they respect that.'

I didn't say a word, preferring instead to give her the thumbs up before turning to look at Dad. 'How's things with you, Dad?'

'Same old, same old, son. Never mind me, what have you been up to?'

'Just the usual. College, a few shifts at the deli each week.'

'You still going to that student union?'

'Hardly ever, got a bit bored with it. We tend to come into town now.'

The waiter approached and took our order. Paul looked at me. 'How're the flatmates? You all still getting on?'

Smiling, I answered, 'Like a house on fire. They're brilliant guys.'

Paul fidgeted with his cutlery.'You think you'll stay in touch after college?'

'Without a doubt, Paul.'

'That's great. I know you were already pals with Greg but that's two new mates you've made then.'

Man, you are so fake, Paul. Turning on the charm offensive in front of her. I can read you like a book. Sooner I get a couple of pints down my neck the better.

The waiter returned with our drinks. Mary raised her glass. 'To family.'

'Family,' said Paul and Gerry.

'Cheers,' I said. *Fucking sham-ily more like.*

Mary took a sip of wine.'So you met any nice girls yet, Connor?'

I stared at her with a deadpan expression. 'I've met lots of nice girls.'

She smiled mischievously. 'Nobody serious?'

I didn't miss a chance. 'Aye, there was one girl I really liked but she didn't feel the same way about me.' I looked straight into her eyes.'You've got to turn your back on people that don't feel the same way about you, haven't you, Mum?'

'Aye, totally. Well it's her loss, son. What a bitch.'

I smiled. 'She's not a bitch. She's a beautiful girl. Timing. Just bad timing. Timing can be really important in life, don't you think?'

Mother smiled. 'Absolutely, son. It's the old sliding doors thing isn't it.' She winked.

Paul pursed his lips, waves of frown lines appearing on his forehead. 'Where's all this philosophical stuff coming from, Connor?'

'Just telling it like it is, bruv.'

Paul eyed me suspiciously.

'Well, I think you sound very mature, son,' she chipped in.

'Here we go, I'm starving,' I said, as the diminutive waiter arrived with the starters.

Paul picked up his knife and fork. 'No way, breaking news … there's another male in Glasgow even smaller than you, Connor.'

I fired a sarcastic smile at him. 'Dynamite comes in small packages, Paul.'

Gerry took a sip of his soup. 'Is that Italian boy still cooking for you?'

'Yeah, his parents own a few restaurants. He'll probably end up running them when he's finished at college. He's so lucky.'

Mary took a break from her food. 'You remember Mrs Paterson that used to live across the road from us, Connor?'

I took a bite of the chicken satay then shook my head.

'You must remember Mrs Paterson. Her son became a copper…'

Placing an empty skewer on my plate, I answered, 'Not got a clue.'

'Well, anyway, she's got cancer.'

'That's a shame.'

'And you know wee Yvonne I've worked with for years? I've spoken about her loads of times. Well her man's got a brain tumour.'

I stopped eating to look at her. 'Jeeso, you're a right misery pervert. Why would I want to hear about stuff like that?'

She shrugged her shoulders. 'Just thought you'd be interested.'

Dad butted in. 'Did you see the game on Saturday, Connor? It was never a penalty, was it?'

I took a large drink from my pint. 'That ref was determined to give us nothing.'

'Aye, you're right. Still six points ahead though.'

'We'll need to try and get to a game before the end of the season, Dad.'

'Aye, son, that'd be good.'

I took aim at Paul. 'What about you, weirdo? You still not into football?'

'Twenty-two overpaid prima donnas running around after a ball while thousands of Neanderthals spout religious bile at one another. No thanks.'

I looked at Dad. 'Never trust a man that's not into football.'

I gave Paul a supercilious grin as Dad laughed at my remark.

I enjoyed the empty silence, refusing to fill it. Waiting on one of my parents to chip in with something. I knew Mum would rack her brain to come up with something interesting to say.

The waiter took the plates away as I ordered another round of drinks. Paul met my gaze. 'So, where you off to tonight?'

I sniggered. 'Never you mind, the last thing I need is you and your saddo pals turning up.'

'As if. We wouldn't be seen dead in the places you frequent,' Paul scoffed.

Wiping my mouth with a napkin, I retorted, 'Are you and big Dougie still going to that place they recite poetry and generally act like ponces?'

'Aye, best pub in the city. Some right interesting people in there. Writers, actors, all sorts. You wouldn't get in *or* fit in.'

I sniggered. 'Aye sure, dead exclusive and fussy when charlatans like you and Dougie get in.'

Mary interrupted us, she'd thought of a question. 'Do you take a packed lunch to college, Connor?'

Fuck me, is that the best she can come up with?

I was saved from the banality by the arrival of the main courses, allowing me some peace for five minutes. Eating in silence, pondering on the merits of our respective dishes, eventually we swapped opinions on them as forks strayed to different plates.

'Have any of your mates decided what they're going to do at the end of their courses?' asked Paul.

'Justin is talking about taking a year off and going travelling to the Far East and India. I reckon big Luca will end up starting in the family business. Nothing concrete though. I'll really miss them if they do leave. They've become like brothers to me.'

'Philosophical and emotional. Careful, Connor.'

'Aye, very good. I'm thinking about trying to get a half-decent job after this course is finished. I'm kind of getting bored with studying now.'

'Good for you, son. You can't beat a bit of work experience. That's the real world,' said Gerry.

Paul and I looked at each other then burst out laughing.

'What's so funny, boys?'

'Mmmmm. I don't think you're best placed to dish out advice on work related issues, Dad,' said Paul.

'Maybe I could get you into the Whisky Bond,' Mother offered, narrowing her eyes.

Paul's laugh echoed through the small restaurant. I was thoroughly disgusted. She genuinely said these things to provoke a reaction from me. 'Do you think I'm doing two years at college ... completing an HNC to end up in a job at the Whisky Bond? Do you even know anything about me? What planet are you on?'

'Oh, it's like that is it? Too good for it, are we? I'm offended.'

'I'm the one who should be offended, as if I'd ever work there.'

'What's up with it?'

'Didn't say there was anything up with it. I'm just hoping for something a wee bit ... a wee bit ... more mentally taxing.'

Dad couldn't handle the ensuing silence. 'Anyway, what's the plans for Christmas, Connor? You and your mates up to anything special?'

'I'm going to Greg's parents' for Christmas dinner then maybe we'll head out afterwards.'

Mary dropped her cutlery on the plate. 'That's great, you can go to a stranger's house for your Christmas dinner but not your own family's.'

'Stranger's house? They're hardly strangers. I'm over there for Sunday dinner once a month. They're really nice people. Cracking cook that Mrs Fullarton.'

'Aaahhh, this just gets better. Cosy wee Sunday dinners. Why d'you never come home for Sunday dinner? Why is that?'

Gerry reached over the table to take her hand.

I looked to the ceiling shaking my head. 'You're causing a scene.'

Her remarks and Paul's irritating pompous ways made my mind up about a swift exit. Happy with my night's work, I stood. 'Right, people, I'm going to head. I'm meeting the boys,' I said, throwing a twenty pound note on the table.

Mother picked it up. 'This was my treat.' She tried to hand it back.

I pulled my hands into my chest, my palms facing her. 'No, it's fine. I've left your Christmas presents with the waiter. Have a nice Christmas.' I shook Paul's hand, gave Dad a hug then Mother was given the same poor offering I had given her on my arrival. Duty done, I couldn't leave quickly enough, bounding out of the restaurant, rubbing my hands together in excitement at the impending night out with my friends.

Eleven

Boredom had set in. Saturday night visits to clubs no longer held the same appeal for me. Sitting in a pub with friends, listening to each other's stories, music playing in the background was something I loved. Clubbing was different. Barely hearing what your mates were saying. The posturing. People pretending to be somebody they weren't. I'm sure some girls only chatted to me to get another friend request on their social network page. *'Sorry, I'm not interested, Connor, but remember to add me on Facebook.'* What is the point? Fucking egomaniacs. *Look at me, look at my wonderful life.* Sure. No interpersonal skills whatsoever but hundreds of 'friends'. Fake. I decided to take an indefinite sabbatical from it. On relaying this to my friends, they'd acted as if I'd committed a heinous crime. Saturday nights out were sacrosanct to them. I soon realised that a quiet night on my own, reading a book or watching a movie, was actually enjoyable. The only downside was when I got woken by the drunken rabble coming home, one of them always hell-bent on giving a blow-by-blow account of the night that couldn't wait until the morning.

I started to think about the future. In a couple of months, we would need to put our cards on the table. Who was moving on and where to? Where did this leave me? If Justin went travelling and Luca left for the family business, would Greg be willing to share a flat somewhere with me? I would rather have slept rough than go back to living with 'her'. *Worst-case scenario would be renting a room in a flat while I got a job to get some money together for a flat of my own.* The thought of us going our separate ways depressed me. It worried me. They'd become my safety net. Stability. Routine. Always there for me. The last two years had been the happiest of my life. The fear of the unknown unnerved me. *Why does it all have to change?*

***

A couple of weeks passed, I found myself becoming more anxious. Calling a meeting under the pretence that the landlord had been in touch wanting an answer as to whether we were staying on, I was rebuffed by the reasoning that they needed a little more time. I was left in limbo to concentrate on finishing the remaining modules of my course. In the meantime, I looked at the costs to rent a one-bedroom flat, and a two-bedroom in case Greg and I teamed up. Comparing the cost between the West End and other areas of the city. I scoured the jobs pages of the newspapers and recruitment sites. I was on a mission, I wanted to be prepared for all possible scenarios. Driven by my determination that I'd never return to my parents'.

On the journey home from college a couple of weeks later, Justin broke the news he was taking a year out. He planned on returning to Rothesay in June to spend a month back home. Bangkok would be his first stop before travelling through other parts of Thailand, then India. A fortnight later as Greg, Justin and I sat in the living room watching *Question Time*, Luca returned from a family visit and announced that his parents wanted him to return to the bosom of the family to start working towards taking over the family business. I grabbed Greg, resting my head on his chest, pretending to cry. 'Please, Greg, please don't leave me. It's just me and you against the world, pal.'

Laughing, Greg shrugged me away. 'Joking aside though, Connor, do you fancy going for a few pints tomorrow and having a bit of a brainstorm about what we're going to do?'

'What do you mean, what we're going to do?'

'Well I thought… Sorry, I assumed, that we'd try to get another flat or look into staying here and getting another two flatmates?'

I let out an enormous sigh of relief. 'Greg, I'm fucking delighted you've said that. I've been worried sick about it. If I had to go back to living with my mum I don't know what I'd do. I'd even ... no, that's going too far ... desperate times call for desperate measures ... I'd even ... I'd even ... move to Rothesay,' I said, lurching at Justin.

Justin smirked. 'You'd fit in a treat there, ya miserable little shit. Oh, I'm sick of clubs. Oh, I just want a wee burd. You're fucking Morrissey in disguise.' He leapt from the sofa, swinging the throw above his head in a circular motion, doing his best Morrissey impersonation.

'That is what I'm going to miss. I love you to bits, Justin. Mon, give me a man hug,' I said, knowing that Justin was utterly uncomfortable with any physical acts of affection.

'Right, so who's in charge of the leaving night then?' asked Greg.

'Leaving *night?* Leaving WEEKEND,' shouted Justin.

Twelve

With the approach of the Easter holidays, Justin asked if any of us had any plans. On hearing we'd nothing planned, he invited us to Rothesay for the weekend. A week later, we sat on a ferry heading over to the Isle of Bute.

'Right, lads, I know it's our leaving weekend but there're a few things you need to know. My dad is English and his name is Rupert so don't start pissing yourselves laughing when he introduces himself.'

I sniggered. 'Can I call him Roop?'

'If you want him to take an instant dislike to you … then yes. Watch your P's and Q's as well. That's all I ask. Mind you're representing me. You know what they say, you can tell a lot about someone by the friends they keep. So, try to act semi-responsible and mature.'

Luca ran his hand through his thick, jet-black hair. 'Don't worry, we'll just be ourselves, pal.'

'No. Please don't. That's what I'm worried about. Act mature and responsible instead.'

Menacing grey clouds raced across the sky as if on fast forward. Turbulent waves slapped the ferry, transforming into white foam. Watching the birds in flight fascinated me. Effortless, wings spread but motionless, riding the wind, scanning the sea below, the gannets prepared to pounce. The seagulls rose and fell, mechanical in motion like someone was controlling them with a joystick. I surveyed the contrast between the powerful version of them in full flight and the frail-looking version as they sat on the sea, bobbing up and down, riding the waves. Like two different species. 'Check how different they look from flying to bobbing about in the sea,' I said, turning to Justin.

Clearing his throat, Justin answered, 'Fuck's sake, when'd you turn into Bill Oddie? You're about the same height, right enough. Mon, upstairs to the upper deck, the view is amazing.'

I couldn't fathom him at times. Shaking my head, I pulled my woollen hat from my coat pocket. 'Sorry, I confused you for someone I could have an adult conversation with. My mistake. So, you're wanting to show me the view from the top of the ship? Will I start calling you Horatio Hornblower?' I shoulder charged him. 'Fuckin island thicko.'

Greg and I stood as Luca said, 'I'll stay here, guys. It's too windy out there; it'll mess my hair.'

'What a pathetic excuse for a man,' Justin snapped.

The three of us climbed the metal stairs, the strange sound of our steps echoing around us. 'This sounds like somebody in a film walking to their prison cell,' I said.

Greg laughed. 'It does, you're right.'

Justin opened the door that led to the upper deck. Greg's neck disappeared like a turtle retreating to its shell. 'No wonder you've got those rosy-red cheeks, Justin. Too much time spent up here. It's Baltic.'

We endured a lap of the deck before we retreated back inside. The fierce wind had battered us into submission, forcing us to scurry back to where we'd come from As we approached Luca, he began laughing. 'Greg, has someone set a banger off in your hair? You look like Boris Johnson.'

Patting his hair like it was on fire, Greg said, 'Aye, very good, pretty boy.'

'So, where are we off to tonight? Where's the place to be for the Rothesay Poss-ee,' Luca said, looking pleased with himself.

Justin popped a stick of chewing gum in his mouth. 'The Golfers.'

Luca looked at him incredulously. 'The Golfers? Surely not. Doesn't exactly sound like a hotspot. I've not packed my Pringle or my Farah gear.'

'Nothing like a shitty stereotype is there. I've lived here for over twenty years, I know where to go.'

Luca folded his arms. 'OK. Fair enough. I'll look forward

to the birdies at The Golfers.'

Greg pulled a face. 'Your patter is rank, Luca. I don't know how you even get the girls.'

Luca slowly lowered his hands from his head downwards. 'This is how I get the girls.'

Greg shook his head. 'I hope René is OK. He's never been on a ferry before. Hope he isn't seasick.'

Sniggering, I said, 'He's already roadsick. If he was an animal, he would be put to sleep.'

Greg nudged Justin. 'Tell Connor what bus to get from the ferry terminal.'

***

We drove along the coastal road speeding away from the town centre. The sea to our left, various detached villas with sea views up the slope to our right. The car climbed the hill heading in the latter's direction.

'How far is it from here?' asked Greg.

'That's it there, fourth house along,' Justin said.

Luca and I, sat in the back, looked at each other, mouths agape. Luca tapped Justin on the shoulder. 'You're a right dark horse. Your dad is called Rupert and your house has got to be worth at least half a million, yet you've pled fucking poverty since the first day I met you!'

'This was my grandad's house. He died when I was a baby and my father inherited the place. We aren't rich or anything. Just the aristocracy of Rothesay,' he said with a laugh.

I elbowed Luca. 'Where there's perception there's deception. It's terrible how we judge each other. Why shouldn't Justin live in a big house like this?'

'Who are you? Lloyd fucking Grossman?' said Greg, 'Just who lives in a house like this?' he mimicked. As he pulled the car onto the sweeping, gravel-covered driveway he continued, 'Why not? Are you having a laugh? Look at him. Listen to him. I'm fucking flabbergasted.'

'Cheeky bastard,' Justin said, putting his hands over his

mouth as he remembered he was back on parental soil.

'Mind your language,' warned Luca.

'Do we even know you? Watch this, he's going in there to talk like he's got plums in his mouth,' said Greg, laughing. He parked the car. 'I'm feeling a bit ashamed of René. He's not used to mixing in these circles.'

Justin got out, stretching his legs. The front door opened. A stunning, older woman with beautiful, wavy, brunette hair and fantastic cheekbones, elegantly dressed in an expensive trouser suit, waved in his direction. 'Hi, darling. Pleasant journey?'

Justin walked towards her. 'Yes, Mother, it was fine thanks.'

Greg turned his head, sharing his disbelief with us. Luca shot out of the car. Justin had barely finished embracing his mother before Luca had made his way up the steps. 'Mother, this is Luca. Luca, this is Mother.'

'Delighted to meet you, Mrs Turnbull,' Luca said, as he placed his hands on her shoulders, planting a kiss on both cheeks, causing her to blush.

She smiled at him. 'Please call me Antonetta.'

Greg and I followed them up the steps. Greg jostled in front me.

'Mother this is Greg.'

Greg took her hand, gently kissing it. 'Nice to meet you at last, Mrs Turnbull. We've heard a lot about you.'

'Hello, Greg. Delighted to meet you. Call me Antonetta.'

'And last, but not least, Mother, this is Connor.'

I shook her hand. 'Hi, Mrs Turnbull,' I said, bashfully looking downwards, unable to make eye contact with her. Her beauty made me nervous.

'What charming young men you are. Please, boys, call me Antonetta. Now make yourselves at home. Anything you need, you only have to ask,' she said, turning to enter the house.

Greg and Luca nudged into each other, Luca whispered, 'I know what I'd ask for.'

She led us to the sitting room where we were met with the sight of a pair of crossed legs in paisley silk pyjamas, a giant broadsheet covered the rest of the person sat on the rococo-style armchair. 'Rupert darling, Justin and his friends are here,' Antonetta said in a sing-song voice.

The newspaper dropped to reveal Mr Turnbull. A ruddy faced man in his early fifties, who looked as if he had lived rather too well. His face suggested a regular diet of game and claret. A magnificent thatch of grey hair, blow-dried and lacquered. He removed his spectacles, folded his newspaper and stood to greet his son and his friends. Justin did the introductions. Our level of enthusiasm for meeting Mr Turnbull differed from the level enjoyed by his mother. Frankly, we were disgusted that such a man got to sleep with Justin's mother every night.

'Let me show you to your rooms, gentlemen,' said Antonetta.

Greg and Luca turned into giggling little schoolboys, pulling faces at each other in response to her offer.

As she led us up the stairs, Greg and Luca were virtually foaming at the mouth, their eyes drinking in the sight of her pert bottom in tight black trousers. Feeble behaviour in my book, they were acting out a scene similar to a Carry On movie

'I've put you all on the top floor, Justin. So, two of you are in this room, and the other two have a room each just along the hallway. I'll leave you boys to decide who's sleeping where,' she said as she left.

I raised my hand. 'I'll double up with someone.'

Greg opened the door of one of the rooms. 'I'll take this one.'

Luca did the same, leaving Justin and me to share.

'Listen, you two saddos,' Justin whispered. 'Stop acting like little pervy boys when my mum's around.' He stuck his tongue out like a panting dog. 'The pair of you look pathetic. I was watching the two of you going up the stairs perving at her.'

'Don't know what you're talking about,' Greg said with a shrug.

'Is it a crime to appreciate the beauty of Antonetta?' Luca

asked.

Justin raised his finger pointing at the pair of them. 'Don't give me any of your bullshit. I'm watching the pair of you.'

'Remember your P's and Q's, Justin,' they said in unison, closing the bedroom doors.

Justin chased after Greg, opening his bedroom door. 'Give me the car key,' he said with his hand outstretched, 'Connor and I will go and get all our stuff.'

'No, it's OK, me and Luca will do it.'

Justin snapped. 'Give me the bloody key, Greg,' he said, trying to keep his voice to a whisper.

Reluctantly handing it over, Greg grinned at the protective son. Walking down the stairs, I said, 'Don't let them wind you up. You know the script. If you show them they're getting to you, they'll play on it. You've plenty of experience winding me up. They're not doing anything wrong anyway. Your mum is beautiful looking. They'll calm down. Don't worry.'

'I hope so. I'm starting to regret bringing them.'

***

The promenade was typical of many British seaside resorts. Decrepit. Numerous empty shops peppered the streets. Greg popped some candy floss in his mouth. 'No wonder you couldn't wait to get away from here, Justin. It's grim.'

Luca joined in. 'Can you believe thousands of people used to come here on holiday, back in the day. Now it's an absolute shithole. You're sorted if you like a bag of chips though. Have you seen how many chippies there are?'

We walked the entire length of the promenade. Justin rubbed his hands in excitement. 'Right, guys, you get the picture, it's grim so let's head to the pub. We're here to have fun. C'mon, let's go.'

Good Friday, half past eight, we swaggered towards The Golfers. My first impression was that it was a typical run-of-the-mill pub. Justin opened the door, the others followed. The place was bouncing. A long narrow space crammed with drinkers of varying vintage. From the barely legal through to elderly couples. 'Jesus, it's like Christmas Eve on the Inner Circle in here,' I said. Everybody looked as if they were enjoying themselves. No posing or posturing. Just having a good time. There wasn't even any music playing. Only voices being swallowed by louder voices. 'What a strange mix of people. Are there not pubs that all the young ones stick to and all the old guys stick to, Justin?' I asked.

'Yeah, there's definitely old man pubs but this pub is where you go if you want a bit of atmosphere. Most of the ones our age come in here.'

Greg returned from the bar with four pints. We all raised our glasses. Justin said, 'Here's to a good weekend, guys.' We took a drink from our pints. Justin put his on the ledge of the pillar that we surrounded, looking at Greg and Luca he said, 'Don't even think about bringing any girls back to mine. No chance. If you go away with someone, fair enough. When you're ready to head back to mine, text me or give my mobile two rings and I'll let you in. OK?'

Greg was getting a kick out of Justin's obvious worries about their behaviour. 'Am I allowed to have a shag in my car? Technically it's not bringing somebody back to yours.'

Justin stared at Greg, pausing before he answered. 'You're on my parents' land. So, no you're not allowed. Fill your boots wherever you want, just not at mine *or* on the grounds.'

I butted in. 'Stop winding him up, Greg.'

Greg sniggered. 'Just cos you've no chance of bringing somebody back, don't back him up.'

Justin periodically bumped into old friends. The same small talk prevailed. How're you liking it in Glasgow? How's college? Have you heard about so and so? A touch of jealousy never too far away because he was only visiting and would be off in a couple of days, leaving them to their little parochial existence.

A couple of hours passed, I stood against the pillar watching my friends. *Check out big Luca, girls fussing all over him*, I thought. *That chat I had with him in my room about 'her'. I love that big guy. Greg's been more of a brother to me than that whiney ponce, Paul. Where's Justin? Oh, he's catchin up with his old mates. He winds me up something rotten but he'd do anything for me. Jesus, what am I gonnae do in a couple of months when this ends*? I was distracted from my thoughts about my friends as I spotted a pensioner sitting on his own, nursing a whisky, a contented little smile on his face. Fancying a chat with him, I strolled over. 'Sorry to bother you, mister, is it OK if I take a seat?'

'Course, son, help yourself.'

'Pleased to meet you, I'm Connor. My mates are over there.' I pointed as we shook hands. 'One of our pals fae college is from here, so we're just through for the weekend.'

'Pleased to meet you, son. My name's Wallace. So, how come you're not over there with your pals trying to get a winch?'

I frowned. 'A winch?'

Wallace laughed. 'Aye, a winch. That's what they called it in my day. A kiss.'

'Oh, a see. A cannae be bothered tonight, to be honest. I was just people watching when I saw you sitting with a wee smile on your face and I felt like having a wee chat with yae.'

'Well I'm glad you did, Connor,' Wallace smiled. 'When you get to my age, the young whippersnappers usually give you a wide berth. What age do you think I am?'

I took my time. 'Sixty-eight?'

Wallace beamed. 'Seventy-four.'

'You look well for seventy-four. You lived here all your life?'

'No, I moved here when I retired at sixty-five. Two years after moving here, my wife, Molly, passed away. So, it's just me now.'

'I'm sorry to hear that. You got any kids?'

'Aye, a son, Gordon. He lives in Edinburgh. He tries to get over whenever he can but you know what it's like. Life is hectic for you youngsters nowadays.'

'Where did you come from before you moved here? Hold on a wee minute, let me get us a drink in. What you drinking?'

'That's very kind of you, son. I'll have a Bells. No ice. No water. Just straight please.'

I went to the bar, ordered the drinks before staring into the distance. My mind wandered to my mum. The barman returned with the drinks distracting me from my toxic thoughts.'Cheers, Wallace,' I said, handing him his drink, then took a seat.

'Cheers, son. Your parents have done a great job; you're a gentleman.'

'Oh, a don't know about that but thanks anyhow.'

'What did you do for a living, Wallace, before you retired?'

'I was a teacher in and around Renfrewshire. I'm Paisley born and bred. Taught technical drawing and woodwork for over thirty-five years.'

'I was so shite at techy, so I was. Excuse my language, Wallace.'

He laughed. 'Don't be daft, son. You don't teach in Paisley for the length of time I did without hearing a bit of swearing.'

'You know what, I've never had a granny or grandad. They died when I was tiny. I'd have loved a grandad or a granny. Aw the stories they've got up their sleeves. Some people think it's boring, but I love it.'

'Uck, that's a shame, son. I'm still waiting on grandchildren myself. My Gordon is a careerist. Well, you've got all that in front of you, son. Marriage. Kids. Grandchildren. What you doing at college?'

'Business, marketing and communications.'

'So, what you fancy doing then? You got something in mind?'

'Na, just see what comes my way. No great plan or that. Plenty of time.'

'But it's always good to work towards something, son.'

'Aye, I know what you mean. I'm terrible for that. I should think about it a bit more. You got any pals o'er here you can go for a wee drink with?'

'Aye, a couple, son. It's difficult though. My pals are still married, so they're not in the same predicament.'

'You like living here though, Wallace?'

Wallace rubbed his chin. Paused. 'Memories, son. Good and bad. I just wish we'd been given more time together here. We only got two years. Listen to me … getting all maudlin. Was that a gin you bought me?' He laughed.

'Hey, don't worry about it, Wallace. I've liked chatting to you.'

Wallace drained the rest of his drink. 'Listen, son – it might only have been a wee five- or ten-minute chat, but that wee chat there has made my week. When you're my age, the only thing you want somebody to give you, is what you've given me. A wee bit of time. You're a good boy.' He stuck his hand out, shaking mine.

'Will you get up the road alright, Wallace? You getting a taxi?'

'No, son, I'm a five-minute walk at most. It's fine. You take care of yourself. And go and enjoy yourself with the rest of your buddies. Life's too short, Connor. Go and grab it by the balls' – he laughed – 'and if you're in here tomorrow, I'll buy you a pint. Deal?'

'I'll hold you to that, Wallace. And don't go playing the old forgetful man's card saying you don't remember me,' I said with a smile. 'One last question before you go. If I'm being too nosy, tell me to beat it.'

'Ask away, son.'

'See just before I came over to your table, you had a wee contented smile on your face. What were you thinking about?'

Wallace took two steps forwards. 'Me and Molly. We were walking along the promenade one day at this time of the year. I know it was this time because we were talking about what happened to the April showers cos it was blowing an absolute hooley. So, we're walking along the promenade and the wind blew Molly's skirt up to her head. She was mortified. The look on her face. That was what I was smiling at.'

He turned and walked to the door, pausing before leaving, he waved. 'Cheerio, Connor. Thanks, son.'

I took a swig of my pint then emitted a large puff of breath. Looking to the ceiling, I shook my head. *Right, Connor, mind the man's advice – Grab it by the balls. Life's too short*. I laughed. *Am too short.*

I've no idea why, but I've often thought of old Wallace. What a cracking old guy. Total shame. Life's not fucking fair for some people. Two wee shitty years of retirement with his wife. Working for thirty-five years, probably getting the piss taken out of him by wee morons like I was at school.

Thirteen

Tapping the beer mat on the table, I flipped it between my fingers. Greg returned from the bar with our drinks. An Australian themed pub, a few minutes' walk from the flat.

'Wonder who came up with the idea that an Australian themed pub would go down a storm in Glasgow, Greg?'

'Agreed. I get London. Glasgow… No.'

'So, I was thinking. This is going to sound strange—'

Greg interrupted me, 'Don't know if I like the sound of this.'

'Very funny. When I think of getting two new flatmates, I just can't picture it. It feels weird, somehow. It wouldn't be the same. I kinda feel it would be disloyal to Justin and Luca. I know it's stupid but that's the way I feel.'

Greg took a sip of his pint. 'I suppose I get that. Let's face it, we're not going to get another Luca, are we?'

'No chance. We won a watch with the big man. I don't know how I'd cope if we ended up with a right pair of untidy bastards or somebody I didn't get on with.'

'Like you get on with Justin! Anyway, I've been working things out. It would be about a hundred and seventy quid each per month on top of what we both pay just now to keep the flat on. If you manage to get a full-time job, with my student loan I reckon we could afford it between us. What do you think?'

'I think we should go for it. If it turns out things are too tight, we could think about taking one flatmate on. Maybe somebody we know who's looking for a room? Plus, we don't need to tell the landlord anything. He's only interested in getting paid every month on time like we've been doing for two years.'

Greg pushed his pint forwards. 'Here's to new beginnings.

Happy days.'

'Cheers. Good times ahead. Right, we've had the leaving weekend so what about the leaving night then…'

***

Luca picked at the plate of food with his cutlery, like a surgeon performing a delicate operation. 'Meatballs could do with a bit of seasoning. The bolognese sauce is spot on. Spaghetti could be a bit more al dente. Well done though, Connor, that's a brilliant effort. We'll make a cook of you yet.'

'Well, it's the last supper, pal. I've eaten like a king thanks to you. The least I could do was try and start the leaving night with a bit of half-decent grub. I've even tried a tiramisu, laden with booze,' I said, rubbing my hands. 'Anyway, I've not had the chance to chat to you. How you feeling about moving back with the parents?'

'Mixed feelings.' Luca sighed. 'You know I play on the whole Scottish Italian thing but family is the be all and end all. I'm glad I'm getting a chance to make things up to them but I'm going to really struggle with getting my wings clipped. I've loved it here with you guys.'

'Don't let him get you aw sentimental, Luca,' said Greg as he and Justin walked into the living room.

I punched Greg's upper arm. 'Can't have a private conversation in here! Listen, there's no doubt about it, I'm going be as sentimental as fuck tonight whether you guys like it or not. The three of you have been like brothers to me.'

Luca smiled at me while Justin looked at Greg, both of them rolling their eyes at me.

'When you've had a family like mine, you really appreciate it when you meet brilliant people like you three who have your best interests at heart.'

'Give it a rest, ya wee wummin,' said Greg.

'Right, I'm going to get us a beer, say a wee toast, then I'll shut up,' I said as I left for the kitchen to a chorus of boos led by Justin.

Handing out the beers, I ushered them to their feet. We

raised our cans. 'To the best flatmates a guy could wish for. I love yiz to bits. Good luck, guys.'

'Good luck,' they repeated, as we prepared for our last night out together as flatmates.

***

The only interview that I'd undergone was an informal interview for the job in the deli, I had no experience of a proper interview. Being fed up after two years of college, securing a full-time job to pay the rent was my only goal. I needed to earn money and quickly. My search for employment dragged me towards one call-centre job after another. The market was saturated with these jobs. The salaries on offer were more than acceptable. Utility companies, banks, insurance companies, and so on.

The first reply I received was from a PPI reclaim company in the city centre. The banks losing the landmark case about mis-sold PPI policies was as far as my knowledge went. At the interview, it was explained to me by the enthusiastic MD that this court case was akin to a dam bursting. There'd be millions of claims throughout the UK. This company, PPI Pro-claim.com, were ideally placed to grab a large piece of this burgeoning market. Great potential for promotion especially for someone with my qualifications, the MD advised. It was obvious to me that the MD desperately needed to fit bums on seats. Weighing up the offer, I thought, Why not? I need the money for the rent and this'll give me a right few quid in my pocket. I've got plenty of time to find my perfect job. This is ideal for now.

Two weeks after the interview, I walked into the new call centre to start my two-week induction. My only worries were about my fellow colleagues. *What will the people be like? Young or old? Will I get on with them? Might meet some nice people. It's a new experience – embrace it.*

My fellow new starts and I were being shown around the office. Entering the main floor, I whispered to a guy whose name I had already forgotten, 'You could get an eleven-a-side football match in here, check the size of this place.' Well over twenty pods, consisting of six cubicles within each pod. Large partitions separated the workers from each other. Designed to quash the sound from your neighbour and any thought of interaction in equal measure. You needed to stand, or turn 180 degrees to see another human being. The partitions and desks were decorated with memorandums, personal photos, drawings by children, calendars, etc. The light was harsh – long fluorescent tubes strategically placed on the cheap-looking, polystyrene ceiling tiles. Water coolers stationed in the four corners. An LED screen on the main wall detailed in-bound and out-bound call data. Calls handled. Calls missed. Everything and everyone scrutinised.

The first week was a real drag. I hadn't ingratiated myself particularly well with Mark, my Team Leader. On the first morning, we sat in a semicircle facing Mark who had instructed us to tell everyone a little bit about ourselves. 'Hi, my name is Duncan … I'm from St Kilda. I have just moved to Glasgow and I'm looking forward to working here.' Having listened to the inane introductions, I decided to add a sprinkling of humour as I introduced myself. 'Hi, everyone. My name is Connor … and I'm an alcoholic.' I gave the reaction it received a nine out of ten when I relayed it to Greg later that night, however, Mark wasn't impressed. I felt I'd been identified as a possible troublemaker. The actual job was going to be a breeze. Mark emphasised the importance of the script that he'd handed out. 'The script is our bible. We stick to it *rigidly*. Verbatim, OK?'

I knew there was going to be trouble ahead between Mark and me. As the week went on, I took an ever stronger dislike to my team leader. "He's a pair of small, rimless specs away from being the identikit of an SS officer. A nasty, heavily gelled, side-shed with a smug look of superiority" was the description I gave to Greg. The second week was more hands on as we practised our telephone skills on each other remotely from the adjoining training room. Encouraged to throw in the odd curveball to analyse how we would react to attempts to deviate us from the script or, as I now called it, 'the Scriptures

According to St Mark'.

Despite my dislike of Mark, I was looking forward to my first proper day and getting settled. A permanent desk. My place within the company. On my first day, I was told that I was now the proud resident of Pod Seven, Seat Three. *Branded like cattle.* No longer Connor Boyd. I became 7.3. I met my immediate neighbours. To my left, Tina: overweight, plastered in make-up and fake tan, eyebrows like slugs resting above her spidery false eyelashes. I was soon introduced to her incredibly loud voice – one that had the ability to cut me in two with the pitch. Worse still, for a female, the words uttered by her tended to be of the strong industrial type. To my right was Duncan from St Kilda. I spent a few minutes in the training room analysing Duncan, privately giving him the moniker, Worzel, because he was a ringer for Worzel Gummidge. It looked like someone had cut his hair with a knife and fork, dangling as it did like straw from a scarecrow. His features were incredibly sharp, a nose that was shaped like a cone party hat, barely visible lips hidden below, and a chin shaped like the letter V. He didn't make much of an effort with his appearance did old Wurzel. His shirt was white a couple of years back and his trousers look like he's slept in them. I felt a bit sorry for him. I knew he'd struggle to fit in. I made a point of being nice to him.

When the first monthly wage slip arrived, I felt great about myself. Looking at it, I thought, *You're a proper fucking adult now, Connor*. Floating out of the office that night, I looked forward to a good weekend. My first month working full-time. A job that, so far, I was enjoying and enough money in my pocket to prevent me from worrying about paying bills or rent. *Think I'll treat Greg to a pizza and a few beers tonight,* I thought.

Fourteen

Our ideas as to what represented a successful night out were markedly different. The club was as dark as one of my moods, the wooden flooring sticky which resulted in Billy Connolly like comedy walking. The air smelt like a toxic cocktail of perfume, questionable body odour, artificial smoke and strong alcohol. Lighting a match would likely engulf the club in flames.

'So, you go into a shop to buy clothes. Great lighting, mirrors, upbeat music. You go in and try something on and if it doesn't suit, you know it doesn't suit because the lighting and the mirrors tell you that. You take it off, hand it back, and say, "No thanks, love, it wasn't a great fit" or whatever. When you go in and try it on, they don't turn the lights down so you can barely see your hand in front of your face and have to take a mad punt on whether it suits you or not. Now, Greg, look around you, it's fucking pitch black in here. Look at the smoke firing out the DJ's box. It's like a scene from The Walking Dead.' I moved my hand from right to left across the scene in front of us like a cheesy game show host showing a contestant what they could have won. 'This is the environment where I'm supposed to meet the love of my life and you're supposed to meet your next conquest.'

Hand over my shoulder but scanning the area for anything that might take his fancy, Greg said, 'Connor, you're too serious, buddy. You work all week in a job that doesn't exactly tax your brain; you're chained to a headset for most of the day. This is where you release the valve from the pressure cooker, not where you dissect the merits of the lighting system. Anyway, you're just using that as an excuse for the mingers that I've seen you pull.'

We were drunk, not 'staggering around, spilling pints, bumping into people' drunk. Just happy drunk, enjoying each other's company.

'Aye, I'm one to talk, Connor. Do you remember that time I pulled that girl that said she went to college with us but we couldn't remember ever seeing her at college?'

'Not got a clue who you're talking about, pal.'

'The one with the eye.'

'They've usually got two eyes, pal.'

'Aye, well this one had two alright, listen to this… So I get chatting to this girl, says she knows me from college. I don't recognise her but I go along with it … use it to my advantage as an inroad. Are you sure you weren't there that night?'

'Just get on with it. I wasn't there; it must have been Justin or Luca.'

'Right, so I'm all over her … she is all over me … I've got the contract out … we've both signed it … we are going back to hers. I'm sent to the cloakroom to get the jackets and I've to meet her at the front desk, you know, where you pay in. So I walk back from getting her jacket … the lights are up and she is waving at me… Fucking hell, Connor! One eye was a nice normal green eye and the other one is like one of those zombie chewing-gum balls that kids love. You know, all grey with veins and shit. God knows what happened to make her eye look like that. I'm no in the habit of carrying eye patches aboot wi me like that Gabrielle. Never mind dreams can come true. This was a fucking nightmare. A mean, I'm thinking there's no way I'm going home with that. Justin looks at me with his biggest smart-arse smile, as if, "How you gonnae get out of this one then?"'

I pulled the pint from my mouth. 'So, it was Justin you were with then.'

'Aye, must have been. So, I'm thinking I'm just gonnae have to put her aff me; let her know I'm no having the eye thing. I elbow Justin and I say, "Where is it you stay again, sexy? … *eye*-Brox? You gonnae use your … *eye*-phone to call us a taxi?"

'She's no daft, Connor. She knows what I'm getting at. She just says, "You're a dick. See me, not my eye" and storms out.

'Now, I'm relieved but the nosy bastards that are hanging around waiting on taxis are calling me all sorts, telling me what a bastard I am.'

I was doubled over in a drunken fit of laughter, tears running down my cheeks. 'I mean, I'm pleading my case, trying to explain that it's not my fault that she has a weird eye thing going on and it was dark so I didn't know until I came back with the jackets, but they're not having it.

'See, I'm weird that way. Some guys would have gone up the road with her and put the eye to the back of their minds and just filled their boots. Say I went back to hers … I could have done it doggy style so I wasn't looking at the eye but it would have haunted me and then the wee man might not have played ball … gone all floppy and before you know it you've got a bad reputation. You go back up the town the following week and some of the girls are smirking at you and one of the mouthpieces says, "Hey Greg, did you ask the DJ to play Sigur Ros?" I'd ask her what she was going on about. "Did you ask for Floppypolla?" and all her posse are fucking cackling like witches. That's probably what would have happened, Connor.'

'And you say that I'm too serious! Are you for real?'

'Always. That's me, alright. Keeping it real. I'm going to the bar. Same again?'

I nodded then engaged in a bit of people watching. Some of the scenes that unfolded in clubs fascinate me. I scanned the dance floor. Looking out for some of the comical sights as some deluded individuals convinced themselves they could really dance. The dance floor was clouded in smoke but it cleared to reveal an enthusiastic dancer who was dancing like he was listening to a faster song than the rest of the dance floor. My head bobbed from side to side as I scanned the bar area wondering what was keeping Greg. *No doubt he's chatting somebody up.* I waited five minutes or so then, losing patience, headed to the bar. Greg was nowhere to be seen. *I'll get myself a drink, he'll show up in a minute.* I saw two girls in the corner arguing, the one facing me was gesticulating angrily, the one with her back to me had her arms outstretched in a gesture indicating that she was trying to reason with her friend. I watched the girl who was facing me storm off, leaving her friend on her own. The friend turned, shaking her head, then wiped her eyes. She leant against the bar as she ordered a drink. I watched her take her drink before walking in my direction.

As she approached, I tapped her arm. 'Sorry, I'm not being nosy or trying to chat you up or anything but I saw you arguing with your friend. Are you OK? My friend's posted missing the now so I was just people watching when I saw the two of you arguing.'

She evaluated me. 'Thanks for asking. I'm fine.'

I smiled. 'That's good.' Becoming aware of how attractive she was, I quickly looked away. Beautiful people make me nervous. Seconds later, sensing she was still there, I looked back at her.

It was clear that she was waiting for me to speak. I felt awkward. My patter and small talk didn't win any awards. I'm pretty self-aware. I know my limitations. So, I just smiled. Her expression was that of surprise that nothing was forthcoming. Eventually, she said, 'Do you know, it's sad really. I stood here waiting on you hitting me with a pathetic chat-up line or some witty banter designed to impress me. And there was you actually just being nice, asking if I was OK. That's bad, isn't it?'

'If it's patter you're after, I'm definitely not the man for the job,' I laughed. 'I was just saying to my friend earlier, look around you, is this really the place where you are supposed to meet the love of your life? Really?' What a stupid thing to say! I chastised myself.

She laughed. 'I totally agree. I'm Laura, pleased to meet you.' She held her hand out.

I shook her hand. 'Eh, oh right. Well. Hello, Connor. I'm Laura.' She giggled at my mistake.

She had her own style. A long, baggy, floral skirt with a long-sleeved, tight-fitting, black top and a pair of worn-looking ankle boots. Her hair was blonde, wavy, chin-length, curling away from her face. Just pure class.

'Do you fancy getting a seat? Just a chat, no strings.'

She smiled. 'Why not.'

We took a seat next to the bar. 'Has your friend left?'

'No, she'll be sat with the creep we were arguing about. She thinks more of two patter merchants than her friend. She'll be down there listening to their nonsense. Can you believe that the one who approached me said, "Do you work at Subway?" I didn't have a clue what he was talking about, so I said, "No. Why?" The sleazebag had a right creepy grin on his face, you'll never believe what he said, Connor. He said, "Cos you've just given me a foot-long."

I burst out laughing. She looked at me, hesitated, then joined in. 'When I say it now, I've got to laugh, I suppose. I'm just bored rigid with daft line after line. It gets tedious. I like a laugh the same as everyone else but not humourless, immature chat-up lines. So, I just ignored him. He was talking utter garbage. I said to Jo that I wanted to move away from them, but she took the huff. I'm too serious, stuck-up and frigid, apparently,' she said with a laugh.

'Difficult, isn't it? When there's two of you and your ideas of a good night are different. Greg and I are best mates. He's a brilliant guy but he loves the chase. I can't be bothered with the falseness of it all. I've not got all the patter like him.'

'Exactly, Connor.' She tilted her head, smiled, looking at me as if suddenly seeing me in a different light. 'So, what do you do?'

'I work in a call centre, capturing new PPI claimants. I only started a couple of months ago, before that I was at college for a couple of years. Greg and I rent a flat over in the West End. What about you?'

'Well, I'm in social services. I love my job. Don't get me wrong, some of the cases are heartbreaking but there's great job satisfaction.'

'Is it not hard to switch off from a job like that?'

'Sometimes. I suppose it's like any other job though. Good days, bad days.'

I finished my drink. 'Can I get you a drink, Laura?'

'Yeah, go on, thanks. Glass of white wine please. She'll have to look for me for a change. See how she likes it.' She smiled. Beautiful dimples, eyes that lit up when she smiled. *God, she is stunning! What a smile, it's turning me into a nervous wreck*, I thought as I walked to the bar.

Ordering the drinks, I puffed my cheeks out. *Don't blow it, Connor. She obviously doesn't suffer fools. Uck, don't be daft. You've no chance anyway. Forget it. She's out of your league. She's only chatting cos her friend has gone AWOL.* I was elated to return with the drinks and find she was still there. Handing her drink over, I clinked glasses with her. 'Cheers.'

'Cheers. So what are you into? What kind of things do you like? Apart from going out at weekends and calling yourself Laura!'

I tapped my fingers nervously on the table. 'What do I like? Well, there hasn't been much time for stuff recently, what with working full-time but I like all the normal things – going to see a film, music, going out with friends, just the usual. What about you?'

'Same really but I like trying new stuff. I try to do something different every couple of weekends if I can. Like last week me and a friend went orbing. Have you heard of that?'

'Yeah, some of my friends have tried it,' I lied, not wanting to come across as stupid.

'It's amazing. What a laugh. It really picks up a bit of speed.'

'Yeah, I'll get around to giving it a go.'

Laura flicked her hair. 'Maybe if you wanted to, Connor, we could go to the pictures or something one night.'

I was so flabbergasted that I couldn't answer. Then, I saw the frown on her forehead. 'Oh. Absolutely. Definitely. Yeah, that'd be great. I'd love that,' I answered, an awful attempt at trying not to appear too eager.

She smiled. 'We'll swap numbers later, OK?'

'Yeah, no problem,' I took a large swig from my bottle of

lager. 'Do you know what I noticed about you that I liked straight away?'

She smiled and gave me a playful push. 'Don't go spoiling it, Connor. This had better not be a cheesy chat-up line.'

'No chance. I don't have any. What I noticed was that you're confident enough to have your own style. Girls are starting to go for the exact same look. It's like a bunch of sheep. Characterless. You have your own look and it's a great look.'

She looked touched by my comment. 'That's really nice, Connor. Thank you.' She paused, then said, 'Sorry, but would you mind if we looked for Jo? I'm starting to get a bit worried.'

'Of course, let's go.' Picking up my bottle, I followed her.

'I think she went over there.' She pointed to the far corner beyond the dancefloor.

We searched for a few minutes before Laura spotted her sat in a corner, kissing a guy, presumably the guy she'd been speaking to earlier. 'There she is. C'mon, and I'll introduce you, Connor.' Standing in front of her friend, Laura put her hand on Jo's thigh. She began to rub it, got no reaction so slapped the girl's thigh instead. Jo opened her eyes, pulled away from the kiss. 'Oh, hi, Laura. Everything OK? And who is this? Are you going to introduce me?'

'Jo, this is Connor. I just wanted to make sure you were OK.'

'All good. You having a good night, Connor?'

'Yeah, I lost my mate but found Laura, so it's a great night.'

'Your mate must be a right shit,' she joked, trying to impress her new friend who looked as if he wished we'd disappear.

'OK, Kelly Osborne, I'll be up at the seats next to the bar when you're done.'

Spotting the resemblance, I laughed. Jo's new friend joined in before he was rewarded with a slap on the chest.

'Bye then,' Laura said, leading me away, both of us

laughing at Jo's evident annoyance.'I know that was below the belt and I shouldn't resort to her level. She can't help herself. She acts so differently when guys are about. She tries too hard. Turns into a show-off. She's a good friend really, just yearns for attention. Oh, I love this song, let's dance,' she said, dragging me towards the dance floor, making it clear that I'd no choice in the matter.

Some people stand out, fascinating you with the way they move, talk, look. Presence, that's what they have. Presence. She danced differently from anybody I'd seen. Eyes closed. As though she didn't care what anyone thought of her. She leant over to me. 'So what are we going to go see at the pictures then?'

'*Hangover Two* is out next week?' I answered.

'Good shout, Connor. I loved the first one. Definitely. That's a plan.'

I wanted to kiss her but couldn't bring myself to try. Unsure of myself. *Maybe she just wants to be friends. Why would she be interested in me?*

She looked at me, as if reading my mind. Smiling, she said, 'You can kiss me if you want to.'

It wasn't a kiss filled with lust. It was beautiful. Gentle. Different.

Fifteen

I lay on the sofa, several cushions propped up behind my head. Placing my book on my lap, I turned to face Greg who was sitting on the armchair to my right, looking through *Private Eye*. 'Greg, what is orbing?'

Greg lowered his magazine, making eye contact. 'You know those massive see-through balls that you go inside, like a hamster's ball and you roll down a hill or whatever. That's orbing. Although I think they call it zorbing.'

'Right. Laura went orbing and asked if I knew what it was. I told her my friends had been before.'

'Yeah, that's a great start. Start as you mean to go on. Daft wee lies for no reason.'

'I didn't want to seem stupid.'

Greg laughed. 'So, you prefer to be a liar than not know what orbing is? She didn't ask you what a knife and fork is. Orbing isn't the nation's favourite pastime you know.'

My face must have bore a nervous look as I patted the arm of the sofa. 'This is pathetic, Greg, but I've never been on a date before. I don't have a clue.'

Greg shook his head. 'It's no big deal. You're going to the pictures. Just watch the film, no wandering hands or chit-chat. Where you meeting her?'

'Going for a coffee before the movie.'

'Right, no doubt you'll get there first. Get yourself a coffee. When she arrives, tell her she looks amazing ... beautiful, whatever compliment you want to give her. Then ask her what she's having and get it for her. Take a seat and chat. Be yourself. Don't try too hard. Easy as that.'

'This is me we're talking about, Greg. You know what I'm like. I'm a nervous wreck. I'm scared I'll blow it. I don't know why she even asked me out.'

Greg looked to the ceiling in exasperation. 'Fuck me, Sadsack. Get a grip. She asked you cos she likes you. Not for a bet. Not cos she felt sorry for you. Not cos she has nothing else to do. There's no point in going if that's your attitude. How many times have a told you about trying to be confident.'

I jumped from the sofa, ruffled Greg's hair. 'You're right. Aye, you're right. Cheers. Right, I'm away to get ready.'

***

The view from the multiplex coffee shop was something to behold. The lights of the city stretching as far as the eye could see. Sat with an Americano at a window seat I looked at the city lights, picking out some landmarks. My attention turned to the cinema. *Wonder what the last film I saw was*? I thought. My nerves affected my thought process. *Forget it, Connor. Just try and breathe properly before you faint. Pathetic. What a state to get into. Sort yourself out.* I scanned the place hoping to find something or someone that would give me a distraction. A bit of eavesdropping on a conversation or trying to decipher the relationship between two people sat together. There weren't many people in and the ones that were offered no possibility for my brain to get sidetracked. Looking back out the window, I felt a pair of cold hands cover my eyes, 'Guess who,' said a female voice I instantly recognised. The hands were removed and Laura took a seat opposite me.

'Hi, Laura. I've got a coffee already. What can I get you?'

'Skinny latte, please.'

I walked towards the counter. *Shit, the compliment.* I turned and headed back to the table. 'Sorry, I meant to say, you look amazing.' Seriously, I was like someone from The Undateables.

She laughed. 'Delayed reaction, Connor? Thank you.'

I felt a pained expression dominating my face. 'Sorry, I'm a wee bit nervous, Laura. This is actually the first date I've ever been on.'

Her face took on the kind of glow that women get when

they've just peered inside a newborn baby's pram. 'Aaawww, that's so nice,' she reached up to grab my hand, giving it a squeeze, 'Just relax. OK?'

'OK. I'll go and get your coffee now.'

She laughed as she removed her scarf, 'OK, Connor. You get me my coffee.'

Waiting on the latte, I felt a hand on my shoulder then Laura's voice in my ear, 'By the way, I forgot to tell you, you look really handsome.' She kissed my cheek. Laughing, I turned and watched her return to her seat, noticing again, how beautiful I found her.

I returned with the latte, feeling more at ease.

Laura sipped her coffee. 'How's your day been then, Connor?'

'Honestly, it dragged in, probably cos I was looking forward to seeing you tonight.'

'That's what's so endearing about you. There's no flannel. You're so open and direct. You say what you think and what you feel. I like that.'

My body relaxed into the chair, her words releasing all of the remaining tension.

'I always try to be straight to the point. I can't stand people that say one thing but do another. There's so much falseness, isn't there? How was your day? Oh sorry, you're probably not allowed to discuss cases with anybody, are you?'

Laura added another sugar to her drink. 'Yeah, that's right, we're not allowed to go into any details about specific cases outside work. It's probably for the best. You need to try and switch off or you'd become a work bore, rattling on about work to anyone willing to listen.'

I placed my cup clumsily on the saucer almost causing it to tip over. 'I'll impose a sanction on myself from ever talking about work because it bores me silly. I wouldn't want to inflict it on someone else.'

'You said you've only started recently after being at college for a couple of years, didn't you?'

I unzipped my leather bomber jacket. 'Yeah. I'd done two years at college and was getting bored with it. Four of us had flat-shared for two years but two of them were moving on. Justin went travelling and Luca went to work in the family business. Greg and I didn't want to move or get new flatmates. It wouldn't have been the same living with new people so I decided to get a job. I needed to earn a wage to pay for the rent. It'll do for now. I've plenty of time to decide what I really want to do.'

'You must have left home pretty quickly then. What age were you?'

'Just turned eighteen. I couldn't wait though. I've always wanted my independence. It's not for everybody but I love it. I couldn't go back to being at my parents'.'

'You got any brothers or sisters?'

'One brother. Paul. You?'

'No, only child,' she said, mimicking a sad face. 'Just me, my parents and a couple of dogs. So, are you all domesticated then, Connor. Can you cook and clean and all that?'

I laughed. 'I'll let you be the judge of that. I'll cook dinner for you sometime. Big Luca, my old flatmate, taught me a few things.'

Laura nodded her head. 'That'd be nice; I'll look forward to that.'

'Jesus, I forgot. What time is it?'

'Quarter to.'

'We better go, the movie started five minutes ago.'

I picked up her coat, scarf and bag, grabbed my jacket and we began to jog towards Screen Three, looking at each other, laughing. The girl at the entrance asked for our tickets. 'Laura, they're in my back pocket, can you get them for me please, my hands are full.' She put her hand in my pocket, I jumped away. 'Hey, cut that out, it's our first date.' I looked at the ticket girl. 'Can you believe that? First date and she is groping my bum.'

Laura handed the tickets to the girl then turned to me, laughing, raising an eyebrow. 'You're worth a watching. You planned that, I bet. Ticket in the back pocket, holding all the jackets. Fly man.'

'You're the groper, not me. I hope you're gonnae contain yourself and let me watch the movie in peace.'

After the movie, I walked her to the bus stop as we chatted about our favourite bits in the movie. We kissed. Waiting on the bus arriving, I asked, 'Are you doing anything at the weekend?'

'Going over to Jo's on Friday but I'm free on Saturday afternoon or Sunday.'

'You fancy doing something then?' I asked.

'Yeah, definitely. We'll have a think about what and where and get something organised, OK?' She leant forwards and kissed me. When the bus finally arrived, I stood and watched her get to her seat. She looked out the window at me. The dimples, the eyes, everything, just her. She waved goodbye as the bus pulled away. I stood there. Smiling. Drinking it in. Buzzing. A few minutes passed before I decided to head home to share how well it had gone with Greg.

Sixteen

Nearly three blissful months had passed since our first date. Texts back and forth. Long phone calls. Numerous dates, eating out together, visits to the pub, generally spending as much time as possible getting to know one another. I couldn't concentrate on work or anything else. Only Laura. Time not spent with her was tortourous. I transformed my room from a typical student's bedroom to something more cosy, homely and female friendly courtesy of the local charity shops. Walls were painted, pictures hung. A massive Persian-style rug covered the awful-looking carpet. I replaced the minging, gold-coloured curtains with something more modern. Nice bed linen, cushions that decorated the bed and a throw – all appeared when Laura came over, then were banished when she left to prevent the wind-up that would no doubt have materialised. I pictured Greg. *'Where's your teddies, Connor? They away on a picnic?'* Mimicking Colin or Justin from the TV, camping it up. *'Oh I dooo love that colour, and what about that throw and those cushions. Simply divine.'*

***

It was Friday night around eleven o'clock. We'd shared a takeaway and watched a DVD. As we lay in bed, our legs entwined, Laura's head resting on my shoulder, her hand stroking my chest, she asked, 'Why don't you ever speak about your family or introduce me to them? You've met my parents.' I had known this was bound to come up at some point. Several times I had tortured myself about it. *What am I going do if she asks me to meet them? I don't want to introduce Laura to 'her'. Mary would find some way of spoiling things.* I put it to the back of my mind, hoping it would never come up.

'It's complicated.'

'Explain it to me then. I might be able to help.'

Struggling to find an answer, I began to fidget, massage my temple. 'I really don't like speaking about my family, to be honest.'

Silence enveloped the bedroom. Awkwardness. Sensing that I'd disappointed her by not sharing my feelings, I rolled away from her body onto my side and faced her. The street lamplight provided enough light to see each other's faces. Our heads rested sideways on the pillows. Looking in her eyes, I said, 'Laura, I promise you, one day, I'll tell you about my relationship with my mother. You know I'm usually straight to the point about things, don't you?'

'Yeah, I know you are; that's fine, Connor. I don't want to push you or seem nosy. I just wondered why you never speak about them or have never introduced me. Would they not approve or something?'

'Are you having a laugh? Approve? They will be in shock when they meet you … in a good way,' I laughed.

She smiled at me. 'We'll see.'

'I love you, Laura. I really love you.'

I hadn't told her before, hadn't planned on saying it. The words had barely escaped when panic set in. Those couple of seconds. What if I'd frightened her off? A huge smile appeared on her face, those beautiful dimples, she put her arms around me and kissed me. Looking into my eyes, she said, 'I love you too, Connor.'

I gently placed my hands on her face, moving her hair to the side, kissing her softly. 'You don't know how much that means to me. I know how lucky I am to have you. I won't do anything to hurt you.'

She clasped her hand around mine. 'I'll hold you to that,' she said with a smile.

On hearing her fall asleep, I leant over to look at her. A humungous smile spread over my face, the smile of someone who can't quite believe their luck. Thoughts passed through my mind like a monkey swinging from tree to tree. I felt transformed. Refreshed. Energised. Those words. Just five words. Words that changed everything for me. My attitude and outlook towards life, my demeanour, my self-worth. My whole being. I'd been desperate for someone to love me. Having found it, I just needed to take care of it. Nurture it.

***

Ambling over to my pod on Monday morning, ten minutes before my shift, I smiled at Tina. 'Morning, how you doin this morning? Good weekend?'

She looked at me, a puzzled expression on her face. 'Wit you so cheery about? Yae get lucky or somethin?' She had an annoying habit of shaking her head from side to side, her tongue peeking out slightly as it rested on her bottom teeth, her eyebrows raised, as she spoke. *She watches too much American Trash TV*, I concluded.

'Luck doesn't come into it, Tina. You had your tan done again? You're looking particularly ... orange.' I laughed. 'Oompa loompa doompety doo, I've had another spray tan or two. Oompa loompa doompety dee, if I have five, I get one for free.' Her evident annoyance at my singing provided me with much amusement.

'Aye, that's better short-arse. Yae worry me when you're being civil. By the way, Connor, you're gonnae need to speak ti Duncan. Wait till you see the nick of him when he comes in. I think he's in the toilet the now. There's at least four people who said to me last week they are gonnae speak to Mark about his Body Odour.'

'That's out of order. Poor guy. I'm not having that. I'll speak to him at lunchtime. Give the guy a break, he's just moved from the middle of nowhere to a big city. He's finding his feet.'

'It's no his feet he needs to find. It's his deodorant. He's rank. Totally barking.'

'You'd kiss him, Tina, I know you would.'

'That'll be fuckin right. He gives me the boak. No chance.' She shook her head. 'Cheeky wee shite.'

'Aaaww for feck's sake,' I said at the sight of Duncan approaching the pod. 'Who shaved you this morning? Edward Scissorhands?'

Tina's deep, manly laugh shot into the air drowning out nearby voices.

'Look at the state of you, Duncan. You've half a bog roll on your face and there's spots of blood on your collar.' I grimaced. 'You not got a mirror in the flat, Dunc? What kind of razors are you using? Or is it garden shears? Fuck me.' I shook my head, feeling a mixture of pity and disgust.

Duncan logged into the system as the calls would start to filter through any minute. 'Connor, ma face is reid raw. Av mak'd a right mess o it,' he said, wincing. His strong accent had us in stitches at times.

'I need a word with you later, when you-know-who isn't about, alright, Dunc?'

'Nae botha freend.'

'Aye. Hullo, this is Duncan from PPI ProClaim.com is that Mrs Watson?'

The madness began. Some days I panicked at the sheer volume of calls, feeling like a sprinter hearing the starter gun as the first of the calls filtered through. On other days, I breezed through it, handling the calls effortlessly, in a rhythmic manner.

Returning from lunch with two cans of antiperspirant, a packet of Gillette razors and shaving foam, I placed them on Duncan's desk. A small note in the bag read,

> *Dunc, a couple of rotten bastards are saying they are going to complain to Mark about your body odour. Don't give them or him the satisfaction, buddy. Head into the bogs when you get a minute and have a right good blast of one of these. Don't be offended, pal, I'm only trying to help you.*

When Duncan returned to the pod a couple of minutes later, I stood while taking the call that had come through so I could see into the neighbouring cubicle. I felt bad as I saw Duncan's small, sad-looking homesick eyes when he opened the bag and read the note. Duncan stood, patted me on the back and mouthed, 'Thanks, neebor, yer a pal,' before he headed to the toilet.

As I finished the call, Mark made an appearance. Everything was done for effect with that guy. He looked at his watch, looked at the Duncan-less seat. 'Mmmmm.' Scanning the floor, then turning to me. 'Where is he?' nodding in the direction of the empty seat.

'Aaaahhh, a visit from the Inner Party, what a pleasure. Is he to be found guilty of committing the crime of visiting the toilet? Are the telescreens set up in the toilet yet?'

Mark's eyes narrowed, his nostrils inflated. 'Get on with your work. Forget the smart-arse literary remarks or The World State will have you in their office for a verbal warning.'

I laughed triumphantly. 'That's *Brave New World*, if you're going to use literary quotes at least get them right.' Mark stormed off with his wounded pride.

'Hi, sir, this is Connor calling from…' I watched Duncan return to his seat and more importantly, I smelt Duncan returning. Smelling like a new man.

'No, sir, I'm not trying to sell you anything. The purpose of my call is to advise you about the PPI reclaim scheme.'

The answer came back, 'Where do you people get my number from? Wipe it from your records forthwith, young man. I am completely and utterly fed up with these nonsense calls, if I wish to purchase windows, I shall do so. If I wish to invest in solar panelling, I shall do so. If I wish to—'

I interrupted, 'I completely understand, sir. Please accept my sincere apologies for wasting a few moments of your afternoon. I appreciate that your time is precious. Enjoy the rest of your day, sir, and rest assured that I, personally, shall not contact your good self ever again. I bid you good day.'

Tina was on her feet, eyeing me like I was an imposter. 'I've sat and listened ti you week after week and never heard yae handle a call like that. Bring back the auld Connor, a think a prefer him.'

She stared at me as satisfaction radiated from me. The perfect embodiment of someone in love. 'Weird. Fucking downright weird,' she muttered while looking at herself in her little portable mirror which she brandished with monotonous regularity throughout the day.

Seventeen

Generally, in relationships one individual holds more power than the other. Laura had less to lose than me. I knew that. No childhood baggage. No scar tissue. She didn't have self-esteem issues. Having a stable family and support network meant the balance of power lay with her. I knew I had to arrange a visit to my parents.' Laura would only get increasingly more curious about my family if I didn't. I had to keep her happy. I felt a real sense of unease about it. Dad had relayed telephone conversations with me to Mum and, like any mother, according to Dad, she was happy and wanted to know all about Laura. In my mind, however, her questions were tantamount to mobilisation.

***

'I can't believe you have made us come out in this weather,' I said, shoulders hunched, head bowed in a futile attempt at deflecting the elements. The wind brought life to a plastic bag, sending it airborne until the branches of a tree interrupted its journey. The bag was eventually set free by the swirling wind, re-joining other discarded objects, like empty beer and juice cans, also brought to life by the powerful, whistling force of nature.

'Don't be a wimp, Connor.' She locked her arm into mine, snuggling into me.

A Saturday morning walk in the park, followed by brunch somewhere, had become a bit of a tradition. Laura tended to spend Friday nights at mine then, after brunch on Saturday, she headed home, much to my poorly concealed disappointment. There was no children's playground or football pitch so the park was mostly used by cyclists, people out for a stroll, and dog walkers. Winter was on its way, we were dressed accordingly. Laura in a grey, three-quarter length coat, battered looking Doc Martens, a Joseph-esque technicolour scarf and a red beret. I wore a navy blue, double-breasted jacket which Greg laughed at, commenting that it made me look smaller than I was due to its length. Black jeans, black Chelsea boots and a beanie completed my outfit. We walked along the side of the park where the river ran. Twenty feet or so through the trees was a rusty-looking fence, various parts of which had been uprooted, remoulded or removed. This provided a good vantage point to watch the river rushing downstream as if racing to make an appointment.

I shouted to Laura, 'Don't lean on that fence it'll stain your coat,' as I pulled her backwards, then manoeuvred her head into my chest. A couple of minutes of quiet reflection followed before I ended it, 'I'm going to organise a visit to my parents to introduce you to them. When suits you?'

'Finally! Does that mean you're sure about me then,' she teased.

'It was fifty-fifty there for a while, but I'll let you hang around for a wee while longer.' I kissed her cheek. 'What you up to tonight?'

'Work night out tonight. We're going for dinner, then drinks.'

'Could you not cancel and we could go tonight?'

Irked at the suggestion, Laura answered, 'No, Connor, I can't cancel. This has been organised for a while. I can't cancel at the drop of a hat because all of a sudden you're in a hurry to introduce me to your mum and dad.'

'OK, fair enough. I just thought that maybe it was more important than a work night out.'

'That's unfair. You're being unreasonable. We can go to your mum's next Friday if you want.'

'Yeah, we'll see. I might be going out with a few people from work on Friday.'

She smirked, 'Oh right … it's like that, is it? Very mature,

Connor. You try and keep your hands off Tina now, won't you?'

So, it's OK for you to go on a work night out, but not me?'

'Course it's fine for you to go on a night out. I didn't say it wasn't. I don't know what's got in to you but I don't like it, whatever it is.' She pulled her arm from mine.

'Sorry, I was being stupid. I'm getting myself worked up about you meeting my mum.'

She locked her arm in mine again. 'Why, Connor? It's a bit over the top. You're introducing your girlfriend to your parents. It's no big deal. The more you make a big issue out of it, the more uneasy you're making me feel about it.'

'You're right,' I said with an air of resignation. 'Right, let's go and eat. Don't know about you but I'm hungry.' I tried to sound upbeat. Internally, I was squabbling with myself about the way I had acted.

The atmosphere between us as we walked to the café was strained. Conversation at a premium. I struggled to think of what to say to restore the equilibrium. 'So, where you off to tonight for dinner and who's going?'

'All of my team are going; there's eight of us. Poor Jordan is the only guy out of the eight.'

'Poor guy? Bet he's loving it. What's he like?' The mention of the solitary male had grabbed my attention.

'Really nice guy. A few of the girls fancy him. No doubt a couple of them will be competing for his attention tonight.'

Despite being unsure whether I wanted to know the answer, I went ahead and asked, 'Is he good-looking?'

'He's not my type but I can see how others find him attractive. He's got a great sense of humour.'

'Well, he better not be fucking sniffing around you.'

Laura turned to face me. 'That's a horrible phrase to use, Connor. There's no need for you to feel jealous. Don't speak like that to me again.'

'Who said anything about being jealous?' I pulled my arm free from Laura's.

'You're acting jealous. You're being a pest this morning. I

wish you'd snap out of it.'

'I don't like chancers, that's all,' I snapped.

She stopped in her tracks, staring at me incredulously. 'You haven't even met the guy. Just because he happens to work in a team with seven females, you're judging him and you've got him down as some kind of lothario. You're being really small-minded.' She shook her head in disbelief.

'OK, OK. I'll look forward to meeting this Gordon guy and making my mind up about him.'

'His name is Jordan *not* Gordon.'

'I know, I was just trying to wind you up.' I grabbed her and cuddled her. 'Sorry for being a moron. I like to think I've done you a favour this morning. I've shown you I'm not perfect. I know you must have been thinking, *Man, this guy is too good to be true*, but now you know I'm human after all.'

She put her hand over my mouth. 'Quiet. Just button it, Boyd. Your mouth has got you into enough trouble this morning. You can make up for it by paying for brunch. Skinny latte, scrambled eggs with salmon for me please. I've got a big night out tonight,' she said, winking at me as she opened the café door. We were met with a blast of glorious warmth and the welcome aroma of coffee and hot food.

***

In the lead-up to introducing Laura to my family I did some thinking. The only way I could describe how I felt since falling in love was this. Prior to meeting her, inside my head there were blacked-out curtains. When she came into my life she swept those curtains wide open to reveal a brighter, better world. I thought about Paul. *It's not his fault that he was wanted and I wasn't. He can't help that. He has a good relationship with 'her' so it's obvious that he's going to stick up for her. I would probably do the same if the shoe was on the other foot. Maybe I should make more of an effort*, I conceded.

'So, meeting the parents for the first time, Laura. Are we nervous?' Greg asked as Laura sat in the living room while I pottered around getting dressed, catching parts of the conversation.

'Have you met them before?' she whispered.

Greg leant forwards. Looked slowly to his left then right, before stage-whispering, 'Yeah, they're fecking horrible people. That's why he's so nervous about you meeting them.'

She pursed her lips together, looking intense. 'Why? What's so bad about them?'

'Just not nice people. Wait till you hear the way they speak to poor Connor.'

A sympathetic look spread over her face. 'They had better not act like that towards him tonight or I'll have to say something.'

'Don't do that whatever you do. I spoke up for him once and his mum threw a glass of red wine over my brand new white shirt. Eighty quid out of Ted Baker. Ruined.'

She placed her hand over her mouth. 'Oh my God, that's awful. What did you do?'

'I couldn't do anything. Gerry got up and grabbed me by the Gregory Peck, told me to get the eff out of his house. I've not seen them since.'

'I wish you hadn't told me this. I don't want to go now. They sound despic—'

'How you doing, Connor?' he interrupted as I entered the living room. 'I was just telling Laura about your parents,' he said with a snigger.

I looked at Laura's pale, horrified face. 'You OK, Laura?' I patted her knee. 'Don't worry they're not as bad as I've made out.'

Laura stared at Greg, her eyes wide. Her face wore a look of dread.

Greg averted his eyes to me. 'I was just telling Laura about the time your mum threw a glass of red wine over my Ted Baker shirt.'

I frowned and looked at Laura, then burst out laughing. 'Don't listen to this idiot, sweetheart, he is having you on.'

Laura pounced from her seat with a cushion, smacking Greg on the head. 'Can't believe you did that,' she said, sighing with relief.

'Sorry, I couldn't help it,' he said, lowering his hands from his face, safe in the knowledge that she'd retreated to her seat. 'You'll be nice and relaxed now though, eh?' He winked as he stood, clapping his hands. 'Right, are you two ready? I'll drop you off at the restaurant.'

***

Greg pulled up outside the Italian restaurant having spent the journey giving me a blow by blow account of his winding up of Laura. 'Have a good night, guys. I'll look forward to hearing all about it tomorrow.'

Standing on the pavement outside the restaurant, I turned to Laura. 'Have I ever told you before you have the cutest little ears I've ever seen. Check the size of them, they're not even adult-sized ears.'

She smiled at me. 'One of the nicest and strangest compliments I've ever been given, I have to say. Thank you.' She kissed me.

Taking her hand, I led her into the restaurant. 'Hi. We have a table booked under the name Boyd.'

'Yes, sir, the other three in your party are here. Can I take your coats?'

'Yes please,' we both replied, before removing our coats.

I led Laura by the hand; looking up I saw my parents' beaming smiles. I smiled back. As we reached the table, my parents and Paul stood. 'Dad, Mum, Paul ... this is Laura. Laura ... Dad, Mum and Paul.'

'Hi, Mr Boyd. Nice to meet you.'

My dad hugged her. 'You too, Laura. It's great to meet you, dear. Call me Gerry.'

'Mrs Boyd, lovely to meet you.' She hugged my mother.

Mum placed both her hands upon Laura's shoulders. 'It's so nice to meet you. Look at you! You're beautiful. I love your outfit.'

'Thank you. You look great too, Mrs Boyd.'

'Call me Mary.'

Paul approached her. 'He's punching way above his

weight,' he said, looking at her and nodding in my direction. 'Hi. I'm Paul.'

'Hi, Paul. Yeah, I tell him that as well.' She laughed as they hugged. 'You really look like your mum, Paul.'

Paul then turned to me and reached out to shake my hand but was taken by surprise as I gave him a proper hug. 'Cheeky b'stard,' I said with a laugh.

I embraced Dad before taking a seat. My buttocks had barely touched the seat before Mum piped up, 'Are you forgetting someone, Connor Boyd?'

Why do parents do that? Calling you by your full name? I stood, peeved at not getting away with it. Hugs over, seated and drinks ordered, the conversation began to flow. I watched Laura with pride as she charmed them by being her usual beautiful, effervescent self. It constantly astounded me that she was mine, sometimes a little voice spoke to me, '*You better appreciate her, boy. I hope you realise how lucky you are!*'

I listened to my mum ask Laura about her job. *The old misery pervert will be disappointed when Laura explains that she's not allowed to discuss her work. She'll be dying to hear some of the miserable cases Laura deals with.* Satisfied that all was going well between them, I turned my attention to Paul. 'How's things with you? What you been up to?'

'I'm good. Uni is going great. I've moved into the student campus now. You should see it. Different class. Everything you could ask for. Lots of nice, interesting people from all over the world too.'

'Not bad for a wee boy fae the scheme,' I said with a laugh.

'When I get my degree and a decent job, I'll be able to say that.'

'Give yourself a pat on the back in the meantime, Paul. You've done great.'

While speaking, I heard mother quietly say to Laura, 'I'm so happy. I've never seen him look so contented and calm.'

I felt my jaw tighten. *Let it go, Connor*. The starters arrived, giving me a welcome distraction. The only sound for a few moments was cutlery touching plates. Laura turned to me.

'You need to try this, it's gorgeous.' She placed a forkful of food in my mouth, causing my parents to smile at one another. Their eyebrows raised.

'Right, enough of that lovey-dovey stuff,' Dad said, teasing us.

'Oh, and by the way, don't think we didn't notice the two of you have a quick peck outside before coming in,' added Mary.

My parents looked pleased with themselves, watching our embarrassed faces as we looked at one another, bewildered at how we had been spotted. The main courses came and went, Mother and Laura chatting away like they had known each other for years. Paul and I conversing properly for the first time in a long time, instead of our previous point-scoring and one-upmanship.

'Laura, you'll need to come over and visit. Maybe we could go to the bingo one night?'

'I don't think that's Laura's thing,' I interrupted.

'Ignore him, Mary. I've never been to the bingo; that'd be good. We'll get something organised.'

I gazed at Laura as she swapped mobile numbers with her. She amazed me. A thought occurred to me. *If someone as kind and beautiful as her could love me, why couldn't my own mother?* Stirring the muddy waters prompted uncomfortable feelings to return. Desperate for some space, I excused myself.

Running the taps in the bathroom, I rested my elbows on the wash-hand basin. Staring in the mirror. Splashing water on my face. Attempting to wash away the negative thoughts. *Fucking plastic. Making out she's somebody she's not. And Laura's falling for it. I knew I shouldn't have introduced her.* Turning off the taps, I looked in the mirror and saw that I'd splashed water all over my shirt. As I sighed, I was aware that all the positivity had been drained out of me by the question that I'd posed myself. I resorted to a coping mechanism that I'd stumbled across recently. I pictured myself standing at a blackboard with a duster in hand. The writing on the blackboard represented the thoughts troubling me. Using the duster, I vigorously wiped the board completely clear. Where this coping mechanism appeared from, I hadn't a clue. I didn't care. All that mattered was it helped. *Right, Connor, an hour and you'll be lying in bed cuddled up to Laura.* The hand dryer dried my shirt a little. Taking a deep breath, I headed back to the table. My mother's smug gaze in my direction un-nerved me.

'You OK, Connor?' Laura asked, putting her hand on mine, giving it a squeeze.

'Yeah, I'm fine. Looking forward to getting a bit of fresh air, to be honest. It's roasting in here.'

'I'll finish this glass of wine and we'll get a taxi, OK?'

I winked at her.

'Connor, you make a lovely couple. Should I be looking out for a hat?' Mary joked.

'Don't be silly. And don't embarrass Laura with daft talk like that.'

Laura tried to reason with me. 'Your mum was only joking.'

I looked at Laura. 'I know she's joking. It's fine.' I turned to Mary, smiled. 'I've not made my mind up about her yet. We'll see how she behaves.'

***

The taxi darted through the city centre streets. The usual sights. Buskers. Beggars. Promotions staff with their false promises. People heading home. The comical sight of the ones worse for wear. The serious clubbers just arriving, ready for a late one. I felt relieved that I was no longer part of that scene.

Laura complimented me on my family, how they'd made her feel so welcome. Commenting on Paul's good points and how Gerry was an old-school gentleman. She turned to face me. 'You feeling better? You looked a bit pale when you returned from the toilet.'

I gazed outside. 'I'm feeling better now.'

'Connor.' Then a long pause.

I knew what was coming.

'Now that I've met your mum, I'm even more confused

what your issue is with her. I don't get it. She seems lovely and she dotes on you and Paul. That's obvious.' She spoke slowly, taking small careful steps to probe.

I turned to face her, but her gaze was fixed straight ahead. 'Laura, I'm surprised at you. You're in social work. You work with people who try and pull the wool over your eyes every day. You shouldn't be so easily fooled. A couple of hours in her company and you think she's wonderful. She's so fucking Machiavellian. Let me tell you, it's all an act with her.' Emphatically, I added, '*I know.*'

Laura fidgeted with her coat lapel. 'I appreciate that, Connor, but I can only take people as I find them. I've always stuck to that premise. I don't listen to idle gossip about people. I know that's not the case with you but you know what I mean. If you give me a reason why you feel the way you do about her then fine. In the meantime, I can only go by how I found her.'

'Don't try forcing me to spill the beans cos I'll just dig my heels in even more. OK?'

Trying to keep my temper in check, I told myself I'd been right all along. It had been a bad idea introducing Laura to 'her'. Any dealings I had with that woman just brought me misery.

As the taxi pulled up outside the flat, I felt a sense of relief. The atmosphere between us felt claustrophobic. Having changed out of my clothes, I popped in and out of the living room, carrying out some chores around the flat while Laura lay watching TV. Whenever I looked in on her, I sensed that the TV was purely a distraction. Her mind was on something else. It made me uneasy. Like sand in an egg timer. It was only a matter of time. Something was brewing within her and it was beyond my control. Carrying in a pile of dirty laundry to the kitchen, I glanced at her, a frown etched on her forehead. When I finished loading the washing machine, I leant against the doorframe of the kitchen. Arms folded, I said, 'I'm going to make a coffee, then we can chat about what's troubling you, OK? Would you like one?'

She half smiled. 'Yes please. How do you know

something is bothering me?'

'I like to think I know you pretty well by now. It's written all over your face.'

In the kitchen, I racked my brain how to best handle the situation. I needed to take back control. I suspected that my mother had mentioned something about the past. If anything was to be said, it should come from me, not that cow. *That's what's bothering Laura, it must be*, I thought. *That cow has said something to Laura about stuff from the past. No doubt it was as soon as I went to the toilet.* The kettle coming to the boil refocused me. I poured the drinks then took a deep breath. Placing the drinks on the coffee table, I snuggled beside her, placing my hand on hers. 'We'll drink these then go to bed and you can tell me what's on your mind.' I wanted to move the conversation to the darkness of the bedroom instead of the blinding gestapo-esque light of the still lightshade-less living room.

As we lay on our sides, facing each other, our faces barely visible to each other, I began. 'OK, what's up?'

She placed her hand on my cheek, stroking it she said, 'You're a straightforward guy. I believe in your honesty. I don't want us to have secrets. Do you?'

'Course not,' I mumbled.

'You said in the living room earlier, I like to think I know you a little. Same here, Connor. I know there's some issue with you and Mary. When you were at the toilet, me and her were chatting. She spoke about where you grew up, then she said "Before we had to leave after all the trouble with Connor." She didn't mean to say it. She apologised straight—'

My false laugh filled the room. 'Good old Mary. Ooops what have I gone and said.' I placed a solitary finger over my lips, rolling my eyes in mock surprise. 'She had no right to say anything to you, Laura.' I sprang upright. 'I was going to tell you about it when I was good and ready. That's her all over. You think that was an innocent mistake she made? Look at the trouble she's caused. Now you're wondering what the hell I done. You're thinking I'm keeping some horrible secret from you. Do you really think that it was just a coincidence that it happened when I went to the toilet? She's forever causing problems. I told you this would happen. Can you understand why I was so apprehensive about you meeting her?'

Laura sighed. 'I don't know what to think, to be honest.'

'This is really difficult for me. The only person that I've told about this is Greg. It happened when I was about fifteen. I've been scared to tell you about it cos I don't want you thinking less of me.'

She put her hand on the back of my neck. 'Whatever you did as a boy has no effect on what I think of you as a man.'

I lay back on my side. I tried to slow my breathing. 'Please remember I was a daft boy at the time. I got in with the wrong crowd. I went off the rails. Things were bad between me and my mum. Things changed at school. Puberty and all that. Loads of different things, all happening at the same time. I got dragged into a situation and couldn't turn back. This boy was a year or two older than me. When I think back, I'm ashamed at how I let him treat me.'

'Aaaawww,' she said, her voice heavy with anguish.

'It's true. He treated me like a right clown.' I couldn't sit still so got out of bed, I sat on the edge with my back to Laura.

I rubbed the top of my head, my hands unable to stay still. 'I was like his bitch. He'd tell me to jump and I'd ask how high.'

Laura leaned over and rubbed my shoulder. 'I'm sure you're being way too hard on yourself,' she whispered.

'So, it started with daft stuff, stealing this and that. I was doing stuff, half hoping I would get caught so it would upset my mum. Suppose, when I think back, I was crying out for attention. Ugh! I don't know.' I threw a pillow at the wall. 'This boy was in a dispute with a family who owed him money. People I should have known better to get involved with but I felt trapped, no way out. It was like being on a runaway train. I couldn't get off, Laura. You can't begin to understand what it was like getting brought up in a scheme like that. You've had a totally different upbringing. Please don't judge me.'

She tried to reassure me. 'I won't judge you, Connor. It

was a long time ago.'

'Zander, his name was. He had a plan to mug the guy that owed him money. The guy had a paper round that made a right few quid. Zander did all these little things that put the frighteners on me. He made it impossible to say no. He gave me a knife and he took me to the tenement where I was to wait and, as the guy came down the stairs, I was to threaten him with the knife and take his money.' I could hear Laura's restless breathing and quiet gasps. Desperate to get this over with, I began to speak faster. 'I asked him and asked him: what if this, what if that? He didn't care what happened though. I was just a fucking puppet. Excuse my language.' My head was bowed, staring at the floor. 'So I done what he asked. But the paperboy treated me like even more of an idiot than Zander did. Total contempt. Basically, he told me to beat it. Even though I had a knife at his back.'

I laughed. 'What does that tell you? A few days before we had arranged to do it, I had gone to the tenement to familiarise myself and to try and get my head straight. A nosy old woman came out of her flat, wondering what I was doing hanging around the back door. She chased me out. So, on the night it happened, I had the knife at his back and the old dear's light comes on. I heard her shuffling down the hallway. I panicked.' I turned to look at Laura. 'What could I do? I stabbed him in the arse three times then ran.'

I closed my eyes as I heard her sharp intake of breath. 'Ohh, Connor, I can't believe he put you in that position. What happened after that?'

'When I think of this bit, Laura, I … I…' I bit my top lip. 'I feel such shame and anger. I went to Zander's uncle's house as agreed. I was in total shock, in a right state. I told him what happened. He didn't seem neither up nor down until he heard me say that the old woman had seen me from the previous visit. I hadn't told him about that. He flipped, threw me against the wall then out the house. Told me that if I ever mentioned his name I would be facing a lot worse than a stabbed backside … I need to get a drink of water. Do you want anything from the kitchen?'

'No thanks.'

Shuffling out the room, my body felt heavy. Wondering what Laura was thinking. I returned to the bedroom and lay on the bed. 'At school the following week we got called to the assembly room. We thought it was for another sex education talk,' I said with a smirk. 'The old dear was in her element, in her Sunday best. She picked me out. That was that. So, you can imagine what it was like next. Police. Social workers. Housing officers. My mum going apeshit. We were a safety concern because it would only be a matter of time before the family of the boy I stabbed took revenge. They were notorious. We were temporarily re-housed at the opposite end of the city. It killed my mum. She'd lived in the scheme all her life. No more contact with anybody we knew in case our address leaked out. Meeting after meeting with social workers doing their assessments for their report to the procurator fiscal. Eventually, me and my dad had to appear before the Children's Panel and I had to show contrition and take a lecture before they confirmed that taking all the social work reports, school reports, etc. into consideration, I wasn't going to a YOI or anything.'

'Come here, you,' she whispered, 'give me a cuddle.' As I cuddled her, she said, 'As if I would think less of you for that. I understand why you ended up getting backed into a corner like that and felt you had no option. I see things like that happening all the time. Peer pressure from the wrong crowd. It must have been awful for all of you.' She stroked my hair. 'So did you miss school for a while then?'

'Yeah. I couldn't take my exams because of all the work I missed. I left with nothing. I had to go to college and do my exams with all the old duffers who mucked up first time ... and Greg. That's how we met,' I said, laughing.

'Connor, that's great what you've done. You could have gone down a different road but you got your qualifications then went to college. I think that's admirable.'

'I just focused on getting my qualifications so I could go to college and move out. Me and my mum's relationship was toxic.'

'Has it not improved since you moved out?'

'Not on my part. Still the same. So, now you know.' I'd told her what I had to. The real reason for my hatred of my mother was under lock and key and would remain there. I refused to even contemplate talking about that.

Eighteen

Never in my wildest dreams could I have envisaged such a traumatic episode in my life turning into something so positive. Yet it had. Confessing about my youthful indiscretion strengthened our love. Respect for my determination to turn my life around. Touched that I'd been reticent about my past for fear of losing her. Relieved we no longer had any secrets. The roots had grown deeper and stronger. As the months passed, Laura gradually stayed overnight more and more. However, too much time concentrating on one specific relationship resulted in others being neglected.
I returned home from work one night, Greg was sat on the sofa, having dinner, a blue plastic dinner tray resting on his thighs. I took a seat. After a couple of minutes' pleasantries about how our days had been, Greg, solemn looking, turned to face me. 'Connor, I've been thinking about this for the last month or so. I'm sorry, buddy, but this isn't working for me anymore.'

'What do you mean? Are you dumping me?' I laughed. Totally wrapped up in my own world, I was unaware of anyone else's.

'No, seriously, Connor. I'm dead happy for you and Laura. It's brilliant to see you so happy but I'm starting to feel awkward in my own flat. As if I'm in the way. We're living different lives now.' He smiled half-heartedly. 'You're happy staying in with Laura watching DVDs, sitting staring at her with your gub hanging open, looking a bit backwards. I'm still going out every weekend, having a laugh. A few of my uni mates have told me about spare rooms going here and there. I think it would be better for the both of us.'

I was taken aback. 'I see.' A short silence followed. 'Shit.

Greg, I'm really sorry for making you feel like that in your own flat. I suppose I've been selfish and got sidetracked with Laura.'

'Don't be daft. You're mad about each other. It's fine. These things happen. This might work out great for you. Have you thought about asking her to move in?'

Taking a sharp intake of breath, I answered. 'No. No chance. She'd never be up for that.' I shook my head.

Greg placed his dinner tray on the carpet. 'Have you ever spoke about it?'

'No. I've never thought about it. It's not like I've been thinking about ditching you so I could move her in. She loves living with her parents. She's totally mollycoddled.'

Greg laughed. 'Not as much as you would mollycoddle her. Would you like her to move in? If the answer is yes, then ask her. What's the worst that can happen. She might say, "No, I'm not ready for that, Connor." Fine. Fair enough. You're probably gonnae see more of her with me moving out anyway.'

'Greg, if she says no, I'm snookered. I can't afford this place on my own. I'd need to look for a one-bedroom flat.'

'What's so bad about that?'

'I hate change, that's what's so bad. Why does everything need to change when things are so good. First Luca and Justin. Now you.'

Greg tried to lighten the mood. 'Can you imagine Laura being here when the four of us lived together? She'd have strangled Justin. You couldn't leave her alone with big Luca. Anyway, it's called progression. You can't hold onto everything, pal. Things change. Chapter One … The Flatmates. Just look back on the brilliant times we had and move on. Your next chapter is … Connor and Laura. Some guys are suited to being single, some guys aren't. You've always wanted to be in a relationship. Enjoy it.'

'Don't laugh Greg—'

'You know I'm gonnae laugh now, don't you?' Greg interrupted.

'You being here is like a safety net for me. I know that's

pretty pathetic but you've always been there for me. Giving me great advice. Solid. Dependable. Like a big brother.'

Greg stood, ushering me up from my seat. He hugged me. 'Big brother will always be watching you,' he said with a laugh. 'I'll only be moving out. We'll still see each other. Still be as tight as we've always been. That won't change if you don't want it to.'

'Course I don't.' I exhaled a long breath. 'Stabbing a guy in the arse, was one of the best things I've ever done. Getting moved to the other end of the city and having to start college to get some qualifications. Without that, I wouldn't have met you!'

We both laughed. As we sat back down, I said, 'Fortune favours the brave, I suppose. Nothing to lose apart from my confidence, self-esteem...' I counted my fingers.

'Don't kid yourself, you never had any of those to lose in the first place, short-arse.'

'Right, I'll ask her and see what she says, then we'll take it from there. I'm going to get my laptop to have a look at what I can afford because I think I already know what her answer will be.'

***

I contemplated the positives and negatives. Waking up every morning next to her. Looking forward to coming home from work every night to see her. Spending more time together. Living together would be such a big step in the relationship. Buzzing at the prospect yet terrified at the thought of her turning me down. My habitual paucity of self-esteem helped provide a plethora of reasons why she would rebuff my offer. *What if this scares her off? She could finish with me. But if I don't ask her I might regret it.* I felt tortured. Pulled in opposite directions. *How am I supposed to know what to do? What's for the best?*

Forty-eight hours later, I stood outside Laura's office, a bunch of flowers in hand. I'd decided on a surprise visit. Hopefully, I'll get a look at this Jordan character. Two birds with the one stone, I thought. Take her for dinner, wait for the right moment. 'Carpe diem,' Greg had shouted to me as I'd left for work that morning. A huge swell of anxiety engulfed me. A bunch of flowers in one hand, a bundle of pessimism in the other. Standing on the pavement, watching the flood of people fleeing the shackles of the workplace, I scanned the crowd. It was like Where's Wally? then, finally, I spotted her. Taking a deep breath I strode towards her. My heart swelled at the beautiful sight of her face lighting up in response to the unexpected visit and the flowers. 'Wow, what a nice surprise,' she said, beaming.

I took a step to my right, flowers stretched out in front of me, pretending to be looking for someone else. 'Here you better take these. My girlfriend hasn't shown up.'

She slapped my arm playfully then kissed me. 'They're beautiful. What a nice thing to do, Connor. You're just a hopeless romantic, aren't you.'

'Hopeless ... aye definitely. Fancy going for something to eat?'

'Check you out. Flowers. Spontaneity. Dinner. I could get used to this.' She took my hand. 'So where do you fancy?'

'In keeping with this hopeless romantic tag you've given me, I was thinking of Luciano's. The first restaurant we went to together.'

'Perfect.'

'Don't go getting your hopes up that I've got a ring in my pocket or something. Look' – I patted my pockets – 'nothing there.'

She laughed. 'The thought never crossed my mind, cheeky. Plus, you know you'll need to do a lot better than that to win my hand.'

I placed my hand dramatically on my forehead. 'I knew it. I forgot the Quality Street. They were the deal-breaker, weren't they? You'll have to forgive me; I'm a bit of a novice at this.'

'Yeah right, Connor. This is your fifth proposal to five different girls. You'd think you would have it down to a fine art by now.'

'Let go of the bitterness. Just because you've never been asked and you know fine well that you'll need to wait till it's a leap year to ask me.'

I opened the restaurant door. 'Ladies first.' I debated on whether to just come right out with it as we took to our seats or whether to pick my moment.

Time can be cruel in moments like this. It was painful. Sometimes, I would rather miss a beautiful moment and instead fast forward to the conclusion. I felt that if I didn't get this off my chest I was going to explode. Drinks, starters, small talk then mains ordered. Still nothing. I had to act. 'Laura, I need to speak to you about something. Don't worry, it's nothing bad. You know sometimes you get bad news but that bad news can lead to something good. Well, I hope that's the case with this situation. I'm waffling. Sorry. Right.' I took a deep breath. 'So, a couple of nights ago, I got home from work and Greg wanted a chat with me.'

'He's not proposed, has he?' she said with a snigger.

Rolling my eyes, I said, 'I feel pretty bad about it to be honest. Greg is wanting to move out. He feels like he's in the way. A bit of a gooseberry.'

'Oh no. Because of us? That's terrible. I thought he was fine with me staying over.'

'Me too. I suppose I didn't think about it though. I can see his point. Greg just wants to party, enjoy the single life. He said we're living different lives now. He was brilliant about it though. So, I wanted to ask you Laura – how would you feel about moving in with me?'

'Wow. I don't know what to say.' She fiddled with her napkin. Folding it. Making different shapes with it.

Eventually, unable to endure her silence any longer, I blurted out, 'Sorry. Just forget I asked. It was silly of me to ask.'

She reached over the table to hold my hand. I quickly raised my arms aloft, like I was surrendering.'Listen, don't feel bad. You don't need to explain. It's my fault. I put you on the spot.'

'No, I do need to explain. I love staying over at the flat, I really do but I'm not ready to move out from my parents'. I love the contrast. I've got the best of both worlds. I get spoilt rotten at home then I get to stay at your place a few nights a week. Please don't be offended. You're not offended, are you?' she asked worriedly.

Desperately attempting to conceal my disappointment, I said. 'Don't be silly. It's fine. I understand.'

'Are you sure? I don't want your feelings getting hurt. I admire how independent you are, Connor, but I just feel that there's plenty of time before the responsibilities of bills and stuff.'

'OK, let's change the subject.'

'Oh, Connor, you're in a mood. It's written all over your face.'

The waiter appeared with the food and offers of parmesan or black pepper, giving both of us a small window of opportunity to gather our thoughts.

As soon as the waiter departed, I answered, 'I've told you I'm not. It's no big deal. I'll just need to get a one-bedroom flat and maybe need to move back over the south side where it's a bit cheaper.'

'But I love your flat.'

'Yeah, so do I but you'll find out in about ten years' time that if it doesn't fit your budget, it doesn't fit your budget. I don't want to share the flat with a couple of strangers.'

She ignored my immature dig. 'I'll help you search for a new flat if you like.'

'No, it's fine thanks.'

She picked up her cutlery. 'Stop trying to make me feel guilty, Connor.'

Waiting until I'd swallowed my mouthful of food, I said, 'I'm not. That's three times I've told you … it's fine.'

'Yeah your words are saying one thing but your face is saying the opposite.'

'I've heard of a mind reader but not a face reader.'

'Grow up,' she snapped.

I fired a false sarcastic laugh in her direction. 'Grow up says the spoilt little girl tied to her mummy's apron strings.'

Laura slammed her cutlery on her plate. 'Look, I'm not going to apologise for the fact that I like living at my parents'. Everybody is different. Get over it. If you're going to keep acting like this, I'm leaving.'

'Sorry for caring. Sorry for being a bit down that my girlfriend is totally against moving in with me.'

'I'm sorry that my Connor's been replaced by Kevin the teenager,' she said, laughing and making eye contact with me, causing me to relent and join in. 'That's better. Tell you what I was thinking though. Do you fancy us going away together on holiday in the summer? I was thinking one of the Greek Islands.

'Sounds great,' I said, feeling like a servant being offered a few crumbs from his master's plate.

Nineteen

Waking for the first time in a foreign country, barely four hours after arriving in Zante, I turned to face Laura, checking she was still asleep. My thoughts turned to the previous day and my first time on an aeroplane. Pretending to take it all in my stride but privately unable to relax until it landed. The feeling of relief as the plane ground to a halt on the runway. The immediate rising of passengers from their seats like a Mexican wave. Suddenly being mugged by the heat as I exited the plane. Unusual exotic smells played with my senses, leaving me annoyed at my inability to decipher the various aromas.

Arriving at the apartments in the early hours of the morning, we'd gone straight to bed. Now that I was awake, my mind refused to go back to sleep. Excitement at being abroad for the first time, looking forward to all the various experiences, getting to spend a full week together – Laura and I. Creeping out of bed, desperate not to wake her, I unlocked my suitcase, grabbed a pair of shorts and a T-shirt, then headed to the bathroom.

The morning sun still rested, saving its energy and power for later when I would discover its full potential. I couldn't keep the smile from my face, bidding people good morning despite having no knowledge of their nationality or their ability to understand me, marvelling at the extensive array of beautiful whitewashed buildings and the sight of an odd blue-domed building that I eventually understood to be a place of worship. Everything seemed so vibrant and colourful to me. I was puzzled by the smell of oregano which reminded me of Luca and which I believed to be an intrinsically Italian herb. Eventually I found what I was looking for, the supermarket that we'd spotted from the bus the night before. In no time, the basket was full to the brim with items for Laura's surprise breakfast – freshly baked bread, various meats, olives, cheese, fruit, tzatziki, coffee, orange juice and honey.

Quietly opening the apartment door, I peered in, relieved she was still asleep. I lay the breakfast out on the table on the balcony.

Sitting on the side of the bed, I began to plant gentle kisses on Laura's cheek until she finally roused from her slumber, smiling up at me. 'I've been out and got breakfast,' I whispered, 'it's all set up outside on the balcony.'

'What? Really?' she mumbled, still trying to fully wake up.

'If you care to join me, madam.' I offered my arm to her as she slowly emerged from the bed.

'Wow, what a lovely sight. Coffee, fresh orange, all this beautiful food.' She kissed me. 'Thank you. This is fantastic, Connor.'

'You're welcome.' I pulled her chair out and we both took a seat. 'It's a stunning place, Laura. So colourful compared to our drab, grey, old city. Wait till you see the water. I've never seen a shade of blue like it. The buildings are beautiful, whitewashed, so clean-looking. And the smells…'

'I don't think I've ever seen you so excited,' she said with a laugh.

'Honestly, I'm buzzing. This is going to be great. What will we do today then?'

'You're going to calm down first! Let me enjoy this veritable feast you've laid out then we're going back to bed so I can properly thank you.'

'I think I'd rather go for a walk, to be honest.'

She lifted her eyes from her food and saw my mischievous smile. She grinned at me. 'Fair enough. Consider my offer retracted.'

I took a sip of my coffee. 'No, it's fine. I've changed my mind.'

'Just as long as I'm not forcing you or anything,' she teased.

'You're so lucky. You get woken to a breakfast like this then you get to go to bed with me. You must pinch yourself sometimes.'

'Yeah, big boy, I'm living the dream.'

***

Laura sat on the sunlounger, her back to me while I applied the lotion. As I dried my hands on the beach towel, she put her earphones on then lay on her stomach. A straw hat covered her head, oversized Chanel-style sunglasses protected her eyes. I sat upright on the lounger, my feet flat on the towel, knees pointing to the sky, surveying the sights, sounds and smells of the beach. Drinking it in. I had finally realised that the seductive smell I'd been trying to identify was emanating from the hot pine trees. Mesmerised by the striking blue colour of the sea, my thoughts wandered to yesterday's boat trip.

The first sight of Smugglers Cove will live with me forever. The most stunning natural sight I've ever seen or will ever likely experience again. As the boat navigated its way around the cove, the humungous, horseshoe-shaped white cliffs that provided shelter to the white sandy beach suddenly became visible. The incredible translucent water. Laura jumped the couple of feet from the boat into my arms causing us both to fall. Her sarong becoming redundant as the water made it transparent. The wondrous sight of the shipwreck planted in the middle of the beach. Learning that the ship had been washed up in the eighties after crashing against the rocks while being pursued by the Greek Navy who suspected smuggling activity. We had returned that morning, this time to take some pictures from the clifftop of the beach below.

'I remember one time, lying in the park with Greg, discussing Australia. Being on the beach at Christmas, opening presents, the for and against. I was against, I thought it would be too alien to me. Since being here, I think the sun has a right good effect on me. I'm wondering if I suffer from that SAD, you know, Seasonal Affective Disorder. What d'you reckon, Laura?'

Quick as a flash, she answered, 'Definitely, Connor. I think you have a chronic case of S A D – Spout Absolute Drivel.' She laughed and laughed, delighted with her line.

'Check you out, gutting yourself at your own patter. On that bombshell, me and my drivel will go somewhere we're appreciated,' I said, laughing. 'I'll bring you back something for lunch.'

'And a nice bottle of Pinot Grigio please, darling.'

'Aye, that's the life, eh? Just send the guy that worships the ground you walk on to get you a bit of lunch and a nice bottle of wine after peltering him. *Yasou, malakas*,' I said, waving goodbye.

While Laura was content with reading a book or listening to her iPod, I preferred to spend most of my day either taking in the sights or going off on my own for a bit of exploring. It was a nervous thing to be honest. I can't sit still. Not being comfortable in your own skin makes you want to be on the move. So, I would stop off for a beer, sample the local cuisine, then I'd return with a sandwich for Laura, excitedly relaying my highlights.

The only negative for me had been Laura's desire to call her mother every single night after dinner. It irritated me. I regarded it as immature. The first night waiting with her, my body language made it perfectly clear I wasn't happy. After Laura challenged me about my attitude, I decided that whenever she went to speak to her mum I'd sit in the nearest bar until she was finished.

On the second last day of the holiday, late afternoon, having spent the day at the beach, we returned to the apartment for a siesta. As Laura slept, lying on her side, her back to me, the sheets at her waist, I stared at her in admiration. Her beautiful, tanned, slender back, her bare neck which I constantly felt the urge to kiss. A curious feeling suddenly overwhelmed me, the only label I could give it was a sense of dread. The power of this feeling frightened me, made me uneasy. Unable to stay still, I leapt from the bed, charging to the bathroom for a shower, hoping to rid myself of the feeling. Scrubbing myself clean from the day's sunbathing, I returned to bed without giving the disturbing feeling another thought.

***

'Christmas and on holiday,' I shouted in Laura's ear, trying to make myself heard above the loud, throbbing dance music. 'The two times you're allowed to act a bit out of character.'

A foolish grin spread across my face as I walked towards the supposed dance podium that was in actual fact a glorified ledge. Clubbers danced on it, twelve feet or so above floor level. Climbing up the ladder fixed to the left side of the ledge I was helped up by the friendly hand of an ecstatic-looking dancer who was keen to cuddle everyone. I danced, looking down at Laura who was doubled over in hysterics at the sight of me on this little health hazard of a temporary dance floor. The dozen or so dancers, deadly serious, trying to outdo each other. Meanwhile, I danced with a huge grin on my face, not taking myself at all seriously, laughing at Laura's reaction. Beckoning her forwards, I pointed to the ladder with my eyes, hoping she'd join me, but she couldn't move for laughing.

Seeing that Laura was staying put, I tried to entertain her by turning to face the dancer nearest to me. Putting on my serious, competitive face, I started to unleash my best moves then stood looking at my rival as if to say, 'Show me what you've got.' This went on for a couple of minutes, only ending when my rival embraced me before offering a fist bump.

Descending the ladder, I was grabbed by Laura as I reached the bottom rung. She hugged me. 'That was so funny. How serious was that guy taking it? I never would have thought you'd have the confidence to go up there.'

'I only did it to make you laugh. It worked,' I said, kissing her.

We finally left the club shortly after five in the morning. Reacting to the early morning brightness like prisoners being released from a sustained period of solitary confinement. Our arms over each other's shoulders, we zigzagged along the road, desperate for bed. We came to a small clearing with one solitary tree shaped like an umbrella. The area was barren with patchy areas of grass and a smattering of wild bushes. Laura grabbed me by the hand. 'Let's have a rest under that beautiful little umbrella tree.'

Lying under the tree with her head on my chest, one hand stroking the parched, coarse grass, I giggled. 'I don't know if I'll be able to get back up.'

'We better watch we don't fall asleep. Just a couple of minutes, OK? Then we'll head,' she whispered.

I sunk my face into her hair, comforted by her individual smell. 'I wish this holiday would never end. I'm dreading going home. It's been amazing. I've loved spending time with you. I'd give anything to remain in this little bubble.'

'Me too, Connor. We'll have lots of other holidays together though. Don't think about home just now, sweetheart,' she said, playing with my hair. 'Let's just enjoy this moment and have a great last day.'

'But it's just so different here. All the senses are invaded with beauty. Colour everywhere, all kinds of aromas to drink in. Back home we are poked in the retina with grey drabness. Our noses are on the receiving end of a two-footed tackle from stale lager and urine.'

'Connor, I don't know if you realise this but you're meant to get the holiday blues when you get back home, not on the second last night.'

'I know, I know – give me a slap. So long as I've got you there'll always be colour. I love you so much, Laura,' I whispered.

She clasped her hand around me. 'You say the most beautiful things at times. I love you too, Connor.'

Those seven days were the best days of my life.

Twenty

'So, how was work?' Laura asked, sitting in the restaurant that Luca's parents owned.

'Not great. I've a feeling poor Duncan is about to get his jotters. That snide little SS Oberführer was on his case again today. He totally ridiculed Duncan's accent, said that's why he's bottom of the entire floor for sign-ups. Cos the customers can't understand him. See, in your office, if the boss was going to speak to someone about performance related issues would they do it somewhere privately?'

'Absolutely, we—'

'Buddy, great to see you.' I stood then embraced Luca.

'And this must be the beautiful Laura that you won't shut up about,' Luca said, hugging Laura then kissing her on both cheeks. 'Really nice to meet you, Laura.'

'You too, Luca. Lovely place you have here.'

'Thanks. Yeah, it's doing quite well. Been pretty busy thankfully.'

Luca was dressed in black, a gold name badge on his shirt: Luca Di Mambro, underneath his name: General Manager. Standing out from the other staff members who wore white shirts with black aprons.

'Looking very sharp,' I said.

'Thanks. So how you enjoying living in bandit country?'

I smirked. 'Very good. St George's Cross, actually.'

'Everything OK, the neighbours and that?'

'Yeah fine. It's not a patch on our old gaff but needs must. You heard from Greg?'

'You know Greg – late night phone calls asking you to go out, the odd text now and again.' He rubbed his hands as he asked, 'Right, what can I get you guys to drink?'

'Can we have a bottle of the Montepulciano D'Abruzzo, please?' Laura answered.

'Great choice! A lady with good taste in wine ... guys, I'm not so sure about.' He smirked as he winked at us before shouting in the direction of one on his waitresses, 'Sophia, can you bring me a bottle of the Montepulciano Reserva please?'

I smiled. 'Girls running after you. Some things never change, Luca.'

Ignoring the remark, Luca asked, 'Have you heard from Justin?'

'I got a brilliant email from him last week. He's in Kandy in Sri Lanka, he attached photos of him riding an elephant, feeding an elephant, washing elephants... Basically ... the elephant man. He's having a great time. He's talking about trying to extend his travels for another three months.'

The waitress handed the bottle to Luca, which he expertly opened before pouring for Laura, 'Care to taste?'

She smelt the wine before taking a small sip. 'Fantastic. Really nice, Luca.'

'Glass of Merrydown for you, Connor?'

'Feck off. Get it poured, waiter.' I moved my glass towards Luca.

'Right, listen, I better go and do some work. I'll pop over now and then when I get the chance. I can highly recommend the sea bass – it's delicious. The wine is on me. Enjoy.'

'Thank you, that's really kind.' Laura smiled at Luca as he darted away. 'Well, he seems a really nice guy,' she said, sipping her wine.

'He is and a right good-looking guy, isn't he?'

'A bit of a pretty boy, not my cup of tea.'

I pulled an incredulous face. 'C'mon, you trying to say he's not really good-looking.'

'He's just not my type,' she answered, her tone indicating she hoped that would be the end of the conversation.

'Don't know why you just can't be honest and admit it.'

She tutted as she shook her head. 'Admit what?'

'That you think he's really handsome.'

'What is this? You're like a dog with a bone. If you think

your friend is an incredibly good-looking guy, then good for you. I'm allowed to have my own opinion. Give it a rest, you're boring me.'

'Why are you so touchy about it? Why are you flying off the handle about it?'

'For crying out loud ... I'm not flying off the handle. I'm exasperated by you constantly asking, sorry, telling me how good-looking Luca is. Stop acting like a moron. What's your problem?'

'I don't have one. It's you that's got the problem – not being honest about thinking that he's a right good-looking guy. Are you scared that you'll hurt my feelings or something?'

Laura shook her head. 'I don't know what your issue is but, if you don't drop this, I'm leaving and you can explain to Luca why I've left.'

'OK, calm down. Ssshhh, here comes the waitress.'

We ordered the food. Laura took her mobile phone out of her bag.

'That's rude, sitting playing with your mobile.'

'I'm not taking any advice on table manners from you, Connor.' Her eyes remained on her mobile.

'OK, I'm sorry. I was being an arsehole. Put your mobile down. Let's chat.'

She finished what she was doing then put her mobile away. Our starters arrived. 'What a laugh in work today – big Tina waltzed in this morning with a fringe. You know I call her an Oompa Loompa cos of her fake tan? Well, with the fringe it is absolutely priceless.'

'That's not nice. You stick up for Duncan but you think it's OK to make fun of Tina. She's probably already really self-conscious; she doesn't need you making immature comments.'

'It's called a joke.'

'I'd like to see how you'd react if the joke was on you.'

'What a waste of a night this is turning out to be,' I moaned, pushing my plate to the side.

'Well you started it – being a pest then slagging off Tina. Sorry, but I find it tedious and immature. This isn't my idea of good company.'

'Fine. We'll finish our mains and head home.'

'Good. I'll get Luca to call me a taxi.'

'What? You always stay over on a Friday. You going home?'

'Yeah, I just feel like an early night now. It's been a long week.'

I folded my arms across my chest. 'Grow up, we have a disagreement and you throw your toys out the pram and run to Mummy. You're just a spoilt wee girl.'

'No, Connor, I just refuse to waste my time with people that act like you have tonight. I'll go home, slip into my jammies, have a nice cup of tea and an adult conversation with my parents.'

'Pathetic,' I snapped. 'Fine. Oh excellent, here comes Luca with the mains.'

Luca placed the plates on the table, 'Sea bass for you Laura. Pizza Diavolo for you, my friend. Enjoy. Can I get you anything else?'

'No thanks, Luca. We're both gonnae get an early night so we'll head after this,' I replied.

'OK, guys. Enjoy your mains.'

We ate in silence. I tried to think of what to say, how to make it up to her. I couldn't find the energy. Not only had I drained Laura, I'd also drained myself.

Twenty-One

The sense of dread that had overcome me in Zante became a regular occurrence. A steel toecap to the cerebral cortex. First thing in the morning, it started. '*Morning, Connor, only me. A long day ahead. It'll drag in no doubt!*' Having a shave, looking in the mirror. '*Careful with that razor, you never know what could happen!*' At work, when Mark circled the floor. '*How you going to pay the rent when he sacks you? You do know he can't wait to sack you, don't you?*' I attempted to shrug it off. Think of something else. It was like a shadow. It was confusing. It deadened my ability to think straight. Needing comfort, I began to ask Laura to stay over more frequently. Matters were made worse when she refused. '*Oh dear, Connor. She prefers a night in front of the telly with her old dear. You've got to ask the question, WHY?*' On the occasions when she did stay over, she had to deal with how taciturn I'd become.

'Is everything alright, Connor? You're really quiet.'

'I'm fine. Honestly.' I cuddled into her as if it was our last night together. Strapped to her like a newborn in a baby sling.

'I don't know why I bother coming over when you barely say two words.'

I would trot out some lame excuse, 'Sorry Laura, I'm just a bit tired tonight,' 'Sorry Laura, I'm just thinking about work.'

Eventually, she asked me outright.

'Connor, are you having second thoughts about us?'

I reassured her. 'No chance. I love you more than anything. I can't believe you would think that.'

Her questioning forced me to try even more desperately to wrestle free from the defeatist thoughts. Without Laura's knowledge, I made an appointment with my GP. Declining the offer of antidepressants, opting for the alternative of one-to-one counselling. I was to receive a consultation telephone call, answer some questions, then a decision would be made on whether I qualified for counselling. Brilliant isn't it? Needing to lay it on thick. Having to beg for help. Keep your fingers crossed that they deem you suitable for counselling. Reliant on some arsehole, probably not even qualified to be making that decision. So, I suffered in silence, waiting on the telephone call. Some days were better than others, but it would rear its ugly head when I least expected it. *'You think some idiot on the other end of the phone is going to help you?'*

The real reason. The driving force behind this repugnant feeling, finally revealed itself to me one Saturday night. Lying in bed, Laura fast asleep, I was gazing at her, trying to count my blessings. Then, it hit me. A bitter, stark forewarning. I believed it to be the sacred truth. Nothing could be more certain. *I'M GOING TO LOSE HER. This can't last. It's only a matter of time.* I rolled away from her onto my back. Fingernails clawing the bedsheets. My breathing became rapid. Leaping from bed, I hurried to the bathroom. Placing the toilet seat down, I sat. My head tucked into my knees, hands clasped behind my head, I rocked backwards and forwards. *What's happening to me*? No matter how hard I tried to reason with myself, this fatalistic force shone like a searchlight in my mind. Like it was the final piece of some esoteric puzzle. *This is the reason why you've been feeling like this.* It mocked me. *This sense of anguish is because YOU WILL LOSE HER! And there's nothing you can do about it.* 'No, fuck no,' I whispered to myself. Rushing to the wash-hand basin, I ran the cold water before relentlessly throwing it over my face. Grinding my teeth. I was interrupted by the sleepy voice of Laura calling out to me, 'Where are you, Connor? Are you OK?'

Turning off the tap, I shouted, 'I'll be in shortly, Laura.' Drying my face, I looked in the mirror at my haunted, pallid complexion. A series of deep breaths, a futile effort at regaining my equilibrium. Leaving the bathroom, crawling into bed, I kissed Laura on the shoulder then rolled over to begin a nightshift of restlessness suffering. Question after question offering no answers. Mental clarity evading me.

***

Forty-eight hours later, I called in sick, then made an appointment with my GP. I described the feelings that were taking over and complained about the fact that I'd been given an appointment to see a counsellor in eight weeks' time. Again, I turned down the offer of antidepressants. The only positive being the week's sick line that I secured. I pondered on whether to discuss how I felt with Greg. It would have been my normal course of action. My best friend. Always there for me. Something in me dismissed it out of hand. The thought of seeking Greg out to discuss it felt like a terrible hardship. The very thought exhausted me. The first three days off work were mostly spent sleeping. Shuffling around the flat as if part of a chain gang. Lethargic. Encompassed by a fog of suffering. Time became meaningless. Not a bit of contact with anyone until Thursday morning when Laura called to remind me about Saturday, asking if I'd bought an evening suit for her work's awards ceremony on Saturday night. This shook me from my torpor. Gritting my teeth, I tried with all my might to regain some shred of normality. I explained to her that I'd been off sick with a virus, that I was starting to feel a bit better and would sort the suit out for Saturday.

Ordinarily, I'd have been buzzing at the prospect of donning a tuxedo, attending an important work night of Laura's. Finally meeting her colleagues. In my current frame of mind, it felt painfully wrong. Everything felt like it was an exceptionally difficult task. The thought of being in a large room full of people, having to engage in small talk, trying to make a good impression for Laura's sake. If it was for anyone else, I wouldn't have gone. This was a big night for Laura though, I knew that. Her work wasn't just a job for her, it was a career. She'd told me all about her high hopes and her lofty ambitions.

***

The double doors of the fashionable city-centre hotel swiped open to a large lobby. A tokenistic tartan carpet covered the lobby. Tourist friendly. A noticeboard on the right directed people to the various function rooms. Waiters and waitresses hurried here and there, making it look like early-morning rush hour. I hurried through a set of white doors, down a hallway. The distant chorus of voices became louder. At the end of the hallway, the space opened to a large rectangular area with a bar at either end. Realising a touch of Dutch courage was required, I headed to the bar furthest away from the main function room. Ordering a double brandy, I lifted the glass. *Please, for one night, give me peace. Let me enjoy this night with the girl I love.* Down the hatch it went. A glorious glowing energy coursed through me. Smiling at the instant effect, I ordered another. *I'm the Ready Brek man*, I thought, laughing as I made my way to the hall. At the entrance to the function room, I spotted a table plan. Taking a deep breath, rubbing my face with two hands, I made my way to the correct table. Seeing Laura sitting chatting to a colleague, I crept up to the side of her and kissed her cheek. She turned, her face lighting up at the sight of me, 'Oh hi, sweetheart. Wow, you scrub up really well, Mr Boyd! Super suave. Loving the hair; very Great Gatsby.'

'One does make an effort, Daisy,' I replied, bowing slightly to her.

'Wow, I could get used to you in this outfit, big boy.' She laughed as she kissed me. 'Let me introduce you to a few of my friends. Everyone, this is Connor.'

Voices shot at me from various directions, like balls from a tennis ball launcher. 'Hi, Connor.'

She took me by the hand, introducing me to all and sundry. A handsome guy appeared at her side. 'Are you going to introduce us, Laura?' he asked.

'Oh hi, Jord. This is Connor. Connor, this is Jordan.'

'Great to meet you at last, Connor, I've heard a lot about you.'

I mustered up all the enthusiasm I had in me. 'Likewise, Jordan.' We shook hands.

If you were to go through my little book of insecurities, Jordan would have ticked the vast majority of the boxes. Significantly taller. More handsome. Better job. According to Laura, a bit of a ladies' man. Charismatic. I knew I wasn't going to like this ponce.

Jordan offered Laura his arm. 'Fancy helping me at the bar?'

'Sure thing, Jord. Won't be long, Connor. You get a seat and get to know some people.'

'What do you fancy drinking, Connor?' Jordan asked.

'I'll have a pint of lager, chanks.'

Jordan let rip with an over-the-top laugh. He stamped his foot on the floor. 'Guys. Guys,' he screamed. 'Did you hear that?' he bellowed at the others sat at the table. 'Connor said, "I'll have a pint of lager, chanks."'

I put on my best fake smile. 'That was a hybrid of cheers and thanks. Chanks.'

'Chanks, Connor. Brilliant,' Jordan said, to the amusement of his sycophantic followers.

I was seething. *What an absolute prick. I'd love to rattle his jaw.*

I took a seat. Scanning the room, I warned myself to keep it in check. *Give that ponce a wide berth.* The woman to my left turned to face me. 'So where do you work then, Connor?'

'Sorry, I didn't catch your name?' I said.

'I'm Siobhan, I work in the same team as Laura and Jord.'

I shook her hand. 'Hi, Siobhan. I work in a call centre dealing with PPI reclaim.'

'Oh, so it's people like you that constantly bombard me with calls about PPI then?'

Smiling, I lifted my hands in mock apology. 'Guilty as charged.'

'Do a lot of people not just hang up on you?'

'Yeah, some are too busy, some are just rude, some think it's all too much hassle or too complicated.'

'Or just a pain in the arse,' she said with a laugh.

'You wouldn't be saying that if I sorted it out for you. Getting you a cheque for three grand within a fortnight.'

'Suppose so. I don't have any credit though so it's no use to me.'

'Well you must be part of the one per cent of the population that doesn't have any credit. Count yourself lucky. Excuse me, I'm off to the gents.'

Fucking imbecile, I thought while I stood at the urinals. *Bet she has a mortgage. No credit, my arse. Hope Laura is at the table when I get back.*

Making my way to the table, I caught sight of Laura and Jordan. Approaching Laura, I kissed her cheek, put my arm around her waist. Marking my territory. Jordan handed me my pint.

'Fancy getting a seat, Laura?' I asked.

'Yeah, let's go. Speak to you later, Jord.'

'See you later, *Gordon*.' I winked surreptitiously.

As soon as we sat, I leant over to Laura. 'I don't like that guy. He is a show-off. A ponce. That was out of order trying to mock me earlier for saying chanks. He couldn't wait to tell the whole table.'

'You're overreacting. That's just his sense of humour. Give him a chance. He's a really nice guy.'

Taking a large swig of my pint, I considered what she'd said before retorting, 'No, I don't like him. And he's too touchy feely with you.'

'Connor, please don't start all that silly immature jealous stuff. Me and Jord are work colleagues, that's it. He's not a ponce, a chancer or any of the things you call him. Dinner will be served soon, then they'll be giving out the awards. I want to hit the dance floor with you later. I've been telling everybody what a great dancer you are.'

I sighed. 'Magic, I'll have a series of amateur Len Goodman's and Craig Revel Horwood's marking me for my dance routine.'

Laura laughed. 'Don't be so serious.' She grabbed the back of my neck. 'C'mon, give me a smile, handsome. I'm loving you in this tux.'

The sound of bagpipes polluted the air. A work colleague of Laura's who I'd noticed earlier at the other end of their table, had his hand on a door as it opened to reveal the lone piper with several chefs carrying large trays resting on their shoulders. As the work colleague was unceremoniously pushed to the side by the procession, I became aware of Jordan's loud, over-the-top laugh. I watched as he pointed before springing from his seat in Laura's and my direction. Laughing in Laura's face, he said, 'Did you see Bob opening the kitchen door there? He asked me where the toilets were.' He continued laughing. 'I sent him to the kitchen … you couldn't make it up. How was that for timing? He tried to open the door just when the piper and chefs were heading out. Everyone was staring at him. So funny.'

Laura slapped his shoulder. 'You're terrible, Jordan.'

I stared straight through him. 'If I was Bob, I'd drag you out of here.'

'Oh, a fighter, are we? I'm more of a lover.' He grabbed Laura and cuddled her. Winking at me. 'Isn't that right, Laura?'

She pushed him away. 'You're a wind-up merchant, that's what you are. Go and eat your dinner.'

I lifted my hand to attract the waitress's attention. I ordered myself another pint and a double brandy. Tucking into dinner, I finally found a degree of peace. Some quiet time to sit and chat with Laura without that twat hanging around. I made a point of drinking the brandy when I thought Laura wasn't watching. When dinner was over, we hit the dance floor. Carrying on as we fooled around to 'Hooked On A Feeling' before the DJ went current with the Black Eyed Peas. The dance floor became the focus for a large portion of the room.

Heading back to the table, I kissed Laura. 'Just popping to the gents.'

I stood at the urinals, smiling. My reservations about the night unfounded. I felt myself nudged forwards, resulting in me pissing all over the place, making a mess. 'For fuck's sake,' I shouted in the direction of the person to my right who'd barged into me.

A switch flicked as I heard the sarcastic apology. 'Sorry, Connor, I didn't notice you there, wee guy.'

Jordan stood at the urinal a few feet away, preparing to relieve himself, a supercilious grin beaming from his face as he looked at me then to his sidekick to his immediate right. I marched forwards and shoved Jordan in the back. I stood waiting.

'You meant that,' Jordan shouted. 'What Laura sees in you…'

He fixed up his zip, about to finish his sentence, he turned to face me. Before he could utter another word, I grabbed him by the throat then headbutted him on the bridge of the nose before taking a step back and landing two quick punches. The sidekick watched, his mouth gaping, before rushing to Jordan who'd slumped to the floor, clutching his nose which was bleeding profusely. I said, 'I've been dying to do that all night. Thanks for giving me an excuse, Gord. Keep away from me and Laura for the rest of the night, OK?'

Quickly washing my hands, I heard somebody from a cubicle shout, 'Everything alright out there?'

'Couldn't be better, buddy,' I answered, taking one last satisfied glance at Jordan as I headed out the door.

Walking towards Laura, I saw her frown. 'You OK? You look a little flustered.'

'I'm wonderful, sweetheart. I'm going to the bar; do you want another drink?'

She twirled her hair around her finger. 'No thanks. Hurry back, we're not finished on the dance floor.'

I smiled, watching her twirling her hair. 'I love you so much. Back in a minute.'

Another double brandy was dispatched. I made my way back with a pint of lager. Relieved to see no sign of Jordan. I took a seat. Wondering where Laura had got to, I took a swig from my pint when I heard a commotion. I turned to my right to see Laura holding a blood-stained serviette to Jordan's nose, his sidekick talking animatedly as Jordan pointed in my direction. I stared at Laura's wounded expression. She stood before me. *She looks like a little girl pleading to her parents*, I thought. 'Did you do this to Jordan?'

Gasps could be heard around the table. 'Oh my God, what happened to Jord,' one woman asked another.

I stood. 'I was standing at the urinal when he came in with his little bum chum there. Jordan barged into my back on purpose, while I was in the middle of taking a piss. I looked over and he was smiling at me, taking the piss, excuse the pun. He's been winding me up all night.'

Jordan remained silent. A voice from the table shouted, 'He bumps into you by mistake and you do that to him? You're such a ned. A wee thug.'

I turned to Laura. With tears racing down her cheek, she screamed at me, 'Just go, Connor. Get out of my sight. You disgust me.'

'But, Laura, he deserved it. He's been winding me up all night. He said he doesn't know what you see in me.'

'Yeah, he's right. Looking at what you've done tonight, I'm wondering the same thing. Please go.' She sobbed as a friend comforted her.

Grabbing my jacket from the back of the chair, I put it on then approached Laura. Her smudged mascara, her distraught face, she looked at me and I saw that she was ashamed of me. 'Please, let me explain,' I begged.

'Get away from me. Please, just go.' Her knees buckled.

Trudging out of the room, glancing backwards on a couple of occasions, I thought, *What a fucking drama. We'll sort all this out tomorrow but right now I need to get to my bed.*

Twenty-Two

On waking the next morning, a highlights reel began playing in my mind. Seeing myself throw a double brandy down my neck on arriving at the hotel. I frowned. *Why the fuck was I drinking brandy?* Laura's smiling face as I greeted her. Dancing with her. Then the image of her holding a serviette to Jordan's bleeding nose. My voice penetrated the mid-morning silence, 'Shit! Oh no. What have I done?'

I sprang from the bed, desperately trying to locate my mobile. Clothes were scattered all along the hallway creating a path that looked like it led to a clue at the end of it. Jacket … nothing. Trousers … nothing. My head felt like someone was playing a drum solo inside it. Hurrying towards the living room, I grabbed the cordless phone. Calling my mobile, I listened for the ringtone. On hearing it ring in the distance, I left the living room, pausing in the hallway. *Kitchen, it's in the kitchen.* I saw it on the table, sandwiched between two empty lager cans. Taking a seat at the table, I picked it up. No incoming messages. As I checked my sent messages my shoulders slumped.

Sent Messages
Yesterday 02.17
Laura
U in yet? U OK or r u ignoring me?
Yesterday 02.03
Laura
I'm really soz but that prixk dservd it. I'm not takin any shite fae a ponce like that. Speak tmorra. Luv u x

Sketchy details began to slowly filter through to me. Getting back to the flat, sitting at the table, drinking a can … but no memory of texting Laura. I picked up my mobile, checked my call log. Attempts at 02.06 and 02.25. Becoming aware of feeling the cold as I sat in my boxer shorts, my bare feet planted on the kitchen tiles, I retreated to bed. I lay the mobile on my bedside cabinet and attempted to plan a way out of the mess. *Fuck's sake, Connor, first things first – get your arse in gear and apologise.* I tried calling but it went straight to voicemail. So, I sent a text:

Sent Messages
Today 10.03
Laura
I can't apologise enuf 4 last nite. I embarrassed u and myself. I know how much work means to u. I will make it up 2 u. I promise. I will apologise in person to Jordan. Please call me or text me. I love u and I'm so sorry. Connor xx

Placing my mobile on the duvet, I rested my head on the pillow, my hands clasped behind. Hoping for a quick response. A positive response. I drifted off into a hazy hangover sleep. Sweating heavily, jerking limbs, jumping between sleep and wakefulness. At four o'clock I stirred, feeling no benefit whatsoever from the sleep. Gulping furiously from a pint of water, I remembered I needed to check my mobile. A text from Laura:

Received Message
Today 13.32
We need to talk. I will be at the flat at 7.

No kiss … nothing. Totally dry. Despair took hold. *I'm well and truly fucked.*

***

After taking a shower, I dressed, tried to make myself look human despite feeling anything but. My hangxiety haunted me. Posing questions I couldn't answer. Guilt-ridden about the great unknown, unable to remember events properly. My mind concocted ever more outrageous scenarios for what had happened the night before, spiralling away from the reality. Paradoxically, I couldn't wait for Laura to arrive and put me out of my misery by telling me exactly what I had done even though I was petrified of her impending decision. Parading up and down at the bay window, looking down at the street below, I grew more and more impatient. Sweat still seeping from my pores, I lifted a magazine using it as a makeshift fan. Needing to satisfy my drooth, I went to the kitchen, poured myself a pint of water and downed it in one go. As I filled it again, the buzzer sounded. I slammed the pint glass on the worktop then strode down the hall to the intercom system. Lifting the receiver, I uttered an apprehensive, 'Hello.'

The voice shot back at me. 'It's me.'

Pressing the buzzer, I waited at the door, listening to her steps as she climbed the stairs.

Her lips were lowered at the corners as if trying not to cry. Puffy eyes like cushions knocked out of their proper shape.

'Hi, Laura,' I said sheepishly, closing the door behind. She didn't respond. I followed her down the hallway into the living room where she sat on the edge of the sofa nearest the door. Her arms were folded. I stood facing her. Scratching at my knuckles. 'Is it OK if I start?'

She nodded her head.

'I'm so sorry for letting you down. My behaviour last night was disgusting. I don't want to make excuses but…'

I paused, taking in her expression, an expression I perceived as detachment. A faraway look. Like she was purely biding her time.

'But, I haven't been feeling great recently, I mean mentally and physically. I was laid low with a virus all week and what with that and drinking too much I think everything came to a head.'

She calmly, almost robotically, answered, 'Is that it? Is

that the best you can do? You assault a colleague and friend of mine, breaking his nose. Humiliate me in front of my colleagues. And you tell me you're sorry you had a bit of man-flu, got too drunk, haven't been feeling great, blah blah blah?'

I stepped forwards, crouched down in front of her, tried to take her hands. She thrust them away as though my attempt at making contact repulsed her. Alarmed at her reaction, I cocked my head. 'You're acting like we're strangers. Why are you being so cold, Laura? I just want to make it up to you. To apologise to Jordan. He didn't deserve that even though he did provoke me.'

She screwed up her eyes as if trying to read a piece of illegible handwriting. Her voice lost its robotic tone, becoming emotional and irritable. 'Are you being serious? Are you forgetting that you texted me last night that the P R I C K deserved it? Do you even know the difference between right and wrong? Let me think' – she placed a solitary finger on her lips – 'why am I being cold? I've had to spend the last few hours pleading with Jord not to press charges against you. Still you persist in not taking responsibility for your actions. Yeah, you were really provoked. He laughed at you because you said chanks. That's it. What else did he do? Go on, tell me.'

'He intentionally banged into me when I was having a pee. Then he mocked me saying, "I don't know what Laura sees in you."'

'Was it maybe just an accident? Was it maybe something to do with you being rat-arsed due to the fact you were knocking back something that looked like sherry or cognac … oh, and in one go as well. I maybe didn't notice but others at our table did. I praised you to the high heavens. My Connor this, my Connor that. Wait till you meet my Connor. What a fool. The first time I introduce you…' She shook her head, closed her eyes, then looked to the ceiling, unable to finish her sentence.

'Please, Laura, I know it was bang out of order. It won't ever happen again. I promise.'

She bit her bottom lip, fighting back tears, she mumbled, 'I know it won't happen again. I can't be with someone who has it in them to act like that. I couldn't trust you. My work means a lot to me. You know that.'

I put my hands on her knees. 'Laura, you know you can trust me. I love you so much.'

'That's the worst part, Connor. That's why this is so, so hard. I know you do! And I love you but you have something in you. An anger. A destructive side. Something that worries me about you. I can't. I just can't. It's finished.' She was finally defeated by the tears that she had been battling against.

I attempted to touch her face, without success. 'You can't do this, please. I'm begging you. You can't throw this all away. Think of all the great times we've had. Not this one terrible night when I acted out of character.'

She tried to wipe away the tears then rubbed her nose. 'But it's not though, is it? You've stabbed someone before … remember?'

'Fuck's sake, Laura. I was fifteen. I knew I shouldn't have told you about that.' I rubbed my temple. 'That wasn't me the other night. You know the real me. Come on. Please,' I thrust my arms wide, my palms facing the ceiling.

'That's the problem, I thought I knew the real you. I thought what happened when you were younger was just a crazy adolescent situation you got trapped in. But when I think of last night on top of what you've done before, I can't trust you. I can't be with someone who has that violent streak. Last night you behaved like the reprobates we deal with through work. I can't be having that in my personal life as well. I'm sorry, Connor.'

Standing, unable to stay still, I scratched and rubbed at various parts of my body. 'Please, Laura. I'll change. I can make this up to you. We can start again, take it slowly, let me repair it. Everyone fucks up at one time or another. People get second chances.' Sensing that she was preparing to rise, I crouched down at her feet again, putting my hands on her thighs. 'Don't make me beg.'

Her look of hurt transforming to pity produced a swell of emotion in me, a lump in my throat that I tried to swallow away. She tried to stand. I pressed down on her thighs, preventing her. As I looked at her, I saw the frightened look on her face.

Removing my hands, I said, 'No. No. You don't think I'd ever hurt you? Laura?'

Her silence hurt more than anything she could have ever said. As she stood, I slumped onto the sofa. Distraught that she could be even remotely frightened of me. All energy sucked from my body. I closed my eyes, refusing to watch her walk out of the flat. Out of my life. Knowing that the mental image would haunt me.

Between sobs, as she prepared to leave, taking one last glance at me, she said, 'I loved you, Connor. So, so much. Don't ever forget that.'

PART THREE

One

An hour or so passed without me moving from the position I'd slumped into on her exit. Entrenched in a state of utter cognitive dissonance. Switching between *I don't fucking deserve this. What a fucking drama queen*, and, *I can't believe I've done this to her. I need to make it up to her*. Unable to cope with the mental turmoil, I dragged myself to my feet, put on my shoes and left for the off-licence. My mind couldn't focus on what had just happened. Alcohol was ingrained at the forefront of my mind though. *Fuck all of them. Fuck everybody. The only thing that can help me right now is a good drink.* I marched to the off-licence, focusing on it like an exhausted traveller in the desert spotting a mirage. My irrational decision-making continued as I bought a bottle of the poison that had led to my current predicament. I chucked in a few cans of lager for good measure.

    Back in the flat, I headed to the kitchen, rummaging through barren cupboards, failing to find a suitable glass for the brandy. Abandoning my search, I grabbed a coffee mug, poured in half a mug of brandy then knocked it back in one go. Wincing, I lifted my left leg off the floor, twisted to the right, my upper body contorting as if I'd been tasered. The lava-like liquid burnt my throat as the numbing process began. Placing the bottle under my arm, I took a can of lager and my mug to the living room and rested them on the two-tier, black pine coffee table. The bottom tier was used for my CD collection. As I sat cross-legged, my memory landed its first low blow of the evening. A reminder of the afternoon I bought the table. Picturing Laura laugh as we continually got lost in Ikea, struggling to find our way out of the maze. When we had returned to the flat, she'd watched me struggle before swiping the instructions from me and assembled the table in no time. I picked up a bundle of CDs.

Blow number two arrived as I looked through the CDs we'd listened to in bed as we fell in love. Reminiscing over the ones she'd bought me, I emitted a long, deep sigh then placed my hand on the crown of my bowed head. This is what it's like to lose the person you love. Reminders here, there and fucking everywhere. Haunting you. Everything you do. She'd only dumped me a couple of hours and already I was being stalked by her fucking ghost. I grabbed the bottle, poured another generous measure which quickly disappeared. *Whoa, this stuff is lethal, but a good lethal*. I laughed as I experienced the first jag from the alcohol.

Leaning my hands on the table, I used it as leverage to stand. 'Right, a little bit of Florence,' I said aloud, sticking the CD in my DVD player. The music began.

'What an opening line! Yesss,' I shouted. 'You grab that fucking happiness, Flo, cos it isnae gonnae last. It'll be out of there like one of those Japanese bullet thingmy trains that looks like a bobsleigh.' I was talking aloud to myself, animated hand gestures thrown in as well. Screwing up my face at the aftertaste of the brandy, I decided to crack open a can of lager. Taking a large gulp, I shook my head like a dog that had just got out of the water. 'Jesus … brandy tasting lager … man, that's vile.' I winced, then took a second swig which was marginally better.

'GENIUS!' I shouted, pointing at the TV. 'The little lamb knifed me in the back earlier, didn't she. Nasty wee wolf in sheep's clothing. Where's my mobile?' I patted my trouser pockets. Picking up my can of lager, I headed to the kitchen where I spotted the phone on the black speckled worktop. Taking the same seat as the other night, I engaged in the same self-defeating behaviour.

Sent Messages
Today 21.23
Laura
I demand anotha chance. Listening to

Rabbit Heart. Who is the lamB n who is the knife. U hav stabbed me in the bak. Wat u got 2 say?

Today 21.26
Laura
Well??? Silence is defening. Takes a bigger person to admit they've made a mistake. Oh Laura dn't be hasty (get it? wee Paulo, oh jenny dnt b hasty)

I finished the can. Punched her number into my mobile. No answer, straight to voicemail. I shouted into the mobile, 'Where are you? Aaahhh, you're playing nursemaid to the ponce. Tell him it'll be his jaw no his beak that gets broke next time. Do you hear me, Laura? Phone me back!'

Sent Messages
Today 21.59
Laura
Grow up. Stop actin so immature. Has mummy bear put u in the bath n put you 2 bed early n took yer mobile away case the big bad wolf texts u?

***

My mobile phone alarm roused me from a drunken slumber. Fiddling frantically with the buttons, eyes closed, trying to end the unwelcome disruption to my sleep. Smacked between the eyes as reality hit hard. That heart-breaking moment when you wake to realise that things have changed. A loved one has passed away ... you've lost the love of your life... Unfathomable anguish. *What the hell do I need to get up for?* Realising I needed to visit my GP for another sick line to prevent unemployment adding to my long list of problems, I rose from the sofa and made my way to the bathroom. Teeth brushed, I ran some water through my hair then left, wearing the clothes I'd slept in.

The all-singing, all-dancing community hub housed GPs, dentists and a children's nursery. It had taken over three million pounds of taxpayers' money, however, accusations of nepotism and cronyism now flew thick and fast. Sold to the people as the bosom of the community, things had quickly turned sour as the 'jobs for the boys' mentality had spread. I sat in the waiting area, still drunk from the previous night, taking in the white sterile surroundings. *It's not the fucking hub that's the bosom of this community, it's the local pub. This is Glasgow. These clowns wouldn't have a clue about the life of the average person on the street. Inept clueless bastards.*

'Connor Boyd, room nine, please,' echoed from the sound system. *They can't even be arsed to come out and greet you now.* I gave the door a polite knock before entering.

My GP irritated me. Sensing a 'pull yourself together', old-school mentality from him, didn't help.

'Well, Mr Boyd, back so soon? What can I do for you?'

I felt like answering, *Fuck all. You know and I know this is all silly buggers. And if you offer me antidepressants one more time, I'm gonnae jump over that desk and strangle you.* 'Well, Doc, things have gone from bad to worse,' I said, laughing nervously. 'I won't bore you with the details but I've split up with my girlfriend. I assaulted her work colleague. My frame of mind is … is … is…' Fidgeting in my chair, my hands dug into the armrests like bird's claws.

The GP sat back in his chair. 'Mr Boyd, have you been drinking?'

I cocked my head. 'How dare you … drinking … of course I've not been drinking at this time in the morning. Drinking! I had a couple of cans of lager last night, that's it.'

'Do you think it's advisable in your current frame of mind to be drinking, Mr Boyd?'

'I think it's highly advisable. See, you don't live in the real world, Doctor Do-Nothin.' I attempted to cross my legs but my right leg failed to latch on to its target causing my shoe to land heavily on the wooden floor. 'Do you think it's acceptable I come here, at the end of my tether, and you try and pat me on the arse, send me away with *zombie* pills.' I raised a finger. 'Not once, but twice. In fact, no doubt today will make it three. Do you think it's acceptable that I have God knows how many more weeks to wait to speak to someone? Just to try and explain that I feel like I'm losing control. You won't have a clue what a dyke is, we used to climb them when I was a youngster. Big concrete squares. Your hands would cut into them while your legs kicked about furiously as yae tried to get leverage that'd get yae to the top. But, you got to a point where you were losing, you were going to fall, you couldn't do anything about it. You were helpless ... had to let go of the concrete and drop to the ground. Sorry I'm not articulate enough to explain it in your language. So, let's just end this charade now. A sick line for a couple of weeks to give me a bit of breathing space would be great. If it's not too much trouble.'

'Mr Boyd, I sympathise with you, I truly do. However, I am not responsible for the machinations of the NHS. I cannot magic up an earlier appointment. We have processes we need to adhere to. Boxes that require ticking.'

I leapt from the chair as if an eject button had been pressed. 'Stick your processes up your arse' – furiously patting my chest – 'I'm a fucking human being, not a machine or a process or...' Out of breath, I returned to the seat.

'Any more outbursts like that and I shall have you removed.' The doctor quickly scribbled on his pad. 'There you go, Mr Boyd. Your sick line. Now hold tight, your appointment with the counsellor will be here before you know it.'

I snatched the sick line, looked him in the eyes, laughing in disbelief. I paused, then shook my head as I stared at the emotionless face looking back at me. Walking out the door, I was overwhelmed by the feeling of hopelessness and nausea.

Two

Four days had passed since she'd gone. Mornings and afternoons spent mostly in bed. Sleep provided a temporary haven. Evenings consisted of drinking as much alcohol as possible. Constantly sending Laura contradictory text messages. The odd voice message *demanding* she return my calls. Ignoring text messages enquiring after me from Greg and my dad. Disappointment as I grabbed the mobile to see a name that wasn't hers. Too much time spent alone, letting thoughts fester. A witch's cauldron of toxic emotions bubbling away.

I awoke around midday. A strong desire to get out of the flat. Do something. Anything. Maybe a walk into town. A bit of fresh air. I showered for the first time in what I believed to be at least five days. The Sicilian lemon shower gel had a similar effect as smelling salts being administered.

Opening the entrance door to the building, I felt the wind on my face. Second thoughts tried to entice me back indoors. I clenched my teeth, took a deep breath and set off. The main thoroughfare that led to the city centre consisted of red sandstone tenement buildings on both sides of the road, interspersed with the odd small shop – newsagents, hairdressers, etc. Enjoying the sensation of my feet pounding the pavements, I tucked my hands in my jacket pocket as I settled into a rhythmic stride. As if marching my sorrows away.

My interest was piqued by a chapel steeple I spotted a couple of hundred yards away. A strange desire to go in and light a candle overcame me. It had been so long since I'd attended chapel that I wasn't sure if they still did candle displays or if every chapel had them. Reaching the chapel, I was relieved there were no cars parked outside which meant no special masses or a funeral. I negotiated the steps leading to the main door and entered. A soothing silence enveloped me. Ignoring the holy water, I strode down the left-hand aisle to a seat in the front row. Familiarising myself with the sights and smells. Five minutes spent in quiet reflection. Images of the chapel I used to attend. Memories of attending with my parents. The charade of them attending together every Sunday. These thoughts irritated me, rousing me to my feet.

Walking slowly to the antique, black, wrought iron construction that housed three long lines of candles. Taking a candle from a cardboard box I put a fifty pence piece in the donation slot. Lighting the candle then placing it in a holder. Gazing at the flame that flickered to the left, fascinated at the small, blue, inner core resting within the larger yellow of the flame. A further halo of light emanated from the flame or was it a shadow? Time came to a halt. Meditating on the flame, aware of it changing colour from yellow to orange then finally to red. Eventually, I returned to consciousness as if I had been prodded on the arm. Shaking my head in bewilderment at the trance-like effect the flame had had on me, I picked up a handful of candles and placed them in my jacket pocket as I walked slowly to the exit.

Certain city centre streets had been changing. For the first time, I noticed the changing demographic. Bookmaker after bookmaker, cheque cashing shops and pawn shops were starting to dominate. Heading down Sauchichall Street, I decided to have a wander in a bookshop. *Perhaps a bit of reading, a bit of escapism will help keep my mind off things.* As I made my way to the bookshop, I spotted a pub on the corner that I'd spent many a good night in. The devious part of my mind, that slowly but surely was becoming more prevalent, encouraged me. '*It's fine, Connor. You deserve a pint or two. That's a good three-mile walk you've completed and a wee visit to chapel into the bargain. In you get, pal.*' My mind made up, I opened the door, headed to the bar and ordered a pint. Looking around, I was surprised at how busy it was for a late afternoon in midweek. Grabbing my pint, I headed to the jukebox, resting the lager on top of it. Two pound coins inserted in the machine, flicking through the collection backwards and forwards with the intensity of someone picking the last six songs they would ever hear. My pint was finished before I'd selected the first three. 'Excuse me, pal. Can you get me another?' I said, lifting my glass in the air. 'I've still got a few tunes to pick here. Don't want somebody nipping in and blagging them from me.'

The barman gave me an affirmative grunt. Having selected another couple of songs I headed to the bar, paid for my drink while constantly staring back and forth at the jukebox, like I was on the lookout for someone on the steal. Selecting the final track, I took my pint and sat at the table next to the jukebox. Smirking as I thought of Greg making a fool of himself one time at the Union. It had been a quiet midweek night. Greg and I invited Luca to the Union for a few pints to thank him for feeding us. Luca and I were at the bar getting the beers in while Greg was at the jukebox. His selections made, Greg walked towards us. The opening bars of his first selection boomed from the jukebox.

'Dooo....doooo....doooo....doooo...
I made it through the wilderness
Somehow I made it through
Didn't know how lost I was
Until I met you.'

The dozen or so students present turned to Greg, smirking and laughing. Luca and I sang at the tops of our voices. The oncoming, puzzled looking Greg, pleading his innocence, mumbling about putting in the wrong code. The happiness I felt soon gave way to melancholy, remembering all the good times. *What's the point of memories if they just drag you down and make you yearn for those days? Be careful what you wish for and all that, to think I was pining to meet someone. Now look at me. A right fucking mess.* When I finished my pint, I ordered another. Contentment should have been my primary feeling. Sitting with my pint, my choice of music on in the background, people watching, however, I couldn't relax, urged on by the desire to be on the move again. A series of quick swigs of my beer, a trip to the toilet, then one for the road as I fired a double brandy down.

The bookshop was only a two-minute walk away. On the way there, I winked encouragingly as I flipped a pound coin into the guitar case of a busker performing a reasonable rendition of 'Wish You Were Here'. Entering the bookshop, I observed the numerous displays of buy one get one free books. Striding to my favourite section, the alphabetical listings of authors, I scanned the rows in search of Kelman. The vast collection of Stephen King novels reminded me of someone mentioning a novel of his, *Rage*, being banned at one point. There was no sign of it so I located a member of staff. 'Sorry to interrupt you, pal. Can you check something for me?'

The female store assistant cocked her head back, probably something to do with the smell of alcohol from my breath. 'Sure thing. What can I do for you?'

'I'm looking for a Stephen King novel called *Rage*.'

'Oh, I'm sorry we don't stock it. You'll get it on the net though … under the name … Richard Bachmann, if I'm not mistaken.'

I thanked her. As I walked away I thought, *Why are we curious about banned stuff or like when a musician dies and everybody suddenly thinks they're a genius and buys their CD? Aaahhh well, back to Kelman.* I grabbed a copy of *How Late It Was* and sat. Twenty minutes or so passed as I flicked through my favourite parts. The alcohol started to take hold, causing a strong desire for food. *I'll head to the café downstairs, get a panini and a wee double espresso.* The lift took me to the ground floor. As the doors opened, the waft of freshly made coffee aroused my senses. Standing in the small queue, panini in hand, I scanned the seating area. Being a little unsteady on my feet, I nudged the person in front of me, offering an apology immediately. The large beanpole figure who wore a trendy flat cap and overly large specs, turned to look at me, his eye movement making it obvious he felt I was invading his personal space. He moved a stride away. Offended by the look, I barked, 'What's your problem? I apologised.'

The beanpole did not acknowledge my existence as I placed my order before moving further away. The barista who was consulting with the girl taking the orders shot a glance at me that I perceived to mean, 'I'm watching you.' Ordering a double espresso, I handed over the panini, moving next to the beanpole who I'd now dubbed Rifkind after an old Tory MP that Dad had a peculiar habit of shouting abuse at whenever he appeared on TV. The surname fascinated me. I mouthed it quietly. 'Rif-Kind. Malcolm Rifkind. Riiiiif-kind.' Suddenly, it became comical to me. Laughing, I said, 'Sorry for bumping into you there, Malcolm.'

So amused at my own petty joke.

Rifkind made eye contact, as if to say, 'OK, please just leave me alone you scary little man.'

'Grande latte with soya milk for Bill,' shouted the barista. Rifkind strode forwards with a big awkward gait, took his drink and moved away as quickly as possible.

'Hi there, if you want to take a seat, I'll bring your panini over,' the girl at the till advised me.

I thanked her as I turned to see where the object of my amusement was seated. Meandering to the table opposite, I removed my jacket placing it over the chair.

'Double espresso for Rifkind,' the barista called.

I laughed aloud at my immature use of the name as I made my way to collect my drink. The waitress walked past me with my panini and placed it on the table.

I tucked into my food, observing Rifkind as the beanpole pulled his Kindle from a black, retro Gola bag.

Growing increasingly irritated, I looked at him. *Fucking sitting in a bookshop with his soya milk and his fucking Kindle. What a clown. Ohhh, look at me, with my trendy hat and specs*. Finishing the panini, I took a few sips of espresso while studying Rifkind. Irrational thoughts buzzed inside me. Unable to help myself any longer I shouted over, 'Hey big guy … BIG GUY. BIIIIIGGGG GUY.' I waved my hands furiously.

Having gained the beanpole's attention, I asked, 'Are you a book lover?'

With a resigned look on his face, Rifkind answered, 'Yes, why do you—?'

Aye, he's even got the annoying posh as fuck Scottish accent that doesn't even sound Scottish and yae havnae a fucking clue which part of the country it's from.

'I'm asking because you're sitting in a shop with thousands of books yet yer sitting glued to an electronic device. WHY? Not … a … proper … book, big guy. Eh, big guy? Why no a proper hold-in-yer-hands. beautiful-smelling book?'

The staff watched and listened with a sense of unease.

'For your information, not that it is any of your concern, I have hundreds of books on my machine. I *cannot* carry hundreds of books physically around with me on my person.'

I laughed. 'On my person! Brilliant. How many books can you read at a time though? See, I don't get this argument from Kindle lovers like your good self, big guy. "Oh, it's just so convenient. Say I'm going on holiday for a fortnight, instead of cramming several books into my suitcase I just take my handy electronic device." That disnae wash wi me. I mean, how many books are you going to read on holiday? Three … four maximum. Hardly a massive inconvenience, is it?'

Attempting to close the conversation, Rifkind offered me a truce. 'We shall have to agree to disagree.' He returned to his device.

Sensing that my target was preparing to leave, I rose from my seat. Slowly edging over to the big guy's table, a mischievous grin settled on my face. 'So, what you reading, big guy?'

My reluctant opponent was losing patience. If it was a boxing match the towel would've been thrown in by now. 'You won't have heard of him,' he snapped.

'Try me, big guy. Don't be so judgemental. Don't judge a Kindle by it's cover. HAAAA! Get it, big guy.' I elbowed Rifkind.

'Luigi Pirandello,' he answered, his eyes darting around, looking for help.

'Never heard of him, big guy. Here, big guy, can you let

me have a quick look, just to see what it's like. Is there not a glare from the screen?'

'I'm busy. I'm trying to read. Now, *please* leave me alone.' Rifkind's voice had become pleading and desperate.

I placed my two hands on the back of the chair next to Rifkind. My anger escalated as my request to see the device was ignored. Swiping the device from Rifkind's hand, I resembled a junkie snatching his latest hit from the hands of his dealer.

Immediately, I balanced it on the palm of my right hand, theatrically swaying from side to side as if a rug was being pulled from under my feet. 'See, if this was a *proper* book, you wouldn't be worried but with one of these…'

Rifkind shot from his seat, stretched out his hand. 'Give it back … right now.'

The barista shouted from her station, 'Is this gentleman bothering you, sir?'

'Of course he is, he most certainly is. Get security.'

'If I accidentally dropped this, with the screen facing down … VAMOOSH! You've lost your hundreds of books, big guy. Wouldn't happen with a book now, would it? I'd be doing you a favour wouldn't I?'

The barista appeared at my side. 'Security are on their way. Hand it back to him now.'

I eyed her badge, Susan, underneath her name: BARISTA. 'Barista … what a *fucking* failure, Susan. Yer parents hoped for a barrister not a barista.' My laugh had a manic edge to it. 'Get it, big guy, get it? Barrister … Barista. That's made my day. C'mon, take a joke, big guy. Simmer down. There's your fancy bit of kit, safe and sound,' I said, handing it back. 'And as for you, Susan, stick to making the coffee ya nosy boot.'

Nonchalantly walking away, I shouted, 'It's been a pleasure, The Right Honourable Malcolm Rifkind. You've made The Right Dishonourable Connor Boyd happy for a few minutes. Chanks a million!'

Three

Walking briskly from one end of the living room to the other, hands in my pockets, I obsessed about my next move. My patience had finally snapped. *How can she just completely blank me out of her life? This isn't on ... no chance! If the mountain won't come to Muhammad, then Muhammad must go to the mountain.* My anger dissipated as I laughed at myself, wondering why on earth I was using the Muhammad phrase. Dressing quickly, I left the flat with a sense of purpose.

    I strode towards the city centre with tunnel vision. It was raining. A gentle sneaky rain. The kind you barely noticed but, if you did, you dismissed it as nuisance value. However, its strength lay in its persistence, slowly but surely it would soak you through. I was unaware of mostly everything around me. An awe-inspiring flock of birds gracing the skies in an orderly collective could have flown directly overhead and I would have failed to notice. My mind was busy weaving pretty patterns of its own. Manufacturing the image of a dramatic reconciliation. Laura leaving the office, walking slowly towards me, throwing her arms around me, telling me what a mistake she'd made. I'd wipe the tears from her eyes and repeatedly tell her I forgave her. She would promise that this would never happen again. When I snapped back to reality, I'd convinced myself that the only possible outcome was a reconciliation. I planned on telling her about the fatalistic feeling that had started to haunt me. How I had convinced myself that I was going to lose her long before I actually did. The way I had allowed this strange feeling of fate to take over and make me act the way I had. *It'll be like giving her the final pieces of a jigsaw, then she'll understand everything, it'll all fall into place.* Excitement coursed through me. My brisk walk became a slow jog. I felt alive. What I felt in my heart was something I had lost sight of. Hope. I convinced myself that there was hope.

Checking my watch, I shivered, realising my clothes were damp. It was two minutes to five. Unable to stand still, I lifted my right foot off the pavement, placing all my weight on my left foot, then changing over to the other foot. Back and forth until I saw the first group of staff members make their way out from the controlled-entry door into the main foyer. I began to focus on looking for Laura. Scanning the foyer intensely. It happened in a split second. As our eyes met, Laura stared at me like a distraught animal caught in the headlights of an oncoming vehicle. She spun around and walked straight back into the safety of the office. I charged through the crowd of people towards the staff door. Desperately pulling at the handle despite being fully aware that it couldn't possibly open. Peering through the slim panel of glass while thumping on the door screaming her name, I flinched as I felt a hand on my shoulder. 'What do you think you're playing at? Where's your identification, son?'

I turned to see the large, broad-shouldered security guard who had a definite ex-forces look about him.

'It's my girlfriend. She's in there and I really need to speak to her.'

'Sorry, you're not allowed in there.' He grabbed my shoulder with one hand and my elbow with the other. 'You'll have to leave, son,' he said, as I was ushered out of the building within a matter of seconds.

Standing on the pavement, I began marching backwards and forwards while furiously rubbing my head. Thinking what to do. Fists clenched. Anger whizzing about within me like when you let go of an untied balloon. *I need to get away from here before I do something fucking crazy.*

Walking back towards the flat, I took my mobile out of my jeans pocket and called Greg. Finally breaking the news to my best friend and asking if he could come over to the flat for a chat and a few drinks. *I need to get all this off my chest. Greg will help me out with some advice. He's always there for me. Not like the bastardin rest of them.*

***

The intercom buzzer roused me from my stupefied state. I dragged myself off the sofa. 'Hello?' I asked in a wearisome tone. 'Alright, Greg, up you come.' I opened the front door then threw myself back on the sofa. In stark contrast, Greg bounded into the flat with his usual zest. Scanned left and right, surveying his surroundings.

'Not a bad wee gaff you've got here, Connor.'

I stared at him then, from nowhere, a tsunami of emotions mugged me. Was it because I totally loved my friend and it was the first time I had seen him since 'it' happened or was it just coincidental? I struggled as best as I could but it was pointless. The horse had bolted. Tears. Face contorted in pain. Shame at letting Greg see me like this. I looked at the floor trying to avoid eye contact.

Greg rushed to the sofa, taking a seat next to me. 'C'mon, buddy, it's OK.' He threw an arm over my shoulder, pulling me closer. 'What the fuck has happened?'

Trying to compose myself, closing my eyes, taking deep breaths; I answered, 'I don't even know where to start, Greg. I've lost the plot. I've lost Laura. I've lost everything.'

'It can't be as bad as that. You got any cans in?'

I rubbed my face vigorously trying to destroy any evidence of manly weakness. 'Aye, in the fridge.'

'Right, I'll go and get us a can and you can tell me everything,' Greg said, as he headed to the hallway looking for the kitchen. Returning with a four deck, he broke one free handing it to me then took a seat on the armchair facing the sofa.

I opened the can, took a massive gulp. 'Check you out sitting there like Carl fucking Jung.'

Greg stood, clinked his can off mine. 'At least you've still got your sense of humour, buddy.'

'Greg, I'm in a right bad place. I'm sorry for bursting your ears with this but I need to speak to someone.'

'You know you can talk to me, mate. Anything. It won't go any further. Just take your time. Begin at the start.'

I rubbed my neck. 'I've lost track of time. I'm struggling … so bear with me. Last week I was laid low with a virus. I forgot that I had Laura's awards thing, fucking penguin suit do.'

Greg sniggered. 'You get the old tux on, ya wee shite? I've always wanted to wear one.'

I sat forward. 'This bastard I've told you about before. Fucking ponce. Justin. He totally tried to embarrass me right from the off.'

Greg put his can on the carpet. 'How come?'

'He asked me what I wanted to drink and I said, "A pint of lager, chanks."'

Greg covered his eyes with his hand. 'Whit the fuck is lager chanks?'

I snapped, 'Aye alright, fuck's sake. I meant to say lager thanks or lager cheers and said lager chanks. So he announces what I've said in front of the whole table. Fucking cackling hyenas all pishing themselves at me. Absolute sycophants for the ponce.'

'Dick.' Greg finished his can and opened another. 'What happened next?'

'Let me ask you a question, Greg – have you ever known me to drink brandy?'

'No, why?'

'When I got to the hotel for some weird reason, cos I was getting over a virus, I thought of hot toddies. Is that what they call that? Anyway, I ordered a double brandy. I threw it down my pipe. It felt like jump leads getting fixed to a car. Energy shot through me. So I got another. I thought of the advert, you know the Ready Brek man with the glow. So, there I am, a raving brandy drinker all of a sudden.'

Greg placed his mobile on the handrest of his chair. 'Weird.'

'So this ponce is way too overfamiliar with Laura. Ends up, I'm in having a slash and I feel somebody totally banging into me, no way is it an accident. I look to my right and he's fucking laughing away with his wee minion. I lost it, done it back to him, planted two crackers on his smug coupon, watched him slump to the ground then thanked him for the opportunity.'

Greg looked at me, mouth agape. 'Oh shit, Connor. You know how much Laura's work means to her. So she binned you right away, I take it.' Greg stood, frustration all over his face. 'You've let the twat win. You must have known he was at it. Sometimes you need to play the long game. Walk away.'

'Fuck off, Greg. I was totally provoked.'

'She ignoring you then?'

'I've tried phoning, left numerous messages. Sent numerous texts. Lost my patience today and went to her work.'

Greg shook his head.

'Wit, you shaking your head at? Have you ever been in love? You don't have a clue, Greg.'

'Thank God. If this is what it's all about then NO THANKS! You're a right advertisement for it, eh?'

I waved my hand dismissively. 'Look, Greg, I'm not in the mood. Away you go; away out with your uni pals.'

'Listen, you, don't take it out on me. I'm here to try and help you. To listen. But I can't just sit and not offer any opinion. Sorry if you don't like it but if I think you've fucked up then I'll tell you so. You want a puppet or a pal?'

'You should have seen her face when she saw me. She couldn't get away quick enough. I know now, after seeing that look on her face … It's over.'

'Listen, Connor, I won't bullshit you. I agree. I don't think there's a chance of her forgiving you. If it was in a club or somewhere other than her work, then maybe, but her work colleague, no chance.'

'I really appreciate you coming over. I'm sorry if I got sidetracked and didn't put enough effort into our friendship recently. I couldn't help it. I'm totally shattered with all this. I'm gonnae have an early night. I'll get you a beer and phone you a taxi, OK?'

'As long as you're sure. Listen, Saturday night – me, you

and Luca … night out. Just like old times.'

'OK,' was all I could muster as I went to get Greg a can and call him a taxi.

Four

Laura,

I'm writing this letter at five in the morning. I've just woke up. Greg was here earlier. I told him about us and about everything that's happened. I needed to speak to someone after seeing your reaction at your work yesterday when you saw me. I've tried texting, calling you, turning up at your work was a last resort. I only wanted to talk. I keep picturing your face, mascara running down it, on the night I ruined everything. Despite everything that was going on around me at that moment, I was looking at your face, the tears running down it and although it was breaking my heart to see you upset and that I was the cause of it, I found something beautiful about it. Your face looked amazing to me, like a stunning painting or something. I suppose that says a lot about my frame of mind these days.

I'm sorry about this being an incoherent rant! I just need to get all these thoughts and words out of my system. I need you to understand as best as I can explain. Don't worry, this isn't a letter begging you to forgive me and for us to get back together. I know we're done, but you and I know that if you clicked your fingers I'd be there in a nanosecond. Cos I'm weak.

Memories are destroying me. Everywhere I go, everything I do, feel or see, I think of you.

The mornings are worst. When I roll over to touch you and you're not there. My mind plays a dirty trick for a split second. It sends the thought that you didn't stay over last night but maybe it's tonight you'll be staying over instead. Then the gut-wrenching reality hits me. How can I get out of bed and function after that? GOOD MORNING! *GOOD MOURNING*.

I miss you so much. I miss your smell. Your kisses. Everything. I go for a walk, I think of us walking in that same spot. I pull out a CD, I remember you bought it for me. You're everywhere. But not *here* where I want you to be, where I need you to be. The safest that I have ever felt in my entire life was when I was cuddled up to you in bed at night. These thoughts are like fucking boomerangs. They just keep coming back. I can't shut them away.

All I wanted was someone to love me. You will never fully understand how it made me feel when you first told me you loved me. You filled a chasm. But the persistent shite reappeared. Sorry, I know you hate me swearing! Your love was light and full of colour. Mine was heavy like a medicine ball. It was dark and it had conditions, stipulations, clauses, etc. I would have walked over broken glass for you. I used to lie in bed at night just watching you sleep. Sometimes I had to fight the tears. What is that all about? Emotions would just drown me. You're truly the most beautiful person I'll ever meet. Those dimples! Maybe it was more than love. Infatuation maybe? I was the happiest I've ever been in my life. The demons, the doubt, the fear all left me. I felt free.

Before I met you, I walked looking down. Everything was down. I didn't notice the beauty around me. Then it all changed. You pulled back the curtains in my mind and let in the light. I looked upwards. I saw with new eyes. But life can't stay like that, can it, Laura? When there is a huge high there must be a low. It's just a matter of when.

So, I began to get a horrible, anxious feeling in my stomach. I would wake in the morning and wonder what this feeling was and why it kept returning. Like nausea, anxiety and fear all rolled into one. Eventually, one night it hit me like a thunderbolt. *Telling* me that I was going to lose you. It was inevitable. Only a matter of time. I tried to fight it but I've been riddled with a lack of self-esteem most of my life. It wasn't even a fair fight. It bullied me. Man is meant to be the master of his own fate but FATE BECAME MY MASTER. I felt helpless.

One afternoon on our holiday, I had to run to the bathroom and get under the shower so that I could compose myself. I think that was the first of the horrible panic attacks. They got stronger and stronger. I'm not feeling sorry for myself here. I'm just trying to explain things to you. And this kind of thing is meant to be cathartic, isn't it? God, I could do with some psychological relief.

None of this makes my actions that night acceptable. If I was thinking rationally I would have seen what Jordan was trying to do and would have just laughed at his pathetic games but I was hell-bent on self-destruction. It felt like it was pre-ordained.

I went to the doctor to explain how I was feeling/thinking. Honestly, it was pointless. I'm still on a waiting list to speak to a counsellor. And that's after passing an audition that proves to them I am worthy. Another reason why I felt HELPLESS.

Whoever said you don't forget your first love is a genius. The way I feel just now it is the only thing that makes sense in this horrible world I'm stuck in.

Laura, I hope you meet someone that you deserve. Someone who will love you in the right way. Someone who will make you so, so happy. I have no anger or ill-feeling whatsoever towards you. The fault lies with me. Within me. I'm troubled. Finding love wasn't the magic fix I naively thought it would be. These demons, shortcomings, whatever you want to call them need to be dealt with before I can even begin to live a happy life. My mind is an agitator. An incendiary device. I need to find the mute button.

Whatever happens, please remember I never meant to hurt you. I'll never forget you.

Thanks for loving me. I didn't think I was ever worthy of it.
Connor
x

Five

The area of the city that we arranged to meet had changed beyond recognition. People spoke of regeneration – sushi bars, barbers rebranded as 'cool chop shops', an enterprise that sold bowls of breakfast cereal for the price of a three-course lunch in most pubs half a mile along the road, artisan bakers charging silly dough for their exotic wares.

I burst through the doors of the pub 'greeting' my friends with, 'Why the fuck are we meeting here?'

Luca and Greg both shot me a look of disgust then stood to perform our usual handshake and hug ritual. They returned to their seats, backs to the window that looked onto the night-time street and the many bars and restaurants dwarfed by imposing, red sandstone, tenement flats. I sat facing them. The darkness hid the soundless rain that fell sideways. Light emanating from the lamp posts provided the only evidence that it was still raining.

'What's wrong? This is a nice boozer,' said Greg.

I pulled a dismissive face. 'You've changed,' I said with a sneer as I walked to the bar. I shouted over to them, 'What you two twats wanting to drink?' Heads turned in my direction, the diction and the volume of my voice was perhaps disturbing in a pub where people were having a quiet civilised drink.

The barman eyed him me with suspicion. 'What can I get you?'

'Three pints of Tennent's, pal.'

The barman looked at me, a supercilious grin beaming from him. 'We don't do Tennent's here.' A false sarcastic laugh thrown in for good measure.

'Aye, right. It equates to one in every three pints of lager drunk in Scotland. Interesting wee fact for you, pal. Feel free to recycle it. Give me three pints of your best-selling draught lager then.'

As the barman began pouring the drinks, I turned to listen to my friends. On hearing Luca explain to Greg that he had some suppliers coming over to the restaurant tomorrow for a 'client-cuddling,' I shouted over to them, 'When did we sign up for wank-speak? I haven't been out for a while but I wasn't aware we'd signed up.'

'Watch your language. I won't tolerate that language in here,' the barman warned.

I frowned at him.'Right, we're in a pub in Glasgow. You have Singer sewing machines all over the place, blackboards depicting goods for sale from various professions that are now sadly defunct. You have the whole pared down *industrial* look going on but you don't tolerate a wee bit of *industrial* language? No Tennent's, no swearing. What about breathing? Do you do breathing in here?'

Greg appeared at my side. 'Calm down, Connor. Go and take a seat; I'll get the beers.'

'No, Greg. *You* take a seat. Is a guy not allowed to give his opinion nowadays?'

Greg walked back towards Luca, shrugging his shoulders as if to say, 'I tried.'

The barman finished pouring the last of the three pints then leant towards me as if telling me a secret. 'Be as opinionated as you like with your friends. No shouting at the top of your voice or using bad language that could offend any of my other customers. OK?'

Snatching a pint, I took a large swig before pulling a face in disgust as if I'd just drunk a pint of evil. 'Aye, OK! Oh sorry, was that too loud? By the way, this lager is as friendly to my palate as your demeanour.'

The barman looked exasperated. 'That'll be fifteen thirty.'

I looked from right to left theatrically, shaking my head. 'Right, where is it?'

The barman refused to play along.

'C'mon, where is it? Where's your mask? You must have a mask, charging five pounds and ten pence for a pint of that shite.' I laughed, raised an eyebrow, shot a smile at him as if, 'what you gonnae do now then?'

The barman looked like he was losing the will to live. 'If you don't like it, feel free to go elsewhere.'

'Charming! What time you on to tonight?'

Running a cloth along the bar, he answered, 'Another hour or so.'

'Good stuff. I'll keep you company until you've finished your shift.' I winked as I returned to my two friends.

Sat opposite Greg, I took another drink of my pint as if I'd completed an eight-hour shift on a building site in the baking sun. Slamming my glass down on the beer mat, I said, 'I've a feeling it's gonnae be a cracker tonight, boys.'

My friends looked at me apprehensively.

Luca offered his condolences. 'Sorry to hear about you and Lesley.'

'Aye, you're that sorry you can't even get her fucking name right.'

Luca put his hand on his forehead, his face contorted at his error. 'I'm really sorry, buddy, I meant Laura. I work with a Lesley. Got a wee bit mixed up. How's things?'

I stared at Luca with a deadpan expression. 'Shite. Absolutely shite.' Noticing Lucas's startled expression, I added, 'Well, you did ask. Sorry, if that's not the answer you were looking for, pal.'

Greg put his pint down and leaned forwards. 'Lose the attitude, Connor. We organised tonight to try to cheer you up, have a few drinks and a few laughs. You've been here five minutes and you've created a horrible atmosphere. We know you're gutted about Laura but don't take it out on the people who care for you.'

'You trying to say *she* didn't care for me?'

Greg looked to the ceiling, closed his eyes and shook his head. 'That's not what I said. Just chill out.'

The three of us took solace in our pints. A battle of wills began to see who would speak first. Luca, the least stubborn of us relented. 'Anyone heard from Justin?'

My arms were folded across my chest. I shook my head.

Greg relayed the gist of an email that he'd received.

'Whose turn to get the drinks?' I asked. 'Whoever's it is, get me another pint of that shite.'

Greg and Luca laughed. Greg stood and threw a playful punch at my arm. 'It's that shite that you polished it off in about six minutes.'

I smiled. 'I'm absolute Gobi Desert. I've got some drooth on me. I'd neck a can of Asda's own brand lager with the thirst I've got.'

As he squeezed past, Greg said, 'Good to see you smile, ya miserable wee tosser.'

I turned to Luca. 'Sorry about earlier. I'm struggling the now. Things are a right mess. But enough of that. How's tricks with you? Still shagging for Scotland?'

Luca was dressed immaculately in a slim-fitting, plain black shirt, blue jeans with a tan-coloured Hermes belt and matching coloured brogues. 'I don't have a minute to myself these days, Connor. The restaurant takes up all my time. This is the first proper weekend night off I've had for six weeks. We're closed on a Monday but that's no use for going out on the pull. I can't complain though. How's things in the call centre?'

'I've been off for weeks. Got a sick line for another week. Just can't face it.'

Luca's face bore a troubled expression. 'Connor, I know everybody will throw their tuppence worth in but you need to remember that in six months this will all feel like a dream. Don't ruin everything while you're trying to get over Laura.'

I offered a fist pump. 'Luca, you're a brilliant mate. You're a great listener. I'll always be grateful for the chat we had about my mum. Honestly, I'm really, really trying.'

'Trying everybody's patience,' said Greg, as he returned with the drinks.

I grabbed my pint and laughed. 'Nosy bastard.'

An hour or so passed. The drink had a relaxing effect on me. The hackles came down. We swapped stories. Laughing like the good times from the past. However, my efforts at temporarily numbing the pain and agitation were futile. Soon,

I was staring blankly into the distance, my mind nagging at me. '*Right that's your time up, I've given you an hour's peace. Now, can I bring your attention to exhibit A: Laura's face on seeing you outside her work.*' Luca handed me another drink, rescuing me from the image. I dragged a small, faux leather, cylinder-shaped bar stool from the table to my left and placed my feet on it.

Greg frowned at me. 'Are you OK?'

'Fine. Why?'

'You've gone a bit quiet.'

'I was just thinking that this bar stool looks like a giant rollo. Didnae realise you were hanging on my every word, Greg.'

Buoyed by safety in numbers as his colleague had arrived to take over, the barman shouted over at me. 'Take your feet off that, someone has to sit on it. They don't want to sit where someone's had their dirty shoes.'

I turned my head in surprise. 'What's your problem? I'm fucking sick of listening to you.' I sprang from my seat, rushing to the bar.

The barman shouted in Greg and Luca's direction. 'Guys, it's up to you whether you want to stay but your friend will need to leave. I'm not taking any more of his nonsense.'

I slammed my fist on the bar. 'Talk to me, ya fucking idiot. Leave them out of it.'

The barman moved to within swinging distance of me. 'Get your jacket and go. Don't make us have to use force.' He placed a special emphasis on his last word.

Raising both my arms, my hands beckoned the barman forwards. 'Go for it!'

Greg and Luca appeared at my side. Luca grabbed me by the shoulders. 'Listen to me, Connor. This is stupid. Let's go.'

I tried to shake myself free. Greg helped Luca as they manoeuvred me like a piece of furniture back to the table and grabbed our jackets.

I screamed and cursed at the top of my voice. 'Stick your fucking, shitty little pub up your arse, you...' My two friends dragged me out like a misbehaving schoolboy being removed from a shop by his parents.

Standing on the pavement, facing my friends, I screamed at them. 'Wit you think yiz are doing? Don't ever embarrass me like that again!'

Greg squared up to me. 'Us embarrass *you*. Are you having a laugh? You've been in a shitty mood since you turned up. I'm sick of having to babysit you. Don't know about you, Luca, but I'm heading up the road. I've better things to do with my time.'

I looked at my watch. 'Fuck off, Greg. Do I look bothered?'

Luca pulled his jacket collar up. 'Listen, Connor, you're not in the right frame of mind. No doubt I'm wasting my breath but you should get yourself up the road too. Greg, you want to share a taxi?'

Greg turned to face the road. 'Yeah, I'll flag *him* one, then we'll get the next one.'

I looked to the sky. 'Stick yer taxi. I'm no sure what I'm doing yet.'

Greg lifted his right arm in the air, using his other hand to whistle at an oncoming cab. 'Fine. You're a fucking drama queen, Connor. Thanks for a brilliant night.'

Luca grabbed me, hugged me, receiving nothing in return. He jumped into the waiting hackney cab with Greg as I looked on.

My paranoid mind directed me to hail a cab and follow them. *Bet they're just ditching me and going for a drink*. I attracted the attention of a taxi, jumped in and ordered the driver to follow the cab in front. Sat in the back I craned my neck left and right, trying to spot my friends' taxi. Passing along the main thoroughfare through a couple of sets of traffic lights, I ordered the driver to pull in. Fancying this area with its little smattering of pubs the most likely place they'd stop if they were going for a drink, I paid the fare and headed to the first pub in the strip.

Walking into the bar surreptitiously, I scanned the place. There was no sign of them so I headed to the next bar. Entering the snug, I ordered a straight Vodka. I'd emptied the glass before I got my change. Walking to the double doors that led to the main part of the pub, I stopped. I hadn't even contemplated what I would do if my insticts proved correct. Striding forwards I pulled the door open just enough to see inside. *DIRTY BASTARDS!* Always go with your instincts. I knew it. I just knew it. My mind ordered me to confront them, but first I strode to the bar and ordered two pints. Talking to myself, telling myself how shabbily I'd been treated, I waited on the drinks. *I'm in the right fucking perfect mood for this*, I thought as I lifted the two pints and headed to the door. Holding the two pints against my chest with one hand I opened the door with the other, spilling lager over my shirt. Striding towards them, I kept my eyes focused firmly on Greg who faced me but was in deep conversation with Luca.

I made an exaggerated noise as if clearing my throat before I said, 'Don't mind if I join you dirty, lying, fucking excuses for pals do yiz?'

Greg looked at me in disgust.

'Wit's up, boys? Thought yiz were heading up the road?'

Luca took a drink from his pint. 'We changed our minds, thought we'd pop in for a quick pint.'

'Don't fucking explain yourself to him,' snapped Greg.

'Aye, you two don't need to explain a single fuckin thing to me. I've got you both a pint, here you go.' Throwing the contents of the two pints at them, I placed the empty glasses on their table then turned to leave.

Greg had thrown himself to the left to avoid the flying liquid. He pounced from his seat, grabbed my shoulder spinning me round to face him. Slamming me against the door, inches from my face, he shouted, 'I've done everything for you, I've been like a brother to you, ya little shite.'

I looked at him with a pathetic clownish grin on my face.

Greg's fist was just under my chin, gripping a handful of shirt. Luca stood at the side ready to step in should things get seriously out of hand. Greg continued his verbal attack. 'Do you think you are the only person that has ever been dumped. You deserved it. You acted like a dick. When are you gonnae stop playing the poor, wee, tortured soul. I'm fucking sick of it.'

'Fuck off. Get … yer … hands … off … me,' I whispered, every word spoken slowly and mechanically.

'Is this how you get your kicks? Do you love playing the *victim*?' Greg annunciated the word disparagingly at me. 'Victim. That's what you'll always be. A moaning faced, little *victim*.'

There are times in life when a word or a statement carries more weight, takes on far more significance. Spoken at a specific time it is elevated to a level way beyond the intention of the person who uttered it.

Victim.

I reacted hysterically. 'I'm not a fucking victim. Get your fucking hands off me,' my arms flailing like an out of control child in the epicentre of a tantrum. When I finally broke free, I screamed, 'We're done, you fuckin arsehole,' as I kicked the door open and fled.

As soon as my feet met the pavement, I turned back towards the pub, placed my hands on the building, bent over and threw up. A foul-tasting acid burnt the back of my throat as I retched and retched until my intestines felt bruised. I felt the anger bubbling inside me like the acidic liquid that had recently escaped from my mouth. This feeling wasn't so easy to dispose of. Straightening myself, I stood at the pavement's edge and scanned both directions for a taxi. Trying to clear my throat, spitting incessantly on the pavement. A taxi finally stopped, I got in and slumped on the backseat advising the driver of my destination. Moisture had formed at the side of my eyes, caused by vomiting. Thought after thought of what had happened scurried through my mind like rodents searching for food. Ill-feeling for everyone spewing from me like the steam from a pressure cooker as the valve is released. *Victim. I'm not a fuckin victim. I'll show him. He's changed since he moved out. Too big for his boots. I don't need pals like that. Sneaking off for a pint without me. They can go to hell.* I checked my pockets to see how much cash I had. Satisfied there was no need to visit a cashpoint. A couple of minutes later, I ordered the driver to pull up. 'Keep the change, pal,' I shouted, slamming the door then storming down the cobbled lane filled with industrial-sized rubbish carts belonging to the various pubs backing onto the lane.

People like me have an uncanny knack for lurching from one diaster to another. A better man, a wiser man would have returned to the safety of their flat to lick their wounds.

As I headed towards my destination I took in the sight of the two doormen. One of them bald. His head resembled a huge boiled egg. A tiny little face was ensconced in the head. The neck was non-existent, merging effortlessly with many chins and broad shoulders. His colleague was taller with short spikey hair, a jutting chin which he had tried and failed to disguise with a goatee beard. The beard just made his chin even more prominent.

'Evening, gentlemen,' I greeted them, rubbing my hands together, 'finishing the night off with a little bit of ornithology.'

'Evening,' the Matt Lucas doppelganger answered. 'On your own, pal? Where've you been?'

Careful to stop a few yards away, aware of the reek of vomit from my breath, I answered. 'A few beers up the West End with friends – pipe and slippers brigade' – I laughed – 'so I thought I'd pop in here for an hour's entertainment.' I winked.

The taller of the doormen smiled at me, returning his wink. 'Good man. Have fun.'

I climbed the stairs, paid my entrance fee, then made my way through the blood-red velvet curtains. Girls paraded about in shorts and cropped vests, taking drink orders. Dancers gyrated on various little stages. The men on their own looked as if even stubbing a cigarette out on them wouldn't get them to avert their eyes. The large groups appeared more relaxed, enjoying their drinks and the camaraderie amongst friends. I took a seat just behind a group of twenty or so friends, hoping a waitress would approach soon to take my drink order. I didn't have to wait long, ordering a pint and a double Camus. My focus switched to the dancers and what their stories might be.I wondered what brought them into this profession? *Never mind what their story is – what the fuck are you doing in a place like this?* I never would have thought I'd frequent a club like this and couldn't fathom why I had ended up drawn to this place.

The drinks arrived, stirring me from my thoughts. Drinking my pint slowly, I sat people watching and eavesdropping on the stag party that was scattered around me. Any attempts at conversation I rebuffed, pretending not to have heard or looking blankly into the distance. My mind, in a rare show of good sense, dictated to me that now was not a good time to engage in any human contact. *Just drink and mind your own business, Connor,* I warned myself.

A disturbance broke out. I watched the big egg-headed doorman and his co-worker shuffle the guilty party down the stairs, wondering what treatment the troublemaker would receive out of sight from prying eyes. I finished my drinks and ordered another pint. The waitress asked me if I'd like anything else. 'Just a pint,' I answered.

'No. Something *else*,' she said.

I shrugged my shoulders as if to say, 'I haven't a clue what you're talking about.'

'Do you want a dance. A private dance,' she whispered.

I examined her face. I stared at her like I was struggling to understand her fully. 'Why not.'

She sat on my lap. 'Great. I'm Chelsea. What's your name?' she asked as she gently manoeuvred her manicured, Union Jack, glitter-decorated fingernails across my neck, sending a shiver up my spine.

'Connor,' I answered, as she kissed my cheek.

'I'll get your drink, Connor, then we'll go through and have some fun.'

I'd agreed without giving it any proper thought. I felt no sexual feelings towards the girl nor anyone else in this place but I wasn't thinking properly.

'Let's go, Connor,' the girl said, linking her arm in mine as I stood, leading me to a small side room. A brown chesterfield in the centre of the room. A small table sat to the side of the sofa. On a table in the top right-hand corner of the room sat a music system. Behind this, the same red curtains I saw on entering the club. I'd no idea what lay behind those curtains. The familiarity of the aroma in the room troubled me, reminding me of a time when Laura had given me a massage using aromatherapy oils.

I sat on the sofa and she handed me my pint then walked over to the music system. An instrumental which I didn't recognise started to fill the room. 'Back in a minute, Connor.' She disappeared behind the red curtains.

I felt myself merging with the sofa. It was becoming a chore to hold my pint so I stretched over and placed it on the table. She emerged from behind the curtains in her underwear, having shed a layer of clothes. I watched her try to walk in a slow, enticing manner in my direction and felt sorry for her. Everything about this seemed sad and pathetic yet I had gone along with it all. The supposedly sexy, atmospheric music, the scent in the room, this poor girl dancing in front of me, removing her bra. Unable to hold it in any longer, laughter burst from my mouth like the vomit I had spewed earlier. This unusual reaction to her removing her bra disconcerted her. She smiled at me as if trying to pretend she was in on the joke too. My continued laughter soon brought her to a halt. 'What's your problem?' She placed her hand on her hip, her head cocked to the side. 'What's with the laughing?'

I tried to speak between bouts of laughter. 'Sorry ... sorry ... it's ... all this,' I motioned with my hand in a sweeping movement.

'What's that meant to mean?' she asked, mimicking my gesture.

'The pathetic music. All this. Why do you put yourself through this charade?'

She bent down for her bra. Putting it back on, she answered, 'Who the hell do you think you are to judge me? This *charade* has paid for me to get through uni. I'm in the last year of my legal diploma. I'll earn more in five minutes in here with you than I could in three hours waiting tables or working in a bar. What do you do for a living?'

'Call centre,' I mumbled.

She laughed at me. 'So, you are sitting there putting labels on me. Probably pitying me. Poor girl, etc, etc. And yet you've just paid *me* about the equivalent of three hours of mind-numbingly boring call-centre work for two minutes of my time.' She fixed her ponytail.

I sat forwards, her words had transformed me. The laughter of a minute ago brought to an abrupt end.

Crossing her arms across her chest, she said, 'Do you see the irony? You're the victim here, *not* me. You.' A mocking grin spread over her face. 'Pathetic.'

I lunged from the seat. 'Don't fucking use that word,' I screamed at her.

'What word is that? Pathetic?'

'Victim. Victim. Don't call me a fucking victim.'

'Everything alright in here, Chelsea?' came a voice from behind.

'Yeah. Just another amateur psychologist that can't handle the fact that they're the *victim*, not me.'

'*Don't* fucking call me that, you—'

My sentence was interrupted by the bulky security man's arms that suddenly engulfed me in a bear hug carrying me out of the room. 'Calm down, wee man. Sssshhhh. Sssshhhh.'

This made me even more irate. 'Don't fucking speak to me like I'm a kid, you big heap of shite.'

'Wee man. Wee man,' he whispered menacingly. 'Any more of this and you'll be going for a big sleep.' His arm wrapped around my neck. The two doormen appeared from the stairs. The bald headed one shook his head. 'What you been up to, pal?'

I couldn't speak. My captor was putting pressure on my throat making me feel sick and faint. 'Bad attitude this wee man has, JD,' the security man advised.

They flanked me on either side then picked me up. My shoes dangled with the toes touching the floor like a ballerina on pointe. As soon as the grip released from my throat, I began to cough, trying to clear my throat. Down the flight of stairs I was carried until we reached the entrance to the club where I was tossed onto the cobbled lane. Pain shot through my elbow as it hit the cobbles. I sprang to my feet. 'Bastards. Fucking bastards,' I screamed as loudly as I could. Pacing backwards and forwards I tried to think what to do. 'Hey, Humpty fucking Dumpty. Ya big, fat, ugly bastard. You need to do something about that temper. Too much steroid abuse. You can't get enough steroids down your pipe can you? And you're still a fat, ugly bastard, aren't you Humpty? What's up, Humpty? Aaahh, that's it – all those steroids have reduced your already tiny little cock to a pathetic looking wee specimen. And that's why you got yourself a job here. Does it make you feel more of a man working here? Does it make up for your tiny, little, steroid-riddled dick?'

The doorman tried a lunge at me but his colleague stopped him. 'Don't, JD, he's not worth it.'

My laugh echoed throughout the deserted lane at the sight of him being held back like a vicious dog on a chain. 'He's HD, not JD. Big fucking Humpty Dumpty. Look at him. A wee pair of dungarees would be different class on you Humpty.'

'You better get yourself to fuck, wee man, BEFORE I FUCKIN KILL YOU!'

The goatee-bearded doorman put his hand on his colleague's shoulders. 'Don't fall for it, JD.'

'Aye, there's a good boy, Chinny Hill. Man, that is a right fucking dangerous chib, I mean chin you've got there. That's a lethal weapon. Wee bit of advice though, Chinny, lose the goatee it's adding even more prominence to that goddamn beast of a chin. Alright, Chinny. Wee bit of advice for yae. Trust me. Bzzzzzzzzz, lose the goatee,' I said, pretending to shave.

Chinny piped up. 'Listen, ya little cretin. You need to look in the mirror. You're a midget with no mates. No bird. Bet you havnae got a job either. Go and crawl back to your wee shithole of a flat or do you still live with yer ma, ya wee misfit.' He laughed, nudged his pal. 'The wee saddo still lives with his old dear.'

I walked a few paces to one of the large industrial bins and pulled out an empty lager bottle throwing it at the two doormen. It smashed on the wall a few feet away.

'Call the police, JD. You're in trouble now, ya wee dick.'

I leant my back against the wall. 'Excellent. Long do you think they'll be? I'm tired, it's been a long day. I'll be pressing charges against that big fucker that tried to choke me.'

Egghead looked at his colleague.'Wit yae reckon it is, Davie? Stupidity. Bravado. Or a bit of both?'

'Aye, bit of both. He's obviously got a right shitty life. In a bad place, chip on his shoulder. Can't believe he hasn't the sense to do one before the polis get here.'

I lifted the bin lid, grabbed a bottle and threw it before grabbing another and throwing that. JD's patience was exhausted, he ran as fast as he could at me. Seeing JD charging at me I fired another bottle which rebounded off his chest as if made of plastic not glass. He grabbed me. 'You could have hit me on the fuckin heid with that, ya little shit.' He spun me around snatching my two arms behind my back before placing his own arm vertically across my back locking my arms in place.

I stretched my neck upwards as I looked skywards and screamed 'Whhhhyyyyyyyyyyyy?' The scream conveyed my suffering and pain with greater accuracy than any number of eloquent words could. A penetrating, desperate plea that would cause a shudder within anyone with a shred of empathy. As I was ushered across the cobbled lane, a police officer's radio crackled. My head was bowed as I tried to catch my breath. Feeling like the epitome of a broken, defeated man, this time in a whisper, I asked again, 'Why?' No hope existed of ever receiving a satisfactory answer.

Six

The turnkey rattled repeatedly on the grey metal door of the holding cell, creating an echo that was only partially drowned out by him slamming the hatch open. My only remaining place of refuge disturbed. A pair of eyes peered through at me as I tried to get my bearings. 'Morning, sleeping beauty. Sort yourself out. Time to go home, unless you fancy another night that is.' The policeman's laugh rang down the corridor as he closed the hatch, heading to the next cell with zestful steps. I dragged myself from the lightweight excuse for a bed. Snapshots from the previous evening flashed through my mind. I felt nothing. Immune to the various incidents. My only concern was getting home.

The turnkey opened the cell door, expelling the darkness, the light emanating from behind him created a messianic effect. 'Ready to go, son?'

'Aye,' I murmured, avoiding eye contact.

I was led down the corridor, through a set of doors which brought us out to the front desk. The administration was quickly taken care of. Forms signed. My belongings were returned. Free to leave. As I stepped into the early morning rain, I recalled that they'd taken a mouth swab from me the previous night. *Why the fuck did they take a mouth swab?* I pondered, walking gingerly towards the nearest main road to hail a taxi home. The falling rain hurt my bones. I felt fragile. Like an animal that had lost a fight and was retreating to its lair to lick its wounds. Heaving a huge sigh of relief, I caught sight of an oncoming taxi with it's *FOR HIRE* sign shining brightly in the early morning gloom. I gave the driver my address then let out an enormous yawn in the hope that the hint for solitude would be taken. Resting my head on my closed fist, I replayed the night's events.

***

I showered quickly as the water hitting certain areas of my body made me wince. After devouring a plate of toast and some strong coffee at the kitchen table, my mobile had finally charged so I switched it on to check my messages. A text message came through:

> **Messages**
> MILK
> Hi Connor. I've bought a little golden Labrador. She's gorgeous. Called her Madge. Taking her for lots of walks to the park. I luv her so much. U need to come over and see her. X

Shaking my head, I typed back my response:

> **Sent Messages**
> MILK
> Aye, I'll get my jacket. Can't contain myself.

I placed the mobile on the table and prepared some more toast. The silence from my mobile disturbed me. I'd expected to receive an apology from Greg. Having had time to process last night's goings-on, I arrived at the notion that I was the injured party. *Fucking bang out of order. No apology. Victim? Victim of a friendship that wasn't what I thought it was.* Pouncing from my chair, I strode down the hall to the storage cupboard. Opening the door, a mop fell forwards rattling my head. I grabbed it, hammered the end of it frantically off the wall before tossing it down the hall as I returned to my search. I found paint and brush and placed them on the wooden flooring. Rummaging through various tools – a hammer, Stanley blade, wallpaper scraper – I finally found the screwdriver. Heading back into the living room, using the screwdriver to prise open the tin of emulsion, I dipped the brush in and began to furiously deface the main wall with graffiti that read:

> MUM: VICTIM = CONNOR
> ZANDER: VICTIM = CONNOR
> LAURA: VICTIM = CONNOR

Rage erupted within me as I stared at my handiwork. Eyes playing tricks as VICTIM = CONNOR stood out like the top line of an optician's letter board, the other names relegated to the unreadable bottom line. Picking up the paintbrush that balanced on top of the tin, I threw it at the wall. Little splatters of paint shot in various directions. Sitting on the sofa I closed my eyes. Thirty seconds or so passed before the brush was retrieved, painting over Zander: Victim = Connor. I began to clean the mess caused by throwing the brush. The other graffiti remained.

***

The following day as I lay on the sofa watching the local news on TV, my interest was aroused by a developing story.

'Good afternoon, this is Sheila Fox reporting from Queen Elizabeth University Hospital where an anti-abortion protest group are holding a forty day vigil. With me I have Gina Campbell-Kennedy, founder of SWEAR, Scottish Women Extending Abortion Rights. Now Ms Campbell-Kennedy, as spokeswoman for SWEAR what do you have to say about this protest by anti-abortion groups?'

'We believe that there needs to be fundamental changes to the Abortion Act 1967. Women need to be given the power to make their own decision where possible. We propose that the current legislation that requires two doctors to approve a termination is outdated and should be replaced. We also advocate decriminalisation and extending the current twenty-four week rule.'

'Dirty, fat, fucking child killer,' I screamed at the television screen. Gina Campbell-Kennedy wore a blue pinstriped suit which accentuated her girth. Her rosy-red cheeks matched her lipstick.

The reporter called her to task. 'Ms Campbell-Kennedy, surely the termination of a pregnancy without the necessary consultation is wrong on several levels?'

'A woman should be able to make her own decision dependent on the various factors in her life. It is her decision, not that of a doctor who knows nothing or very little about that individual's life.' Her smug, laissez-faire attitude enraged me.

The reporter adopted a different tack. 'You must have something to say to the people who believe that increasing the twenty-four week period is morally repugnant and medically dangerous.'

A supercilious look adorned Ms Campbell-Kennedy's face. 'It's not my place to speak for these groups. I act in the interests of SWEAR and we believe that the current act is archaic and in need of modernisation.'

'I'm afraid that's all we have time for. Thank you, Ms Campbell-Kennedy,' Sheila Fox reported.

I threw the remote control at the screen, the batteries popped out landing on the carpet. Grabbing my mobile, on autopilot, I called Greg. 'Did you see that fucking cold-hearted boot on the news there about the Abortion Act?'

Greg answered, 'Are you for real? You cause all that trouble, then call me as if nothing happened? You don't even say hello … or apologise. You just launch into some story that I don't have a clue about.'

I terminated the call. *Can't believe I forgot that I wasn't speaking to that jumped-up dick.* I called my father. 'Dad, you watching the news? Did you see that bitch that's campaigning to extend the abortion timeframe and decriminalise it?'

'Hello, son, yeah, I saw it. Disgusting. What happened to life being precious? How's things? You've not been in touch for a while.'

'Somebody ought to teach her a lesson, Dad. Bet she doesn't have kids or even want them. Imagine a baby over six months old being terminated. He or she is a proper living thing at that stage. Fuckin disgusting to even consider that. Can you imagine that, Dad?'

'Are you OK, Connor? You sound a bit … a bit … highly strung or something.'

'Aye, I'm highly strung, Dad. It's a fucking disgraceful idea.'

'Did you hear your mum got a dog?'

'I need to go, Dad, there's the door,' I lied, ending the call.

Grabbing my laptop from under the bed, I headed to the living room and took a seat on the sofa. Entering the name 'Gina Campbell-Kennedy' into my search engine. Various articles within numerous local and national newspapers appeared. Skimming through them, I absorbed little snippets of information from them as if building a profile. A question and answer session provoked me into shouting aloud. 'Aye right, you really look like you go for a two-mile early morning run in Queens Park!' My attention turned to Laura. Using a different email address and separate social media profile I'd set up when she blocked me, I perused her page. She had taken to posting information about her morning runs using an app that showed where she ran, how far and for how long. I studied the pictures she had posted but it caused too much pain to see her face. The memories of our time together. All the things I was no longer able to do with her. Slamming the laptop shut I lay back down on the sofa.

Seven

Pedalling furiously, I zigzagged through the pedestrians making their way over the Clyde Bridge to the south side of the city. A bike and a cycle jacket for thirty quid courtesy of an advertisement in Gumtree. The plans spawning in my mind had directed me to make the purchase. However, before my plan could be executed, I had unfinished business to take care of. Like a stereotypical movie depiction of an erratic American paperboy I jumped off the bike as it slammed against the tenement, both wheels still spinning. Sprinting up the stairs, I knew there was no way back. Rattling repeatedly on the door, Dad eventually answered, his face covered in shaving foam, holding a razor. 'Connor, what a—'

I barged by him, down the hallway, into the living room. Dad followed a few paces behind. 'What's up, son? What's going on?' he mumbled, trying to avoid swallowing the shaving foam.

'Where is she?' I pleaded.

'Your mum?'

'Aye, ma *mum*.'

'She's at the park with Madge.'

'Wit? Who the fuck is Madge?'

Dad laughed. 'The dog.'

Shaking my head I sped down the hallway through the front door and down the stairs. Jumping back on the bike, I heard Dad shout from the window, 'Connor … Connor, come back.'

Passing through the park gates, I pedalled along the path looking in every direction for her. Through the tunnel of trees, I thought about how quiet the park was, probably due to the frequent rainfall. Over the bridge to the far end of the park that spread out before me, I braked hard, grinding to a halt, my back wheel kicking to the right. I watched Mother in the far corner throwing a stick into the trees. Fawning over the little dog that answered to the cry of Madge. For me, it was a surreal sight, watching her shower the little dog with affection. *She's a total stranger to me. Mother? Some fucking mother. Look at her showing that fucking dog more affection than she's shown me in all my life.* Ramming my front wheel up and down in anger off the path, I began to pedal in her direction. My breathing became more audible as I ground my teeth. On seeing me pedalling towards her, she let out a strange excitable laugh. I jumped from the bike as it skidded on the grass leaving it's mark on the wet surface. 'Connor, has something happened? Is it Paul?'

There was an intenseness in her pale blue eyes. 'No, it's not Paul. It's me. I want to ask you a question.'

Visibly relieved, mother replied, with a smile, 'Ask away.'

Her demeanour puzzled me.

'Do you have any regrets?'

She cocked her head. 'What's wrong, Connor? You're worrying me.'

I stamped on some broken branches causing me to slip slightly as the wet ground and slippery branches gave way. 'ANSWER ma question.'

Picking up Madge, holding her to her chest protectively, she answered, 'I don't know what's got into you. Is it Laura? Have you and Laura split up?'

'Aye, we've split up. You'll be happy about that though, won't yae? Cos you tried your best when we met, your little slip of the tongue when I was at the toilet. You're fucking conniving and I can see straight through you. I know more about you than you think I do.'

Mother slowly stroked her little dog's head. 'Is that so? Me too, Connor.'

I took a single step forward. 'What do you mean by that?'

'Just what I say. I know more than you think I know. Let me ask you a question, Connor. Why do you think Paul and I are so close?'

'Because he's a fucking weasel. And a sycophant. He's blind when it comes to you. That's why.'

'No, I'll tell you why. Me and Paul are cut from the same cloth. Whereas you and your pathetic excuse of a dad have more in common.'

I clapped my hands.'Finally showing your true colours, Mary.'

'Plenty more where that came from, s*on*. But go on, you've come here with something on your mind. Say it.'

I was struggling to think straight, this wasn't part of the plan. I stared at her open-mouthed.

She smirked at me. 'Show some balls for once in your life. Tell your mother why you came here in a dishevelled mess and in such a hurry. It's written all over your face. SAY IT!' She kissed Madge's head. 'I'll do it for you then, Connor. You're too late. I've even ruined this for you. You shouldn't have left it so long.' Her grin transformed into a callous, wicked sneer. 'That day you came home from school early. She nodded her head in time with each word she uttered. 'You … *heard* … me.'

'Fuck. No. No. That can't be right.' Her words hit me like a surprise punch to the gut. I dropped to my haunches, my chin tucked into my chest, two hands clasping the back of my head. 'No. Please no. You fucking *knew*? I don't…'

'What don't you? Do I need to spell it out?'

Rising to my feet, storming forwards, I grabbed her by the shoulders. 'You evil fucking cow. Why?' I shook her vigorously, her pet barked, trying to defend its mistress.

'Why? You heard why.' She leaned nearer, close enough for me to smell the coffee on her breath. 'I wanted to leave *him*. I was trying to find the courage. Sorting it all in my head, I was making plans, then you happened. YOU! ruined everything. Carrying you for nine months broke me. I didn't want you or your dad. Then, when you arrived, it was even worse. The fucking spitting image of your lazy good-for-nothing dad. All that Catholic guilt like a cancer growing in me for years. All because of YOU!' She stabbed a finger at me.

I grabbed her finger and with my other hand slapped her face. She made no effort to evade the slap. 'That's us even.' Her teeth gritted, staring at me furiously, she said, 'Don't think of doing that again.'

I took several steps backwards. 'But I was an innocent wee baby. What could I do about you wanting to leave him? What could I do about looking like my dad? None of this was my fault! I didnae stand a chance,' I pleaded breathlessly, pausing to collect my thoughts. My arms and hands stretched towards her. 'LOOK AT ME! Look at the state that carrying this fucking burden for years has left me in. Now you add on another layer of mental torture as if it doesn't mean anything. Aye, listen boys, you know that issue with my mum from when I was a wee guy? Well, I heard her tell my dad she wanted an abortion and she greets herself to sleep at night that I was born cos it meant she couldnae leave my dad. Well, it gets better, lads, she actually *knew* that I knew and she despises me for not digging her up about it until now. She blames *me*' – I patted my chest twice – 'for being born and for having the temerity to look like my dad.' I scratched my head. 'Do you even realise how warped you are?'

She picked something out of her jacket pocket and fed it to Madge. 'Life's tough, Connor.'

I couldn't stay still, my arms were flailing around as I turned this way and that, the wheels in my head turning, trying to process her admission. 'But what about all the stuff getting Dad and Paul to speak to me about the way I was treating you?'

Mary shrugged her shoulders. 'I didn't ask them to. They did that of their own accord. Poor Mary … her Connor speaking to her like that. I just played along.' She smiled nonchalantly.

'You're a cold, heartless cow. How did you know I heard you?'

Looking at me as if I was an imbecile, she said, 'It didn't take a genius to work it out. I thought I heard a noise at the time but put it down to paranoia. Within a few days your behaviour totally changed towards me. You're an open book, like your dad. I could see the hatred spewing from you that time you came home after apparently falling off the bus. You underestimated your old mum. Gerry was stupid enough to put it down to you being a teenager. I'm not so stupid. I channelled all the pain inside me anytime I needed to. Remember, when the police brought you back. "I don't know what to do with him, officers." The tears. What a performance! *You* got to feel the pain I'd felt. I've lost the best years of my life because of you and your dad. You have no idea what it felt like being ready to leave him then becoming pregnant and unable do anything about it.'

I shuddered at the sight of her snarling face, her nose scrunched, teeth resting on her bottom lip.

'Imagine something growing inside you that you don't want, knowing it has resigned you to at least another sixteen years of a loveless marriage. I'd have left and taken Paul but there was no way I could have left when you came along. I didn't want to be anywhere near you. I've been hell-bent on staying with him the last few years to make you suffer as much as I have, safe in the knowledge that it was poisoning you. No more. It's done.'

I covered my face with my hands as if to make it all go away.

Madge was trying to wiggle free from her mistress's grasp. 'C'mon, my wee Madge. Be a good girl now for Mummy,' she cooed. 'The irony of you being on the other side of the door hearing my truth all those years ago then fast-forward to the day you moved out. If only you saw the smile on my face when you closed the door after whispering those words in my ear about enjoying my freedom etc.'

Shaking my head furiously, I suddenly felt faint.

Mother smirked. 'I just kept giving you rope to hang yerself. Organise a wee family dinner, knowing full well you'd ruin it. And guess what that succeeded in doing? Pushing me and Paul closer and closer and you and him further and further apart.'

She patted the dog. Shedding one emotional mask for another, she eyed me with a mixture of disgust and pity. I desperately wiped the tears away. 'You were supposed to look after me! You're my mum!'

Her pale blue eyes looked translucent to me as she answered, 'In name only. I don't feel like your mum and you don't feel like my son.'

'You're fucking sick in the head' – I jabbed my finger in her direction –'I won't let you get away with this. I *refuse* to be your fucking victim. I promise you this' – I wiped my nose and eyes with my sleeve – 'I'll get my revenge. That's a promise, you're a fucking, evil, old bitch.'

I mounted the bike. As I began to pedal, she shouted, 'Thanks, Connor, I've waited on this day for years. Run to your dad if you want. He's all you've got. I'm free. I'm leaving him. Paul is all I need.'

Eight

Six o'clock the following morning. Sat at the kitchen table, drinking from my mug of coffee, I felt a sense of focus I hadn't experienced for some time. The sense of directionless had been shed. I revelled in this new sense of purpose. Approaching what lay ahead as if heading into work for a mundane run-of-the-mill shift. Paradoxically, it was the calmest I'd felt for what seemed to me like an eternity. *It'll be over soon.*

Picking up the black rucksack which I'd packed the previous night like a regimental soldier preparing for inspection, I walked down the hallway and opened the front door. Unlocking the padlock from my bike, I placed it in the rucksack. The homely aroma of a fry-up wafted from a neighbour's door, reminding me of weekend mornings from childhood. Mother's face appeared in my mind which led to flashbacks from yesterday. I closed my eyes, took several deep breaths, tossing the images from my mind. *Focus, Connor. No distractions. No sentiment. No more being the victim.*

Opening the controlled-entry front door to the block of flats, I walked with my bike into the early morning mist. A cacophony of birds tweeting and chirping, making early morning demands. The noise seemed more acute to me than normal, making me wonder whether the poor visibility had something to do with it. Perhaps not being able to see as clearly made the everyday background noise more noticeable. I tried to put the visibility issues to the back of my mind as it created doubt. *You sure it's safe to cycle in this, Connor? How are you going to spot anyone coming? Are you sure about this?* Mounting the bike, I set off, attempting to pedal my doubts away. Cycling along the canal-side, a blanket of mist hovered over the water making it look like a scene from a Japanese B-Movie. I imagined some kind of creature emerging from the water, roaring and scanning for its victim. As I cycled onwards, the overhead conditions improved slightly, so I stuck to my planned route. Arriving at the southbound cycle path entrance to the tunnel I pressed the button to gain admittance. Scoffing inwardly at the futile attempt to prevent undesirables from entering with their alcohol and spraypaint.

On entering, I was mugged by various stenches. From urine to a musty dampness. Momentarily deliberating on whether to turn back and re-evaluate my route, I decided to press on. The claustrophic, low-ceilinged, concrete tunnel had been initially whitewashed but was now layered in grime. A variety of graffiti adorned the walls. Gangs marking their territory. Sectarian bile. Namechecks destroyed by derogatory comments added at a later date, from questioning parenthood to sexuality. Wall lights created straight lines of light on the roof of the tunnel barely a foot away from my head. Metal railings separated cyclists coming from the opposite end of the tunnel. Anxiety reared its ugly head, making my skin prickle. Sweating profusely despite the dank, cold conditions. Pedalling as fast as possible, desperate to escape this tunnel that was beginning to resemble a manic scene from one of the many nightmares I'd experienced recently.

Eventually a window of early morning greyness appeared in the distance. Gradually becoming bigger and greyer. A portal to freedom and open spaces. My breathing returned to normal as I enjoyed exaggerated breaths of fresh air like I'd just come up from underwater. Cutting through the streets, more and more early risers appeared. *Off to put a shift in then home to their families. Just normality. Everyday life. How could it not be me. No, not wee Connor. Fucking cursed.* I was released from my thoughts by the cry, 'Watch where yer goin, ya clown. Yae nearly knocked mi o'er' as a supermarket worker emerged from a block of flats.

Pulling to a stop, I checked my watch. Satisfied I was on track, I flipped my water bottle from the frame, taking a swig before replacing it and setting off again.

Five minutes later, I was at the park gates. Two great stone pillars on top of which sat what looked like lanterns. The branches and leaves on the trees immediately inside the gates looked like they were stretching to protect the pillars and lanterns, as if covering their eyes from the horrors to come. I pulled out the cycling jacket I'd been given with the bike, putting it on over my black hoody. Looking like a die-hard cyclist out for an early morning spin in weather most wouldn't contemplate, I cycled slowly into the park. Watching and listening. Scanning the area like a bird of prey. Patient. Looking like someone in love with the great outdoors. Just pedalling. Admiring the flowerbeds. A dog barking loudly in the distance sharpened my senses. Past the boating pond. The great glasshouse. Paths branching off in different directions. Park benches peppered along the path. Making my way down the tree-lined path with a rusty fence on my right, I saw her coming towards me from around a hundred yards away. *Imagine being so stupid to have an app on your social media site that shows the world where you run everyday and at what time.*

Stopping at the next bench, pulling up my hood, I pointed my front wheel in the direction I'd just travelled from. With my back to her, I wriggled free from my rucksack, placing it on the handlebars then unzipping it. Delving around inside it, I felt her pass me. Counting to five while hanging my rucksack from a handlebar, I pedalled towards her, catching up in a matter of seconds. Five yards from her, I jumped from the bike and grabbed her from behind placing my hand over her mouth as she ground to a halt. The heat from her mouth on my palm. My thumb lodged against her cheekbone, fingers on her jawbone. An arm pinning her shoulders to my chest.

I leant my mouth towards her ear, whispering, 'Watch your thoughts. They become words. Watch your words. They become deeds. Sticks and stones can break your bones. WORDS,' I gritted my teeth, 'CAN FOREVER HARM YOU.'

Removing my hand, her mouth hung open as she tried to catch her breath. I dragged the Stanley blade from one side of her cheek past her open mouth to the other cheek. Her faint scream immediately drowned by me stabbing furiously inside her mouth, her tongue. A gargling sound as though she was gargling the blood like a mouthwash. The smell of blood, the unexpected thought that it smelt like iron. She dropped to the ground with a strange animal-like whimpering sound. Removing my jacket, I quickly wiped my hands while returning to the bike. Unzipping the rucksack, I stuffed the jacket and Stanley blade inside. As I sped off, the sense of calm surprised me. If asked at this moment, 'What do you feel?' My answer would have been, 'Nothing. I feel absolutely nothing.'

***

Arriving back at the flat after committing the act that registered as nothing more than taking a stand, I stripped before throwing my clothes straight into the washing machine. Then I took a shower. Sat in the shower, arms clasped over my knees, my chin tucked into my chest, the water hit the back of my head before parting over different parts of my body. Eyes closed, a satisfied grin, enjoying the sensation of the water like fingertips caressing my neck. No thoughts, purely enjoying the water on my body. My body clock was all out of kilter. One late night after another, drinking in an effort to numb the pain, still in bed into the afternoon – it all meant that the early morning rise was catching up with me. Drying myself, I meandered towards the bedroom, naked, longing for sleep. Erasing the brief thought of how nice it would be if Laura was there to cuddle up to. Lying in bed, I stretched over to the bedside table and grabbed my wallet. Stroking the photo of Laura. *I loved you so much. I wish you hadn't hurt me. Now you'll know you were right about me after all.* Placing the treasured photo back in the wallet, I shoved it back on the table and let sleep come to me.

Drenched in perspiration, the bedsheets clung to me like an additional layer of skin. A foostie odour permeated the bedroom. The most satisfying, unbroken sleep I'd had in months.

My eyes tried to adjust to the deep, penetrating darkness – the bedroom window faced onto the back court with no means of light. Rubbing my face with both hands, I stretched my arms and legs, letting out a satisfied breath. Picking up my jogging bottoms from the bottom of the bed, I put them on and walked down the hallway into the kitchen. Filling a glass with fresh orange, I poured it into my mouth, the tangy juice causing me to suck my cheeks in and shiver. My tongue no longer felt like an old, arid doormat. Returning to the bedroom, I turned on the bedside lamp, my eyes twitching furiously, adjusting to the new conditions. Picking up my mobile I saw six missed calls from Dad and one text message.

> **Messages Received**
> Today 21.02
> Dad
> Have u heard from ur mum? I'm worried. Think I heard her going out with Madge b4 work. When I got up Madge wasn't here? She hasn't come in from work and I've just spoke to Carol from her work. She didnae turn up today?? That's not like her Connor. Phone me!!!

I shook my head. 'Poor bastard. Welcome to my world, Dad.' I threw my mobile to the bottom of the bed.

***

Forty-eight hours passed since my moment of retribution. One trip to the shops, purchasing everything I needed. Temporarily retreating from society. Mobile switched off. Empty cans of lager lay on the carpet, a dirty plate on the bedside table that had ousted the previous occupant to the carpet, the lampshade lying at a peculiar angle.

The vast majority of time spent in bed. Episode after episode of my favourite programme, *Breaking Bad*. Walter

Scott, arms folded, curiousity aroused by the scene unfolding in front of him.

The knocking on the front door alarmed me. Pursing my lips, I wondered why the intercom hadn't buzzed. Another bout of knocking. Aptly dressed in black, a V-neck T-shirt and jogging bottoms, I folded my arms across my chest, wiggled my toes and waited. Another bout of knocking. A short pause. Reaching for the remote control I pressed the mute button. Whispered voices. A rattling on the door, this time knuckles replaced by a closed fist pounding on the door. I slid out of bed, reaching under it for my trainers. 'I'll be a minute,' I shouted, as I slipped my feet into the trainers. Walking to the door, I took a deep breath. 'Here goes,' I whispered under my breath.

Opening the door I was faced with two police officers flanking a middle-aged man, his blemished face looked as if it had been attacked by a purple marker pen. 'Connor Boyd?' he enquired.

'Unfortunately for me, yes I am,' I answered walking back into the flat.

The three men followed me. 'My name is D I Jackson; I'm investigating the serious assault of a fifty—'

Pulling my jacket from the wardrobe, I interjected, 'I know why you're here, let's not go through all this. Let's just get it over and done with at the station.' I slipped my jacket on.

Jackson was not amused. 'Listen, you jumped-up little prick, let's get one thing straight, I'm in charge here, not you. There's a poor woman disfigured… You could play a game of fucking noughts and crosses on her face and you swan about as if nothing's happened. Get him cuffed.' He nodded to the accompanying officers.

Ushered down the stairs, I turned to the officer to my right. Laughing in his face, I said, 'This isnae the first time I've been frogmarched down the stairs by a pair of dicks.'

The officer looked straight ahead, poker-faced, refusing to acknowledge my existence.

A hand on the crown of my head pushed me downwards as I was tossed into the back seat of the police car. D I Jackson sat to my left, the officer I had insulted to my right. The other officer got into the driver's seat and started the engine.

A few minutes into the journey, as we pulled up at a set of traffic lights, I stared out of the window. A group of secondary school boys were skulking around outside a chip shop. The large, overweight bully held another boy by the neck and dragged his knuckles up and down the boy's skull. Another boy slammed his open hand under his friend's bag of chips, shouting, 'POW!' knocking the bag out of his hand, chips flying in all directions. My memory switch was flicked as images of that fateful day returned to haunt me. My mother's poisonous words. The boys I watched through the car window were around the same age as I was when it happened. When everything changed. This feeling I was currently experiencing had returned with monotonous regularity throughout the years. Haunting me. As much a part of me as my limbs. *Nobody should ever be made to feel like ... like they're...* I searched for the correct word. *That's it. Worthless.*

'I'm Connor Boyd. And I'm a worthless fucking nonentity,' I whispered, as the car pulled up outside the police station.

Epilogue

Her Majesty's Prison Service is a wonderful institution. It would blow your mind – the things readily available to us. Every drug that you can imagine. Forgive me, I've lost my freedom, not my sense of humour. Can you believe that the one thing that potentially might have saved me, the help that was so elusive on the outside, is so readily available in here? Talking to a professional about my life has rescued it. My counsellor has taught me so many things. Like the meaning of remorse. I have taken full responsibility for my mistakes and accepted that I was not to blame for other people's mistakes. I have looked within at the impact that my poor decisions had on the individuals affected. A letter to my victim has been sent expressing my utmost remorse and offering a sincere apology. I have learnt to forgive myself. Tooled with some effective coping strategies I really think I can make a difference, perhaps work with young offenders. Greg, the wind-up merchant that he is, calls me the born again christian. I'm just glad we've patched things up after the way I treated him. I have read a lot and tried to educate myself. I chose not to let time be a noose around my neck, instead I befriended it. People say, you only get one life. I disagree. At this moment in my life, I am Connor Boyd III. The first version of me died on that day when I was thirteen years old. My former self died after several sessions with my counsellor. My name is *still* Connor Boyd ... but I am on a journey. A journey with the firm intention of becoming a better man. A good man. Despite everything.

Fantastic Books
Great Authors

CROOKED CAT

Meet our authors and discover
our exciting range:

- Gripping Thrillers
- Cosy Mysteries
- Romantic Chick-Lit
- Fascinating Historicals
- Exciting Fantasy
- Young Adult and Children's Adventures
- Non-Fiction

Visit us at:
www.crookedcatbooks.com

Join us on facebook:
www.facebook.com/crookedcatbooks

Printed in Poland
by Amazon Fulfillment
Poland Sp. z o.o., Wrocław